THE REMEMBERING

THE REMEMBERING

BOOK THREE OF THE MEQ

STEVE CASH

BALLANTINE BOOKS

NEW YORK

A Del Rey Trade Paperback Original

Copyright © 2011 by Steve Cash

Published in the United States by Del Rey, an imprint of The Random House Publishing Group, a division of Random House, Inc., New York.

Del Rey is a registered trademark and the Del Rey colophon is a trademark of Random House, Inc.

ISBN 978-0-345-47094-2

Printed in the United States of America

www.delreybooks.com

2 4 6 8 9 7 5 3 1

Original design by Susan Turner

For Chloe, Colin, Zoe, and Scout

ACKNOWLEDGMENTS

I want to thank the true believers: Cody and Allison, Star and Mike, Sydney, Linda, and John. I also want to thank Betsy Mitchell for every question and suggestion. She was my "other" voice and she was always right. Lastly, I want to thank Tom and Frances Bissell. Inside their hearts and souls, I know they are Meq.

THE MEQ

Aitor Zezen (B. 426 BC) / Itzia (B. 311 BC)

begat

Yaldi Zezen (B. 172 AD)
Yaldi Zezen / Xamurra (B. 201 BC)

begat

ZIANNO ZEZEN (B. 1869 AD)

Umla-Meq (B. 1005 BC)
Sister – Eder-Meq (B. 998 BC)
Geaxi Bikis (B. 51 BC)
Unai Txori (B. 217 BC)
Baju Gastelu (B. 299 BC)

Opari (B. 1310 BC)
Sister – Deza (B. 1313 BC)
Trumoi-Meq (B. 1117 BC)
Usoa Ijitu (B. 412 BC)
Nova Gastelu (B. 1894 AD)

Xanti Otso – the Fleur-du-Mal (B. 356 BC)
Mother – Hilargi (B. 897 BC)
Father – Unknown
Uncle – Zeru-Meq (B. 901 BC)

Ray Ytuarte (B. 1783 AD)   Susheela the Ninth (B. 3061 BC)
Sister – Zuriaa (B. 1790 AD)
Mother – Ikerne (B. Unknown)

Previously, in *The Meq* and *Time Dancers:*

From the introduction of the electric lightbulb to the supernatural light from an exploding nuclear bomb, Zianno Zezen, or Z, has been witness to these events, and yet he remains in the body of a twelve-year-old boy. His human friends and family are changing, aging, and dying. But Z is not human. He is something else, something older. In his heart and mind, now more than ever, he knows what it means to be Meq, living inside Time and history, to be part of it, and still be outside of it—a stranger, a seeker . . . a survivor.

In Book One, *The Meq*, Zianno's adventure of self-discovery led him to understand the significance of the Stone of Dreams. The ancient black rock with its mystical hypnotic power over all other animate beings was passed down to him from his father, and his father's father, and so on, going back millennia to the Time of Ice. Four more Stones are known to exist: the Stone of Silence, now carried by Nova Gastelu; the Stone of Will, carried for the last two thousand years by Geaxi Bikis; the Stone of Memory, carried for nearly three thousand years by Umla-Meq, also known as Sailor; and the Stone of Blood, carried even longer by Z's one true love and Ameq, Opari. As Sailor once told Z, the carriers of these Stones must endure, and it is essential that all five Stones are present at the Gogorati—the Remembering. Why? No one knows for certain, but the Meq have always speculated that the Stones have something to do with their origins, and possibly their future. At the end of Book Two, *Time Dancers,* very few Meq are left alive, and it is possible, nay probable, that Z's friend and mentor, Sailor, has been incinerated by the nuclear bomb over Nagasaki. The Fleur-du-Mal, the cruel Meq assassin and nemesis of Z and the others, is alive and well, and it is known that he has captured and imprisoned Susheela the Ninth, the Ethiopian Meq whose existence was once thought to be only a rumor. She has been alive for five thousand and six years and is by far the oldest among them. The Fleur-du-Mal is sadistic and completely unpredictable. What will he do next?

It is late 1945, World War II is over and the Cold War has just begun. The Meq and their secrets, powers, and "abilities" will be sought by the Soviets and the Americans. The Remembering is just on the horizon, less than seventy years away. Since the Time of Ice the Meq have always believed they know the *when* . . . but they still do not know the *where*. The mystery must be solved in time, and Zianno may be the only one who can solve the ancient riddle.

BOOK
THREE

PART I

Coincidence is God's way of remaining anonymous.

—ALBERT EINSTEIN

I

LABEZOMORRO

(COCKROACH)

When the people are gone, when the trees are dead, when the animals are dead, when the sky is poisoned, the earth blackened and the rivers and seas fouled, the cockroach will be there. He will survive. He will be awake, hungry, scurrying in darkness through holocaust and nightmare—an elegant, six-legged silent witness and ancient sentinel. He will be waiting for you there. He will be among the survivors. Underground, in the wall, at the back of the cave, the cockroach will be there.

It was 11:09 in the morning, August 9, 1945. Forty thousand feet in the air, the enormous cloud began to break up and spread across the sky in swirling whites and grays. Below it, the Urakami Valley and the city of Nagasaki were invisible under the dark mass at the cloud's base. I hadn't moved or blinked or said a word for seven minutes.

"Are you deaf and mute, Zezen, or have you not seen death before?"

I turned slowly and looked up to the top of the castle wall. The Fleur-du-Mal stared down at me. His hair hung loose, down over his shoulders. His green eyes were hard and bright. Then the huge, wrought-iron gate to the castle began to swing open. The old hinges sounded like giant fingernails scraping a giant blackboard. "Come inside, Zezen," he said, "and leave the body of the woman inside the gatehouse, if you wish."

He waited for me to reply. I said nothing. Finally, he shook his head and said, "Have it your way, then, but the wind is shifting."

I looked back toward the cloud, which was breaking up rapidly. "Why should that make a difference?"

The Fleur-du-Mal raised his head and laughed. His brilliant white teeth gleamed against the sky. "Radiation, you idiot," he said. "Gamma, alpha, and beta radiation. That was an atomic bomb."

"What is an atomic bomb?"

"Come inside and I shall explain it to you. Otherwise, you will likely die. I doubt the Meq have ever faced a nuclear explosion, let alone what that insidious cloud contains. Or would you rather stand there and find out for yourself?"

I looked down at Shutratek's lifeless body. One eye had opened, so I leaned over and closed it, then stood and stared again at Nagasaki. Sailor and Sak had been on their way to a location near the Nagasaki railway station, close to where the Urakami River runs into the harbor. None of it was visible now. The whole city was silent under the blackness. I didn't move. I couldn't, I was frozen.

"They are all dead, Zezen," the Fleur-du-Mal said from above. "All of them—Zuriaa, Susheela the Ninth . . . Sailor and the Ainu. All of them."

I spun around. "You knew Sailor and I were in Nagasaki?"

"Please, Zezen, do not insult me. Of course, I knew. I knew the very hour of your arrival and I have been well aware of every one of your clumsy attempts at locating my many *shiros*." He scanned the sky and the horizon, then added, "Your time is up, Zezen. I am closing the gate. *Adieu, mon petit.*"

He disappeared from view and the massive gate began to close. I glanced once more at Nagasaki and knew the Fleur-du-Mal was right. They were all dead, all of them. A wave of nausea passed through me. I thought of Sailor and felt a sudden sense of loss and despair I had only felt once before, on the day my own mama and papa died. Sailor was so much more to me than I even realized, more than a friend or a teacher. He was irreplaceable. Behind me, I heard the screeching of the hinges and looked back at the gate. It was almost closed. I half dragged, half carried Shutratek through the opening and just in time. The gate locked into place. I laid Shutratek down on the stone floor inside the gatehouse, then looked up to see the Fleur-du-Mal standing next to me. I tensed instinctively. He could have easily slit my throat at any moment.

He sensed my fear and laughed bitterly. "Sometimes I worry about you, *mon petit,*" he said. "Your nervousness is palpable. I am not going to harm you." He paused and smiled. "Now, follow me inside. *Rapidement!*"

"What about the woman?" I asked, nodding toward Shutratek. The Fleur-du-Mal had already started walking. He stopped abruptly and sighed, shaking his head from side to side. "She is dead, Zezen," he said. "She will not be less dead by taking her inside the *shiro*. Leave her. Tomorrow, or perhaps the next day, when the air is safe, you may do with her what you wish. That is my final thought on the subject."

The Fleur-du-Mal turned and continued walking toward two heavy wooden doors directly under the lowest roof of a five-tiered wood and stone tower. Both doors were covered with iron straps, ancient protection against battering and cannon fire. The *shiro* was a magnificent structure and compound. I stared up at the five tiled roofs, one piled atop the other. I felt numb and strange. Sailor was dead along with an entire city full of people. Everything was surreal. I got to my feet slowly. The Fleur-du-Mal had said it cold and with a cold heart, but I knew he was right about Shutratek. I could not help her now and he gave me no choice. But what was I doing? Only a few hours ago I had set out to trap

and kill him. Now I was agreeing with him and about to become
a guest in his house. And why hadn't he killed me when he had
the chance? Nothing made sense anymore. I followed the Fleur-
du-Mal across the courtyard without another word.

Inside the *shiro* it was dark and cool and completely silent. I could
see several windows off to one side, but they were all shuttered.
There was no furniture, except for two hand-carved wooden
chairs sitting against one wall. The Fleur-du-Mal locked the reinforced doors with a long iron key bigger than his own hand, then
turned to me. "This way," he said, motioning me toward a stone
stairwell that led only down. He reached up and removed a
screened lantern from the wall and lit it. I paused at the top step.
"Please, you first, Zezen," he said with a slight grin. "Youth before beauty," he added, laughing.

    He held the lantern high over our heads and we started down.
After ten steps the stairwell turned ninety degrees, then again after
ten more steps. With the Fleur-du-Mal at my back, I expected to
feel the net descending, the prickly feeling of fear I nearly always
felt in his presence, but I didn't. I felt no fear whatsoever.

    "Where are we going?" I asked.

    "You shall see soon enough. Keep walking," he said without
emotion.

    Finally, three stories beneath the ground floor of the *shiro*, our
descent ended. We were standing on the stone floor of a long hall
that led to our left and right. The Fleur-du-Mal pointed the
lantern to the right toward a heavy wooden door, which was reinforced with iron straps like the doors above. As we approached,
the door opened slowly and a short, middle-aged Japanese man in
Western dress was standing in the doorway. He wore extremely
thick, round glasses, making his eyes look as big as walnuts behind

them. He was not surprised to see us and he did not look at us as ordinary boys. He knew we were Meq, I could sense it.

The man smiled wide. "Hello, mister. Yes, hello, yes? Hello, hello."

"Out of the way, Koki," the Fleur-du-Mal told him. "Bring us tea."

"Yes, yes," the man answered. "Tea . . . hello, yes?" He was still smiling and staring at me.

"Hello," I said. His smile widened. His teeth were stained brown and he smelled of tobacco.

"Now!" the Fleur-du-Mal said firmly.

"Yes, yes," the man replied. He glanced once more at me, then turned and scurried away into the depths of a huge room with Persian rugs covering the stone floors and elegant tapestries and modern paintings covering the walls. The room was brightly lit and looked warm and inviting. It was filled with Spanish leather chairs, English oak tables, and Belgian lamps. Greek, Roman, and Egyptian artifacts and sculpture were everywhere. There was nothing Japanese about it.

"You are staring, Zezen. Are you not well?"

"No, no, I was just . . . I mean, I didn't expect . . ."

The Fleur-du-Mal laughed loudly. "Quickly," he said. "Inside, and make yourself comfortable."

I stepped into the room a few paces and looked back over my shoulder. He was locking the door with the same long key he'd used on the other doors. "Who is that man?" I asked.

"Pay him little mind," he said, dismissing the thought with a wave of his hand.

"But who is he?"

The Fleur-du-Mal paused and sighed. "His formal name is Naohiro Nishi. However, I refer to him as Koki, an abbreviation for *Kokkuro-chi*, the Cockroach."

"The Cockroach?"

"Yes . . . it is a long story and not worth explaining. Simply stated, he owes me a debt, or shall we say his family owes me a debt. I need him for various services when I am in Japan. And there you have it. Please, take a seat. Koki will be out shortly with tea. You look as though you need it, *mon petit*."

"What did you do for his family?"

The Fleur-du-Mal stared at me with piercing green eyes and I noticed that not only was his hair longer and hanging loose, but he was also missing his ruby earrings. "If you must know, nearly eighty-five years ago, I saved them all from certain death. Now, that is quite enough said on the subject."

I sat down carefully on one of the leather chairs and watched him. He moved gracefully, lighting screened lanterns on the wall and various candles strewn about the enormous room. I didn't know whether to believe him or not. I had never known the Fleur-du-Mal to save anyone except himself from anything.

"Did you realize, Zezen," he said from the far end of the room, "this entire space was once used exclusively as a torture chamber and prison?"

I waited a moment. I glanced over at the locked, reinforced door. "And now it isn't?" I replied with the greatest irony I could muster.

He laughed and then disappeared somewhere in the shadows, saying, "I must change into something more comfortable. Relax, *mon petit,* and enjoy your tea."

I remained motionless for several moments and closed my eyes. I tried to relax, but my mind kept returning to the white light of the atomic bomb and the rising, ugly, swirling, black cloud over Nagasaki. It was death on a scale that was unimaginable. Suddenly

I began to tremble and shake, first in my hands and fingers, then all over my body. I opened my eyes wide and attempted to stand. My legs wobbled and buckled and I sat back down. Images of Sailor being burned and blown apart turned over and over in my mind. I couldn't make them stop. I heard myself moaning, "No, no, no, no." I stood up again and forced my legs to move, walking in a tight circle. I stared down at the pattern in the Persian rug beneath my feet. Every part of the beautiful woven design seemed to move and change shape, turning into flaming dragons and demons, all with their tongues out and eyes bulging from their sockets. And they were screaming, screaming and howling with laughter. I put my hands over my ears to make them stop, yet they only got louder and louder. Then I felt someone touch my shoulder. "Mister, hello, mister," a voice said. I opened my eyes and saw Koki's smiling face. He was pointing toward a small cup filled with steaming liquid, sitting on an end table next to the leather chair. "Tea," he said, then added, "Hello."

"What? Oh, yes, of course." My voice was dry and raspy, and I cleared my throat. "Thank you, Koki, thank you." He nodded once and bowed modestly, then started to leave again. He was nearly out of sight before I said, "Koki, wait!" He stopped instantly and turned to face me, still smiling. "Please," I said, "please . . . don't go. I mean, have a seat, I'd like to . . . to . . . I have a question for you."

He walked back toward me slowly. His smile faded and he seemed hesitant, even fearful. He wouldn't come any closer than ten feet. I motioned for him to take a seat in one of the chairs, but he ignored the gesture and kept his distance. I saw his face twitch once and his hands began to tremble slightly. My own trembling had ceased. "Do not be afraid, Koki," I said. "I would never hurt you. Do you understand?"

At least thirty seconds of silence passed and his eyes never left mine. Finally, in a soft and barely audible voice, he said, "Yes, mister."

I sat down in the leather chair and asked him again to take a seat. Shaking his head back and forth, he refused and stayed where he was. I picked up the cup of tea with both hands and blew on it, then took a sip. He never blinked and never looked away. "Do you know what has happened, Koki?" He made no response. "Up there," I said, pointing at the ceiling. "Outside . . . to the south . . . in Nagasaki . . . do you know what has just happened?"

He seemed confused and looked up. "Nagasaki?" he asked. He was blinking rapidly now.

"Yes. Do you have family in Nagasaki?" The question confused him even more and he glanced back over his shoulder, then looked up again. I tried another question. "Do you know what happened in Hiroshima three days ago?"

"Hiroshima?"

"Yes, Hiroshima. Do you know about the bomb, the atomic bomb?"

Koki stammered and muttered something to himself, but never answered. Instead, he began rocking from side to side in a rhythmic motion and turned his head toward the wall. He moved back and forth in perfect time, and seemed to be staring at something, or into something, or possibly nothing. I thought I heard him humming deep inside—a last chant or lost prayer.

Before I could ask him anything else, a voice behind me said, "I am afraid Koki is not aware of current events, Zezen." It was the Fleur-du-Mal and I had not heard him approach. Walking into view, he was wearing an elegant silk kimono, cut to his specifications. His hair had been pulled back and tied with his familiar green ribbon and he was once again wearing his ruby earrings. He sat down casually in a chair opposite mine. He let a slow grin spread across his face, then continued. "Let us say, Koki does not get out much."

I ignored the comment and looked back at Koki. He was deep inside his trance. "Where is he staring?" I asked.

"Most certainly at Goya," the Fleur-du-Mal answered. "Koki has been fascinated with Goya for years."

I followed Koki's gaze toward the stone wall. Five paintings hung in a row—three by Pablo Picasso from his classical style of the twenties, and two by an artist unfamiliar to me. I walked over to get a closer view of the paintings. The artist's name was Candido Portinari and his style had the influence of Picasso, but definitely not Francisco de Goya. Nor were there any Goya paintings, drawings, or prints anywhere on the wall. There were only the five paintings and one unusual object attached to the wall with iron clamps—a human skull. I glanced at Koki. His hands shook and he rocked back and forth and his eyes never left the skull. I turned to the Fleur-du-Mal. "I see no Goya painting."

"Not 'painting,' Zezen. Goya. Koki is staring at the skull of Francisco de Goya." The Fleur-du-Mal paused, grinning, then added matter-of-factly, "In 1899, during an exhumation in Bordeaux, it seems to have gone missing. At the time, and at the very least, I thought Goya's head might serve as an interesting conversation piece." He paused again and looked at Koki. "Alas, it has not."

Before I could make a response, or even form one, the Fleur-du-Mal spoke firmly to Koki in Japanese, repeating the same phrase three times, which included one word in English—"chess." Seconds later, Koki came out of his trance and calmly walked out of the room without a word. The Fleur-du-Mal's voice and words had been a key that unlocked something in Koki's mind, almost as simple as coming out of a deep hypnotic state with three claps of a magician's hands, and very similar to the way all Giza respond to the Stones.

Once Koki was out of sight, the Fleur-du-Mal said, "He is an idiot . . . an idiot savant . . . but an idiot nonetheless."

"What do you mean?"

"I will explain later. I believe it was the atomic bomb you most wanted explained to you, was it not, Zezen?"

"Well . . . yes." I hesitated, thinking again of Sailor and Sak— all of them. "What is it?"

The Fleur-du-Mal laughed to himself. "Ironically, or perhaps not, it was Koki's brother, Tsuneo, who *explained* the fundamentals of a nuclear explosion to me, in the fall of 1940, shortly after he returned from his studies in Germany." He waited for a response, but I said nothing. "All right then, *mon petit* . . . let us begin with the atom itself."

To my surprise, the Fleur-du-Mal was an excellent teacher. As he elaborated the fundamentals behind the physics of what we'd witnessed over Nagasaki, all of it theory until now, he made certain I clearly understood each principle before he continued. He mentioned Albert Einstein several times and I was reminded of New Year's Eve, 1918, high on a ridge at Caitlin's Ruby—the last time I saw old Tillman Fadle and the first time I heard Einstein's name. Looking up at the night sky, he told Geaxi and me that Einstein was after "what gets through the cracks."

Geaxi asked, "You mean the light?"

Tillman Fadle answered, "I mean that what turns *on* the light."

In half an hour the Fleur-du-Mal had explained everything and I was left speechless, wondering at what the Americans had done, technologically and morally. The consequences were staggering. It was now a brand-new world, a world led by a species capable of wiping out all living things in the blink of an eye. He finished speaking and leaned forward in his chair. He put his

hands on his knees, as if to rise, then paused and glanced at me.
For a moment he seemed to be thinking the same horrifying
thoughts as me. He smiled faintly, then walked over to the skull
of Goya and stared at it with his arms folded and his legs spread.
Goya stared back with empty eyes. Over his shoulder the Fleur-
du-Mal said, "There are only three questions worth asking, *mon
petit*. Who are we? Why are we here? And how shall we conduct
ourselves?" I said nothing. He walked a few more paces to his
right and stopped in front of the two Portinari paintings. A full
minute passed in silence, then I heard him talking and mumbling
under his breath. I could only understand a few words. He said,
". . . irrelevant now . . . tired of it . . . *juste mon genie . . . juste mon
genie*." Suddenly he turned on his heels and stared at me. He was
smiling and his ruby earrings reflected the light of the wall lamp
just over his shoulder. "In what do you believe, Zezen?"

"In what do I believe?"

The Fleur-du-Mal rolled his eyes and sighed. "Yes," he said.
"Do you not understand the question? And, please, do not insult
me by answering 'the Meq' or something equally obsequious."

I was surprised, but not dumbfounded, and the answer came to
me immediately. I didn't even have to think about it. I looked in
his green eyes and said, "I believe in—"

"Chess, mister!"

The Fleur-du-Mal and I turned in one motion. It was Koki
and he was holding a chessboard with all the chess pieces aligned
on top in their proper positions. The chessboard was made of ma-
hogany and the pieces were carved from jade and ivory. The
whole set looked ancient and valuable. Koki's glasses were sliding
down his nose and there was a trickle of drool running out the
corner of his mouth. He seemed excited.

"Put the chess set down on the table, Koki," the Fleur-du-Mal
said gently. "We shall play later. I promise." He led Koki's eyes

over to me. "M. Zezen and I are going to play first," he said, smiling, then looked back to Koki. "Bring me sake, Koki. Hot sake—make sure the temperature is correct. We shall play chess after that. Now go," he said, waving his hand toward the recesses of the huge room. He waited for Koki to exit, then turned and glanced at the chess set. "India," he said, looking back at me. "The set came from Vishakhapatnam. I saw you admiring the craftsmanship. It was a . . . gift from someone."

"A gift from whom?"

The Fleur-du-Mal either didn't like the question or didn't want to answer. He frowned and nodded toward the table. He cleared his throat and said, "Shall we play?"

"All right," I said. He asked which set of pieces I preferred and I chose the jade. As he swiveled the board to position the jade pieces in front of me, I said, "By the way, my answer is Opari."

"Your answer? What do you mean?"

"My answer to the question, 'In what do you believe?' My answer is Opari."

The Fleur-du-Mal never said a word and made his opening move, P to K3.

We played several games throughout the afternoon, or what I assumed to be the afternoon. Three stories underground, it was already becoming difficult to judge the passage of time. In each game, the Fleur-du-Mal played quickly, moving pieces in a reckless disregard of strategy. He would surrender his queen early, then his rooks and bishops, almost everything. He seemed to be interested in one thing—the endgame. Only when his king was down to two or three allies would he begin to pay attention. Then he would methodically take the offensive and eventually spring his trap and checkmate me, no matter how many pieces I had left. I couldn't beat him. The Fleur-du-Mal won every game.

He also talked incessantly while he played. Even as he was losing piece after piece, he asked question after question, the first of which was, "Aside from you, *mon petit,* and poor Sailor, how many survived the avalanche at Askenfada?" I told him the truth. I said Rune Balle had been killed. All the Meq had survived. "What a shame," the Fleur-du-Mal said with a snide smile, but his words didn't ring true. His true reaction had been *relief.* He had been relieved to hear that the Meq survived. Though it was gone as fast as it had appeared, I had seen it in his eyes and I had never seen it there before.

Later, as I was rearranging the board after yet another loss, he asked if I still carried "that odd little rock." I glanced up to see if he was being facetious, but he seemed genuinely curious. I continued to sort the pieces and answered, "Of course."

"Would you mind if I examined it briefly?"

I usually would have said no without hesitation; however, under the circumstances, I saw no reason to refuse. I knew the Stone of Dreams had no effect on the Fleur-du-Mal and we weren't going anywhere for some time. I reached in my pocket and felt the cold surface of the Stone in my palm. I pulled it out and tossed it across the table. The Fleur-du-Mal caught it with one hand, then looked over at me and smiled. *"Merci,"* he said. He stood and began pacing the room, turning the ancient, egg-shaped black rock round and round in his fingers, observing every tiny striation from every possible angle. Finally, he came to a stop and looked at me. "The Stone of Dreams, no?"

I said nothing, but nodded my head once.

He continued walking, then halted again abruptly. He had his back to me and he was facing the wall. "Pray tell, Zezen," he said over his shoulder, "what do you suppose is the true nature and purpose of these ugly, ridiculous rocks?"

"I—"

He spun around before I could answer and tossed me the Stone, laughing. "You do not know! Do not even attempt an answer." He glanced away from me, toward the wall in the direction of Goya's skull. "No one knows the answer . . . no one."

"Perhaps we'll find out at the Remembering."

"The *Remembering*?" he said, then laughed out loud several times. "That is even more ridiculous, Zezen. None of you have ever had the slightest clue in determining its location. The Egongela is as unknown to the Meq as it ever was. Your time is dwindling, and after what we witnessed this morning, the Stones and the Remembering are now insignificant and obsolete. Even Sailor would have realized this fact, Zezen. You must scrape the scabs from your eyes and see this world for what it is. There is no viable future for the Meq . . . not in this world, and not without the Sixth Stone. Sailor knew this . . . Sailor alone among you knew this to be true.

"The Meq are doomed for several obvious and gradual declines, Zezen, including the absence of large numbers of Meq offspring, and the total absence of twins and multiple births. I am certain no one has mentioned this, have they? And I would, if I were a betting man, make a hefty wager that Sailor, Trumoi-Meq, or any of the rest of them, including my uncle, has ever mentioned the psychotic rage and jealousy that can appear in the Meq *after* they have crossed in the Zeharkatu. No, I bet not, these are facts the Meq do not want to face." His green eyes darkened. "Yet I have witnessed this fact in my own life, in my own father and mother."

I had never heard him say anything about his family before and I seized the opportunity. "Zeru-Meq told us you . . . you killed your father when you were only twenty-two months old. He said he came into your house and saw your father standing over your mother, who was already dead on the floor. Then he said you killed your father, using telekinesis and a kitchen knife."

The Fleur-du-Mal smiled. "I am afraid my uncle suffers from limited vision." He walked in even, slow paces toward one of the Portinari paintings hanging on the wall. He stopped, paused, straightened the frame a fraction of an inch, then turned and asked, "What makes you think I did not kill them both?"

The question stunned me. I listened but didn't respond. I slipped the Stone back into my pocket, then finished arranging the pieces to begin a new game. "What did Susheela the Ninth tell you about the Sixth Stone?" I asked. "I know you seek it."

His green eyes flared and he unconsciously reached for something inside his kimono. It was his stiletto and simply touching it seemed to relax him. He walked calmly to his chair and sat down slowly. He surveyed the chessboard and turned it around, so that the ivory pieces were in front of me. He said, "The black witch is . . . *was* . . . of no help whatsoever." Then the Fleur-du-Mal looked up at me and almost whispered, "Your move, *mon petit*."

After a few more games, I had to quit. I was exhausted. I kept seeing the flash of the atomic bomb over and over in my mind, and I couldn't concentrate or listen to the Fleur-du-Mal another minute. He talked incessantly about the Meq, the Giza, the nature and flaws of war, the landscape of North Africa, the temples and people of southern India (particularly the women), and the futility of all vendettas, including his own against my grandfather, Aitor, and Carolina and her family. The way he spoke wasn't quite regret, but it was as close as the Fleur-du-Mal could get. He told me he would miss Sailor infinitely more than he ever would

Zuriaa. He said her insanity had spiraled out of control while in
Japan. And during our last game, he even recited a poem, which
he claimed was a Provençal Meq song from pre-Roman times.
The song went like this:

> Not age nor death
> not war nor wealth
> shall ever be enough
> for me to be reconciled
> with what lives safe inside
> and yet is wild
> what is and was
> and yet still is—the child.

As soon as I was checkmated, I said, "I'm finished. I'm hungry
and I need some rest."

To my surprise, the Fleur-du-Mal agreed. "Yes, you are right,
Zezen. We need food and we need rest. The Japanese will be sur-
rendering within days. They must, they now have no choice, and
I . . . we . . . must be ready to leave. Nagasaki and Japan itself,
pour moi, will no longer serve as, shall we say, a port in the storm."
He paused, then stood and faced the far end of the cavernous
room. "Koki!" he said loudly and firmly.

Before Koki arrived, I asked, "What is an 'idiot savant?'"

"Ah, yes," he said, and looked down at the chessboard. "But
perhaps, Zezen, you should see for yourself. Please stay where
you are."

Koki walked toward us mumbling. I think he was saying,
"Hello, yes" over and over, as if he were rehearsing the lines. He
had a funny little gait, sort of side to side. He reminded me of a
Japanese Charlie Chaplin. His glasses sat on the end of his nose
and they were nearly fogged over. He was carrying a fresh pot of

tea on a bamboo tray and the spout was directly under his chin, sending steam up to his glasses. He took extra care setting the tray down, then wiped his runny nose with the back of his hand and nudged his glasses back in place. He could barely see, but he picked up the pot and leaned over to refill my cup.

"I'll do that, Koki. Thank you, anyway," I said, taking the pot from him carefully.

"Koki," the Fleur-du-Mal said with a grin, "would you like to play chess now?"

Koki nodded his head without expression. He was rocking gently back and forth. "Yes, hello," he said. A new trickle ran from his nose and he wiped it again with his hand.

The Fleur-du-Mal reached into his kimono and withdrew a blue, embroidered handkerchief, which he handed to Koki. "Sit here," he said, giving Koki his seat in front of the jade pieces. "M. Zezen will be your opponent." Koki sat down and stared at the board. He glanced at me once and I smiled. He smiled back, exposing his stained teeth. "Your move, Zezen," the Fleur-du-Mal said, "and play as fast as you are able—Koki only plays at one speed."

I was puzzled, but I made the common opening, P to Q4. That was the last move I made with any comfort or assurance. Koki played so well and so fast, I never knew what hit me. I could barely keep up. He had me checkmated easily in no time at all.

"Play again," the Fleur-du-Mal said, "and try harder."

We played again and it was worse. Koki had my king trapped in five moves. He was brilliant. I'd never seen the combination of moves and strategy he used, and he played with lightning speed. "I give up," I said. "You are an amazing, wonderful player, Koki. I can't beat you."

Koki smiled. "Yes, hello," he said softly, then he said it again.

"Koki can destroy a grandmaster in the same fashion," the

Fleur-du-Mal said. "I have seen him do it on several occasions.
I cannot beat him. I never have. He is the best chess player I have
ever played and I have played around the world for two millennia." The Fleur-du-Mal was standing between Koki and Goya's
skull on the wall, probably to keep him from being distracted.
"Naohiro Nishi, my Koki," he said, "has a very rare and curious
madness. I have never seen it in the Meq; however, I have seen it
appear in the Giza for centuries in various forms. I believe the
current term for it among the Giza is 'autism.' It is a generalized
and convenient term, just as they are using the absurd word
'schizophrenia' for a thousand different, beautiful, and unusual
states of mind. They have little imagination and they have learned
less about madness. Nevertheless, Koki is incapable of living in
open society on his own. His uncanny ability to play chess better
than anyone in the world has no meaning or significance to him.
Koki merely likes to play, but no more than he likes to smoke cigarettes. They are equally important activities and routines." The
Fleur-du-Mal paused. He watched Koki trying to wipe his nose
with the handkerchief. Using his hand had proved more efficient.
"Come, Zezen. Follow me and we shall eat, although I apologize
in advance for the lack of variety. The war has made it somewhat
difficult to serve proper fare." He waited for me to stand, then
headed for the other end of the room and a long dining table
barely visible in the shadows. "Koki! Bring the fish soup from the
kitchen, with steamed rice and those tiny eels we had yesterday."
Halfway across the room, the Fleur-du-Mal smiled at me. His
teeth were dazzling white. "You will love the eels," he said.

I'm not sure how a day like August 9, 1945, is supposed to end.
For me, it finally ended on a single bed in a small room with stone
walls and no windows, my "apartment," according to the Fleur-

du-Mal. Lying in the dark with my eyes wide open, I tried imagining that in St. Louis the day had ended quietly, just another sultry night among many others in a long summer, perfect for a slow walk in Forest Park or a baseball game at Sportsman's Park. I wondered how the Cardinals were doing in the pennant race, and I wondered about Jack and Star and Caine and Willie, and especially Carolina. I thought about her age and suddenly realized she was now seventy-five years old. Impossible, I thought. I wondered about Opari over and over, then thought of Ray and Nova, Geaxi and Mowsel, Zeru-Meq, everyone and anyone . . . anyone but Sailor. I could not think of Sailor without seeing the white flash again, and the horrific cloud that followed and filled the sky. I knew if anyone had survived in Nagasaki, for them, August 9 would never end. I let my mind go. My thoughts formed and dissolved at random, reeling and rebounding through time, people, and places. Eventually, I drifted off and fell into a dream. It was a dream of immense power, and as puzzling as a lone footprint on a deserted island, which is exactly where it began.

I stood barefoot in the sand. I didn't feel the sun on my back, but I knew it was behind me. I turned to face the sea and saw two dolphins rising out of the blue water in a graceful arc and falling back with barely a splash. A fat, yellow sun sat low on the horizon; however, I had no sense of sunrise or sunset. I held Papa's baseball in one hand and wore Mama's glove on the other. I knew the Stone of Dreams was still intact and stitched inside the baseball, and Mama's glove looked exactly the same as it had in 1881, yet I felt no sense of paradox. In fact, I felt no sense of anything. I was myself then and I was myself now, but not quite; I was not living, or I was reliving—no, no . . . *I was about to live.* I was certain of it. I looked down and focused on a single child's footprint in the sand. It was nearly my size, only slightly wider with fatter toes. I was perplexed. The imprint was made too far from where the beach met the underbrush for there not to be another. How did it get there, and why only one? How was it possible? I looked down at Papa's baseball in my hand and something or someone compelled me to look up the slope of the beach toward the dense green tangle of jungle and the jagged peaks and cliffs above and beyond. Suddenly I knew what I was supposed to do. My purpose was to deliver the Stone of Dreams to someone who was waiting for me. Without thinking I shouted, "Opari!" A second later the sky began to darken. I looked back toward the sea just in time to catch the low-contrast bands of light and dark racing across the water. In front of the sun, the moon was gliding silently and gracefully into place. It was the *Bitxileiho*—the Strange Window. I turned and ran up the slope, and as I ran I also realized this was the end of the *Itxaron*. The Wait was over and there would be a "crossing" like no other, but for whom? I kept running and running. Then came totality and utter darkness. "Opari," I whispered, and woke up. The dream, in reality, probably lasted only a few seconds, but I spent the rest of the night lying on my single bed, motionless and staring up at nothing.

The next day began with two sharp knocks on my door, followed by a small voice, "Rice, mister." I sat up and lit the candle next to my bed, then slipped on my shoes and walked the short distance over to the door. It wasn't locked because there was no lock. The only doors with locks were the "front" door and the one leading off the great room to the Fleur-du-Mal's private chambers. I swung the door open and immediately smelled tobacco. Koki's smiling face was staring back at me. "Good morning, Koki," I said. The big room was silent and dim behind him. "It is morning, isn't it?" Koki looked at me, saying nothing, rocking side to side and smiling. He was holding a bowl of steamed rice topped

with a few slivers of carrot and mushroom. My question seemed
to have no effect. Suddenly he shoved the bowl at me, almost
hitting me in the chest. I grabbed the bowl with both hands just
before he let go of it. "Hello, mister," he said, and walked away
repeating "hello" over and over. "Koki—wait!" I said, but it was
no use. He never turned around. I watched him walking with his
odd little gait and realized why Koki probably wouldn't and
couldn't turn around. Turning around, reacting, was not in the
plan, the pattern . . . the practiced routine. Responding to me
would have meant *change,* an extremely difficult and frightening
complication in Koki's world.

I left the door open and ate the rice and vegetables sitting on
my bed, staring through the open doorway into the darkness of
the great room. The rice was good, under the circumstances, but
it wasn't enough. I had my appetite back and the rice only made
me think of more and better food in a better place. I thought of
St. Louis and Carolina and Jack and Star and Caine . . . in her
kitchen . . . sunlight streaming through the open windows . . .
Ciela is cooking, laughing . . . the Cardinals are on the radio . . .
Opari is holding my hand . . . all of us . . . laughing . . . her eyes
are dancing, laughing . . . Opari . . . Opari. In the next moment
I had my first thought of escape. I would not wait to find out
what the Fleur-du-Mal had in mind. I knew I had to get out of
the *shiro.* I only had to find the means.

The rest of the second day went much the same as the first, as
did the third and fourth days. Electricity to the hills in the vicinity of the *shiro* had not been restored since the bomb dropped.
Three stories below ground level, my time was spent keeping the
wall lamps lit in the great room, listening to the Fleur-du-Mal
continue to expound on everything from consciousness itself to
the habits and habitat of the red-cowled cardinal. Often, and
without explanation, he would retire to his chambers for hours at

a time, then reappear just as suddenly. He constantly dispensed
warnings, opinions, and proclamations about the Meq. Some of
them were absurd, but all were fascinating and revealing, even
confessional. He did most of the talking while Koki and I listened. And we played chess. Over and over and always with the
same results—the Fleur-du-Mal beat me and Koki beat both
of us.

Without a radio, I had no idea if the Japanese had surrendered
or not. If the Fleur-du-Mal had any access to current events, he
never mentioned it. For me, the great room became more claus-
trophobic by the hour. I missed the sunlight and longed to
breathe fresh air. The Fleur-du-Mal, however, seemed in no
hurry to leave. He was enjoying himself. Every day he wore a different, exquisitely embroidered kimono. He was gracious and
generous, a perfect host. He even offered me a complete set of
clothes, which I needed badly. They were his own and had never
been worn. Smiling, he said, "You might as well take them. They
are out-of-date, American, and of marginal taste and quality . . .
precisely your style, I should think, *mon petit*." I smiled back and
welcomed them, and they fit perfectly. Then, on the fifth day,
everything changed quickly, beginning with the simplest event. It
was only for a brief period and it was late in the day, but it made
all the difference.

Koki and I were in the middle of yet another game of chess.
The Fleur-du-Mal was not with us. He had been locked inside
his chambers for at least two hours. The game was going the same
as all the others. Koki would lean forward in his chair, make his
move quickly, then sit back and start rocking, never saying a word
and staring down at the chessboard. Occasionally, he would drool
out the corner of his mouth, then wipe his chin and adjust his big
eyeglasses all in one motion. We were entering the endgame and
I only had six pieces still on the board, none of them my queen.

Koki had trapped and captured her within his first ten moves. My king was doomed again and I knew it. Just as I started to move, all of the half-dozen hand-wrought Belgian lamps scattered throughout the great room began flickering with light. They were each electric and in seconds the flicker became a solid flood of light. The *shiro* finally had electricity. Koki expressed no emotion and showed no awareness of the change, or it simply didn't matter to him. He continued rocking and staring at the chessboard, waiting for me to move.

Then I heard the music. The sound was faint, very faint, and scratchy like a phonograph record. I focused my hyper-hearing and located the source. It was coming from deep within or behind the stone walls, somewhere between the Fleur-du-Mal's private chambers and Koki's small apartment.

"Koki," I said, "Koki, do you hear the music?"

Before he knew what he was doing, Koki raised his head and smiled. I could see every one of his stained teeth and even smell his breath from across the table. "Yes, mister," Koki said. "She likes the music, hello." A second later he realized what he had done and it scared him. His smile dropped instantly. He bent his head down and resumed his frozen stare at the chessboard, rocking back and forth and moaning slightly.

"Who is 'she,' Koki?" I asked. "You said 'she.' Who is 'she'?" I asked again, but I knew I wasn't going to get any more responses. Koki had retreated completely into himself and the chessboard.

Somehow, I had to find a way to gain Koki's conscious awareness of me without frightening him away. I had to become real in *his* world, not he in mine. As I thought about the problem, I listened closely to the music. I hadn't heard it in years, but I knew the piece. It was one of Solomon's favorite symphonies—Gustav Mahler's Symphony No. 1 in D Major, the work Mahler himself originally titled *Aus dem Leben eines Einsamen,* "from the life of a lonely-one." I thought back to the many times in Carolina's home when Solomon would play the symphony on the phonograph while we were reading or doing other things, such as playing chess. And then it hit me! There might be a unique way to break through to Koki's world. It was a long shot, but I remembered something Solomon had shown me one rainy day when we were listening to Mahler and I was beating him soundly in a game of chess. I had him down to six pieces. Solomon slowly surveyed his remaining pieces, laughed to himself, and then proceeded to checkmate me in six lightning-quick, seemingly irrational moves. I asked him how he had done it and he said Emanual Lasker, the great German champion, had shown him a series of moves, an endgame progression that he called the "Davidsstern," or Star of David. Solomon said the progression would only work in a particular situation and it would probably only work one time against a grandmaster because a grandmaster would never forget the progression once he had seen it. I looked down at the positions of my six remaining pieces on the chessboard. I was in luck. Each piece was in the exact position Solomon's had been. Six crazy, unlikely moves later, I glanced up at Koki. I cleared my throat and said the magic word—"Checkmate."

Koki stopped rocking. He was drooling and his eyeglasses had slipped down his nose, but he didn't wipe his chin or push up his glasses. He only stared at the chessboard. He showed no emotion or expression on his face or in his eyes. He didn't even blink. He just stared down blankly, as if he had simply come to the end of a long sentence and there was nothing left to read. The Fleur-du-Mal had told me that ever since Koki was a boy, since he first learned the rules of the game, he had never been checkmated. Somewhere behind the stone wall, Mahler's symphony began the second movement. Koki raised his head and looked directly into my eyes. He wasn't smiling, but he wasn't afraid.

"Hello, Koki," I said. "My name is Z."

Koki was about to reply when all the electric lamps in the great room went dark and behind the stone wall the music stopped playing. Electricity to the *shiro* had been cut again. We still had light in the great room, but very little. I looked around and only two candles were burning in the wall lamps. Ten seconds later the door to the Fleur-du-Mal's private chambers burst open and the Fleur-du-Mal stormed into the great room. Mumbling and cursing in French, he walked over to a long table against the wall and found a box of candles. Methodically he proceeded to light every wall lamp in the room. Then he walked over to where Koki was sitting and stood behind him, stroking his hair gently from behind. *"Tu me peles le jone,"* he said in a low, bitter voice. Koki stiffened in his chair. The Fleur-du-Mal leaned in closer to Koki's ear and said something in Japanese, then added, "Tea, Koki. Now."

"Yes, mister. Hello," Koki said.

I couldn't be sure, but I thought Koki glanced once more at me before he rose out of his chair and walked out of the room, wiping his chin and adjusting his glasses as he shuffled away.

The Fleur-du-Mal straightened his kimono and turned to take his seat. I quickly and quietly cleared the chessboard. I didn't want him to see the final positions of my game with Koki, or know anything about what Koki had partially revealed. I also decided not to mention the Mahler symphony unless the Fleur-du-Mal brought it up. He knew I possessed the ability of hyper-hearing, but perhaps he didn't know it could extend through stone walls.

Sitting down, he snarled, "Your Americans have complicated my life, Zezen!"

I watched him before I made any reply. As usual, he was being sarcastic, but there was a bitterness and fury in his eyes that reminded me of the Fleur-du-Mal I had always known, not the "gentleman host" he had been recently. And he looked more than angry—he looked dangerous. Slowly I began to reset the chessboard. "I don't believe I have ever considered them *my* Americans," I said.

"You were born there, no?"

"Yes, of course. You know that."

"Then they are *your* Americans." The Fleur-du-Mal paused and crossed his legs, leaning back in his seat. He looked small in the big leather chair. Both of us did. He glanced down at the chessboard.

"Do you want to play a game of chess?" I asked.

"No, *mon petit,* no games. Today we speak of the Meq!"

And that's what we did, only there was no "we" in it. The Fleur-du-Mal took off on another harangue about and against the Meq. He started talking and didn't stop for the next three hours. During that time, Koki brought us tea twice and I got my confirmation that I had broken through to him. On both occasions he glanced at me as he left the room and smiled widely. He had never looked at me before without first being addressed. The second time I winked at him and he smiled even wider, and I knew I was now a part of "Koki's world."

Listening to the Fleur-du-Mal, I waited for the right opportunity to confirm something else—the identity of the "she" Koki had inadvertently exposed. I had an idea of her identity, it could only be one person, but somehow I had to confirm the deception without the Fleur-du-Mal being aware of it. After three hours, I finally got my chance. He was ranting on about the Stones and how he believed they were directly related to consciousness in a specific manner the Meq have either long forgotten or never understood at all.

"This is the ultimate knowledge," he said, "and the Sixth Stone *is* this knowledge, Zezen. Mark my words! I tell you the knowledge is there!"

I was looking down at the chessboard. "It is a shame Susheela the Ninth is no longer available," I said.

"She is useless," he muttered.

I looked up instantly. "What's that?"

He only paused for a heartbeat. "I said she was useless, completely useless, of no consequence, unnecessary. She will not be missed." He paused again and smiled slightly. "Moreover, there are others who may be of assistance."

"Others? What do you mean, 'others'?"

He didn't answer and I didn't persist. I had what I wanted. It wasn't much, but it was enough. While he continued his rambling monologue, I let my mind drift and hatched a plan. It also wasn't much; too obvious, a lot of luck involved, and it all hinged precariously on the unknown reaction of one person—Koki. Still, it was a plan and I was out of options.

The day ended with a simple meal of miso soup and a half-dozen steamed dumplings, during which the Fleur-du-Mal railed once more against the United States, warning of the perverse nature in the power they now possessed. "Even with this power," he said, "believe me, they would stop at nothing to possess the power of the Stones . . . and the ones who carry them." On and on he went, leaping from one thought to the next. Finally, we said good night and I walked into my room alone. In the great room, I heard the Fleur-du-Mal still talking and extinguishing the wall lamps one by one. The last thing I heard him say was, "Process, Zezen, the answer is in the *process*."

The night couldn't pass fast enough for me. I tried not to think ahead, but it was no use. I worried all night about what was wrong with my plan. I was gambling on so many unknown factors. I went through every contingency, and there were many, yet

I still didn't have an answer for the very first problem—the exact words in my first question to Koki. It would make or break the plan. I was already dressed and sitting on the edge of the bed when I heard two sharp raps on my door, followed by the familiar, "Rice, mister." As I was walking to the door, the answer came to me—*a question wouldn't work, it had to be a statement!*

I swung open the door. Koki was smiling and rocking back and forth. He held a candle in one hand and a bowl of steaming rice in the other. His brown eyes were huge and watery behind his glasses, and he was looking directly at me. I let a moment pass, then said the words evenly, one by one, "Take me to the black girl, Koki. Now."

Koki nodded his head up and down. "Yes, hello. Yes," he said without hesitation. I waited for him to say something else, or turn and move. He didn't. Then I realized he had no idea what to do with the rice. His "routine" had not yet been completed. I reached for the bowl and set it down inside my room. "Thank you, Koki," I said. "Now, take me to the black girl."

We started toward the back of the great room, Koki leading the way and staying close to the wall. His candle was the only light in the room and as he shuffled past Goya's head, I glanced at it and stopped. Koki walked on a pace or two before I said, "Wait, Koki." Then, for some unknown reason, I reached out and dislodged the skull from the iron clamps and put it under my arm. "Keep going, Koki," I said. He was staring wide-eyed at the skull and moaning. "It is all right, Koki, it is all right," I repeated. "Keep going."

At the far end of the great room we walked through wide double doors into the kitchen area, then beyond and through a smaller door into Koki's apartment. The room stank of stale tobacco and the scent of sardines. He pushed back a curtain in the corner of the room and opened a heavy wooden door reinforced with three iron straps. The door led to a dark stone passageway. There was a flimsy string of electric lights along the wall, but the electricity was out. I found another candle in the room and lit it, using Koki's candle. He walked ahead of me. The air in the passage became cooler and slightly damp. We took two right turns and passed by three doors, all reinforced in the same manner. At the fourth door, Koki came to a halt. The door was no different from the others except for a long iron key hanging from the wall next to the door. Koki spun around and grinned. "Hello, mister. Yes."

"Yes," I said, grinning back, "yes, Koki, yes!" I handed Goya's skull over to him and said, "Hold this." Koki's mouth dropped open, but he nodded his head and began rocking back and forth, holding his candle high in one hand and Goya tight against his chest with the other. I slipped the ancient key off the hook and inserted it in the lock, then turned it once to the right and heard the click. I pushed on the heavy wooden door. The hinges groaned and creaked from the weight. I held up my candle and took a step inside. I could see a Persian rug beneath my feet, but that was all. Then I heard a match being struck and a small bloom of flame flared in the darkness. In its light I saw her sitting on a bed ten feet away and looking up at me. She lit a candle next to the bed, then looked back at me. She wore black cotton pajamas and slippers. Her hair was cropped close to her head, and her skin was as black as her pajamas. She wore no jewelry, but her eyes sparkled in the candlelight like two brilliant green emeralds. In one second I knew in my heart and mind that she was much, much older than all the rest of us. Susheela the Ninth.

"*Ta ifi dite ifsaah, dite kaa mabayisa,*" she said softly.

I took another step forward. "I'm sorry, but I'm not familiar with your language," I said. "Do you speak English?"

"Most certainly," she answered, smiling slightly and reminding me a great deal of Opari, not only in her features, but also in her speech and manner. She rose to greet me. We were exactly the same height. "My words were these," she said. "'And the light shineth in darkness, and the darkness comprehend it not.'"

"My name is Zianno Zezen, Egizahar Meq, through the tribe of Vardules, protectors of the Stone of Dreams, and I have come to take you out of here." I looked into her intensely green eyes. Inside her gaze there was a deep calm and stillness I had never seen before in anyone's eyes. I was sure it was this utter and complete serenity within her that had frustrated the Fleur-du-Mal to the breaking point. "I know who you are," I said, "but what do I call you?"

"Long ago, in my youth, I was called 'Sheela.' Would that do?"

I smiled and told her that would do just fine, then I told her we must leave immediately.

"I understand," she said. She grabbed a few loose items from the table next to her bed, shoved them into side pockets in her pajamas, and reached for a light shawl draped over a chair, but nothing else. She turned to me. "Shall we?"

I paused at the doorway. In the passage Koki was still rocking and holding Goya tight. Behind me, she asked, "Do you know of a secret exit?"

"Not exactly, but I'm pretty sure *he* does." I nodded toward Koki.

"Koki?" she asked, raising her eyebrows. "You are depending on Koki?"

"Yes. If I know the Fleur-du-Mal, there is another exit from this level of the *shiro*, a hidden one, probably dating from when the level was used as a torture chamber and prison. That's what would have attracted him to the property. I'm betting Koki knows where it is."

"And you believe Koki will lead us to this exit? He is not capable of such behavior."

"He is today." I pulled the door shut and placed the key back on its hook. "Koki," I said, "show us the way out . . . the other way." Koki looked at me and acknowledged me, but didn't respond. He seemed confused. I reached out and took Goya's skull from him. I was worried I had scared him and fear was the last thing I wanted him to feel.

Suddenly Susheela the Ninth stepped forward. *"Dedoko,"* she said quietly. *"Dedoko . . . kakushigoto . . . kakushigoto,* Koki."

Koki wiped his chin, pushed his glasses up, and grinned. His stained teeth looked black in the faint light of the candles. "Yes, hello," he said, and turned around, shuffling away through the darkened passage, not waiting for us.

I glanced at Susheela the Ninth. "I don't know what you said, but thank you . . . Sheela."

She smiled at hearing her childhood name. "I told Koki you wanted the *secret* exit, and you are welcome . . . Zianno."

"Call me Z," I said, then motioned her ahead of me. "Shall we?"

Koki picked up the pace and we walked by three more doors before the passage came to a T. We took a left and stopped in front of another door, which resembled the others in every way, except that when Koki opened the door there was no bedroom or cell inside. This door led to an iron spiral staircase winding up and disappearing into darkness.

"Yes, hello," Koki said.

"Hello, yes, Koki!" I replied, glancing up. "Follow me." I held the candle high. Susheela the Ninth fell in behind me and we started up. After climbing one full revolution, I looked down and noticed Koki still standing at the bottom of the stairs. He hadn't moved. Then I realized he couldn't. Climbing up and out of the *shiro* was too much for him. He had done what he was told, but leaving the *shiro* was out of the question. Tomorrow he would likely forget that he had helped at all. Tomorrow he would remember nothing about the incident, including Susheela the Ninth and me, and yesterday, for Koki, was inconceivable. He was looking up through the steps of the spiral stairs, watching us. He wiped his chin once. "Good-bye, Koki," I said. "You play a great game of chess."

His face widened into his biggest grin and he nodded his head, however, I'm not sure he comprehended a word. "Yes, mister," he said. "Hello."

I glanced at Susheela the Ninth. Her smooth black skin was shining in the glow of the candles. "Let's go," I said, and started climbing, almost running up the spiral stairs. With every step I thought of Opari—her eyes, her lips, her voice. I decided not to stop until we got to the last step, wherever it might lead. Behind me, Susheela the Ninth kept pace easily.

After what I guessed to be five or six stories, we came to the top of the spiral. The final step led directly to a low and narrow hallway about ten feet long and lined with cedar. At the end of the hallway was a square window with louvered shutters. I pushed open the shutters and looked out. We were three stories above the courtyard, and the only way down was across and over the curved, sloping roof of the third tier, then a drop to the second tier, then the first tier and on down to the graveled courtyard. If this had been an "escape hatch" in the past, it had not been a good one. We crawled onto the tiled roof and carefully made our way to the edge. I looked up and breathed deeply. The early morning fresh air felt cool and wonderful. Below us, to the south and west, fog spread over the Urakami Valley all the way to the sea and beyond. Nagasaki was not visible.

We took turns hanging and dropping from tier to tier, and each time, I tossed Goya's head down to Susheela the Ninth before I dropped. When we reached the courtyard, she asked, "Why do you carry this skull? What is its significance?"

"I don't know," I said, "I mean . . . I'm not sure." It was a stupid answer, yet it was true.

As quickly and quietly as we could, we covered the distance to the gatehouse and gate, which was locked. I paused long enough to look inside the gatehouse. It was empty. Within the last five days, someone had removed the body of Shutratek. Just then something made me turn and look back at the *shiro*. For a split second, in an open window on the highest tier of the stone tower, I thought I saw two green eyes staring down at me, but they disappeared instantly. Susheela the Ninth was already over the gate and waiting for me on the other side. Could it have been the Fleur-du-Mal? Had he been watching us from the beginning? Was he letting us escape?

"Why do you hesitate, Z?" she asked. "We must make haste."

"Sorry," I said, shaking my head once and tossing Goya to her. I scrambled up and over the gate. In another minute, the *shiro* was out of sight and we were on our way out of the hills and down to Nagasaki.

We ran, walked, and ran some more. I had no certain destination in mind, but unconsciously I was heading toward the railway and Urakami Station. Even in the hills, we passed many people, some with nothing, some with their meager belongings piled on a wagon or cart. Whether young or old, man or woman, their faces and expressions were devoid of all feeling and life. None of them paid any attention to us. We were invisible to them. They were living and walking, yet their eyes were dead. I kept thinking of Opari to keep from thinking about Sailor and Sak. I could not imagine the kind of unspeakable mass destruction and death these pitiful people had witnessed. I knew many were also dying from radiation as they walked, and for those who lived on and survived, even into old age, life would never be the same.

At one point, we paused to rest in a small open-air shrine by the side of the road. We sat on one of two stone benches inside. Below us, the morning fog blanketing Nagasaki and the Urakami Valley began to slowly burn off and dissipate.

Susheela the Ninth turned to me. "Who is this one you think of repeatedly, Z?"

Her question startled me. "What? How did you know what I was thinking? I never said a word."

"It was unnecessary. Your heart and mind were shouting."

I stared at her with brand-new wonder and respect. As far as I knew, this was an "ability" no other Meq had ever possessed. "Is it mental telepathy? Is that what you did?"

"Not quite; however, it is an ancient trait common to my tribe. Another form of communication, if you will—older, simpler. The trait has been a great aid in my survival."

I looked long into the emerald green eyes of Susheela the Ninth, once again amazed at how little I truly knew or understood about the Meq. I cleared my throat and said, "Opari. Her name is Opari . . . she is my Ameq."

"I see." She paused and glanced away, then smiled to herself. "Opari," she said slowly, one syllable at a time. "A beautiful name. I believe it means *gift* in the Basque tongue. Correct?"

"Yes."

"Where is Opari now? I do not suspect she is near."

"No, she's nowhere near, and I give thanks for that. As far as I know, before the bomb, she was still somewhere in China."

Susheela the Ninth dropped her smile. "Bomb? To what bomb are you referring?"

I looked out over the thinning fog. Spreading out below us, the Urakami Valley or what was left of it was gradually becoming visible, and it was worse than I imagined. "He didn't tell you? The Fleur-du-Mal didn't tell you what happened five days ago in Nagasaki?"

"No. Xanti never speaks of the Japanese war. He only speaks of Mahler, and painting, and the Sixth Stone, of course. Now, what do you mean, Z—'before the bomb'?"

The fog had almost cleared. From our angle in the hills, it now appeared that all of Nagasaki had been annihilated, leaving nothing but a sprawling black scar, a dead zone of vast proportions. "Look there, Sheela," I said, "look down there and try to conceive of a bomb causing that devastation in a split second, a single bomb with the power of a thousand suns. Eight days ago, the Americans dropped the first one over Hiroshima. Five days ago, they dropped another one on Nagasaki." A few moments passed. "I knew someone . . . someone who was in Nagasaki."

"Yes, I know," she said.

"You know? How could you possibly know that?"

"Never mind," she said. "What do they call this bomb?"

"An atom bomb . . . they call it the atom bomb."

She gazed out and down at the nightmare of Nagasaki in the distance, then rose to her feet without changing expression. "Take us down there, Z."

For the next forty-five minutes, Susheela the Ninth and I did not speak, not to each other or to anyone else. Nor will I speak of it now. I will not desecrate the countless missing souls of that place, or the burned and broken bodies and vacant stares of the survivors. We walked among and through a true hell on earth. Without realizing it, I dropped Goya's skull somewhere along the way. Even if I tried, there are no adequate words for what we saw, and it must never happen again.

Incredibly, the Urakami Station was open and trains were running. No plant, tree, or structure anywhere near the station had survived. I looked up and the giant statue of Shofukuji was gone forever. The stench of death was ever present all the way to the entrance. Suddenly, in my mind I had a "vision" of the Fleur-du-Mal. He was sitting in his kitchen with Koki, polishing various pieces of ancient copper kitchenware and listening to Mahler's Symphony No. 1, and he was grinning. His perfect white teeth sparkled. I blinked several times, then cleared my eyes and continued walking. Not twenty feet away, the bloated carcass of a dead horse was the last thing I saw as we entered the station.

Once we were inside, Susheela the Ninth seemed to slow down and lag behind. I thought nothing of it and walked ahead five or six paces, then just as suddenly as the "vision" had come, I felt an extremely strong presence jolt my mind and body like a live current. The presence was Meq and very familiar. I never thought I would feel his presence again, or see him again, but this one had surprised and amazed me many times over. I turned the corner and there he was. He stood with arms crossed, leaning casually against the tiled wall, waiting. He wore a cone-shaped straw hat pulled down low on his forehead. When I approached, he pushed the hat up slowly and shook his head from side to side, as if he were slightly annoyed with me. It was Sailor.

"You are late," he said.

"I am?"

"Yes—we must hurry. The train to Kobe and Osaka leaves in less than five minutes."

Susheela the Ninth walked up silently beside me. Even though she was a black girl in black pajamas, people passing by paid no attention to her or to us. Nagasaki was too grim and surreal for us to be noticed. I gazed into Sailor's eyes. He had never looked so good, and his "ghost eye," which ever since the death of his Ameq, Deza, had been a gray, swirling cloud was now absolutely clear. "I thought you were—"

"Dead?" he finished.

"Yes. How in the world—"

"I will explain later," he said, then glanced at Susheela the Ninth for the first time. "Now we must move, and move quickly."

"Sak?" I asked.

Sailor shook his head back and forth once.

"But—"

"I am somewhat like the cockroach, Zianno. I shall survive, regardless of the circumstances."

My mouth dropped open. "You know the *Cockroach*?"

Sailor gave me a quizzical look, then shook his head and led the three of us away toward the trains, talking about a merchant in Osaka as he walked. He reached for Susheela the Ninth's hand and she gave it to him without hesitation. Somehow, I knew he had been expecting her. As we were buying our tickets, Sailor turned to me and whispered, "No, I do not know the *Cockroach*. The only cockroach with which I am familiar is an insect, and to the best of my knowledge, unable to speak." He paused for a heartbeat. "Do you happen to know a cockroach that speaks, Zianno?"

I smiled, following him through the turnstile. I thought of Koki still deep inside the *shiro* in the hills above Nagasaki, probably smoking a cigarette or playing another game of chess, wiping his chin and pushing his glasses up the bridge of his nose. By now, I was sure Koki had completely forgotten Susheela the Ninth and me and what he had done for us. Whether or not the Fleur-du-Mal had allowed it to happen became moot and meaningless. Sailor stopped and waited for an explanation. I walked by Sailor and whispered, "Yes. Yes, I do know a cockroach that speaks," then added, "he is a good friend of mine . . . and the best chess player in the world."

2

ZORI
(LUCK)

Luck, like beauty to the eye, is truly in the mind of the believer. Consider the tale of the Basque shepherd who one morning left to tend his flock. By midday, while crossing one of the highest and most treacherous passes, a sudden blizzard blinded them for hours. When the storm passed, the shepherd found a lamb stranded on a precarious ledge. As he crept out to save the lamb, he dislodged a hawk's nest hidden in the cliff. The angry mother hawk flew at the shepherd and plucked out his right eye with one sweep of her talons. The shepherd lost his balance and grabbed for the lamb, dragging them both over the ledge. They dropped nearly twenty feet to another ledge and rolled over as they landed, crushing the shepherd's left leg and making it useless. He cried out in agony, but miraculously crawled off the ledge with the lamb. Using his walking stick for a crutch, he was able to gather the rest of his flock and make his way out of the pass and down to the meadow near his home. He later lost his leg and wore an eye patch for the rest of his life. Whenever asked to recount that horrific day, the shepherd would always smile and gladly tell his tale, ending with the words, "It was the luckiest day of my life." Then with a quick wink of his one good eye, "After all, my friend . . . it could have been night."

The train was crowded and chaotic. Sailor led the way, followed by Susheela the Ninth, then me. We slipped through and around each person like sleight-of-hand magicians, barely touching anyone or even being seen until we'd already passed. Sailor and Susheela the Ninth were ancient masters of the trick, and I was getting better. Inside the train the air was stifling, even though every window was wide open. We squeezed into a narrow seat at the rear of our compartment, along with an old woman carrying a pumpkin in her lap. The pumpkin was wrapped in a ragged blanket, and she had the saddest eyes I'd ever seen. She saw the face and hands of Susheela the Ninth and asked Sailor in Japanese if the great bomb had turned the girl's skin black. Sailor waited a moment, then told her, yes, it was true, the bomb had done it. The answer satisfied the old woman and seemed to confirm something in her mind. She glanced once more at Susheela the Ninth, then looked away from us for the rest of the time she was on the train.

I turned to Sailor. He anticipated my question and answered before I said a word. He spoke in English, but low so only I could hear. "Luck," he whispered. "In a word, Zianno, it was simply luck that I survived. I was in the right place at the right time, while Sak was in the wrong place at the wrong time. The circumstances could have easily been reversed. But now is not the right time or place to tell you everything. Later, Zianno, later."

Our train headed north and east, changing routes and making several detours. Just minutes before noon, we made yet another unscheduled stop in a small station near Kurashiki. As the train came to a halt, Sailor and I leaned our heads out the window. The station was filled with people, but they weren't waiting for the train. Every single person on the platform or inside the station was gathered around the loudspeakers. Many had their heads bowed in reverence. Then the Japanese national anthem, "Kimi Ga Yo," began playing through the loudspeakers. When it came to a close, an announcer said the next speaker would be the Emperor of Japan. Sailor turned his head and gave me a quick look of disbelief. We both knew this had never happened before. The voice was thin and high-pitched. *"To our good and loyal subjects,"* the Emperor began. *"After pondering deeply the general trends of the world, and the actual conditions in our Empire today, we have decided to effect a settlement of the present situation by resorting to an extraordinary measure."* At the end of the speech, it became evident Japan had surrendered unconditionally. In twenty-six hundred years, Japan had never surrendered to anyone or any country. No one in the crowd or on the train shouted or cried out with joy. Many were confused from the courtly language, some were praying, but most were sad and in tears, including the old woman next to us. She stared down at her pumpkin and held it even tighter. I only had one thought—World War II was over.

Sailor looked at me, whispering between his teeth, "We must leave these islands!"

I whispered back, "What about the Fleur-du-Mal? In case you didn't know, he's still alive and well."

"The Fleur-du-Mal is no longer relevant," Sailor said, exchanging subtle glances with Susheela the Ninth. He had not yet addressed her by name and she had barely spoken. "We have everything we want from him," Sailor added. "The Fleur-du-Mal has become obsolete, Zianno."

I didn't respond, but I didn't agree. The Fleur-du-Mal had lied to me about Susheela the Ninth and her existence. He could have also been lying about everything else, including the "futility of vendettas." And though the Fleur-du-Mal may or may not be relevant, I knew he would never be obsolete. In a few minutes our train began to pull slowly out of the small station and continue on to Osaka. I watched the fields and tiny farms pass in silence. The Japanese countryside was beautiful. It was the middle of August and the grasses and trees were deep green. I let my mind drift away from war and the Fleur-du-Mal and thought about St. Louis and Forest Park . . . and Opari.

• • •

Once we were off the train and walking the streets of Osaka, it became much easier to go unnoticed. The great city had been devastated in several areas from heavy incendiary bombing, and after the Emperor's speech many people seemed almost in a state of shock. We did see a few patrols and truckloads of drunken soldiers driving wildly through downtown, crashing liquor bottles in the street and screaming that the war would go on. Most people simply watched them, unmoved and unaffected. Finally, just after dark, we found the address Sailor had been seeking. The house was on the south side of the Dotonbori Canal in the Minami section. Sailor said we were looking for a man named Katsuo Gidayu, the last in a long line of masters in the art of Bunraku, or traditional puppet theater.

"Do you know this man?" I asked.

"No," Sailor replied.

"I don't understand. Then why are we here?"

"Do you remember the dinner we had many years ago in St. Louis, Zianno, when Solomon and I recalled our first meeting in Macao?"

"Yes, of course. Solomon said you were 'too easily found.'"

"Well, what can I say? He may have been right. The point is, I told you I was waiting for someone."

"I assumed it was Solomon."

"It was not Solomon for whom I was waiting. I was waiting for Takeda Gidayu, Katsuo's father. The Gidayu family has, how shall I say, *assisted* the Meq on several occasions throughout the last three centuries. Takeda and Geaxi were especially good friends." Sailor paused, removing his odd straw hat and surveying the crowded street. "I am hoping he told his son about us. If so, we can be assured he will help us."

"What if he didn't?"

Sailor ignored my comment and knocked softly on the door.

After several moments the door opened and all three of us were looking into the beautiful dark eyes of a girl exactly our height. She gazed back at us, glancing at Sailor and me, then staring at Susheela the Ninth. I was certain she had never seen black skin before.

In Japanese, Sailor asked, "Is your father here?"

The girl focused on Sailor. "No," she answered. "My father is dead. He was a soldier."

Sailor waited a heartbeat. "I see," he said. "Are you alone? Is there no one else?"

The girl paused and looked hard at Susheela the Ninth again. "My grandfather is here."

"Is his name Katsuo?"

Suddenly, from somewhere inside the house, a booming male voice asked, "Who wishes to know?"

"I do," Sailor said.

A middle-aged man appeared behind the girl. He was tall, well over six feet. "Who are you, boy?" the man asked. His hands and long fingers were resting on the girl's shoulders.

Sailor then did something unique and unexpected. He had not been wearing his star sapphire because the ring would have drawn attention to us. Instead, he had kept it hidden inside his pants pocket. Never losing eye contact with the man, Sailor held his index finger, his ring finger, out to his side. Then, using his "ability" of telekinesis, Sailor made the ring move slowly out of his pocket. Silently, magically, the ring traveled into the air and over to his hand, where it slid down gently and into place on his finger. *"Egibizirik bilatu,"* Sailor said. "I am Umla-Meq, a friend of Takeda Gidayu."

The big man's eyes widened and so did the girl's. He backed

away a pace or two and bowed deeply from the waist three times. It was a formal, courtly gesture and the girl seemed confused. She watched her grandfather with an open mouth, as if she had never seen him do such a thing. "I am Katsuo Gidayu," the man said, "Takeda Gidayu's son." He looked once at Susheela the Ninth and me, then back to Sailor, and I knew he knew we were Meq. "I am honored by your presence," he said. "How may I serve you?"

Sailor smiled slightly. "We need shelter."

"It shall be our pleasure . . . for as long as you need it, sir."

"Please, formalities are unnecessary, Katsuo. You may call me 'Sailor.'"

"Yes, sir, if you so desire."

The girl was pulling on her grandfather's arm. He bent over so she could whisper something to him, which she did. When he straightened up he told Sailor his granddaughter, Ikuko, was foolish and unsophisticated, but if it would not offend, she had a question for the black girl.

Speaking flawless Japanese, Susheela the Ninth responded to the man herself, saying, "Yes, most certainly, and it would not offend." She looked directly at the girl, who was still clinging to her grandfather's arm. "You may ask me anything, Ikuko, anything at all. What do you wish to know?"

The girl relaxed a little and said, "Are you from Africa?"

Susheela the Ninth smiled wide and laughed, reminding me again of Opari. "Yes . . . yes I am," she said. "Have you ever heard of a land named Ethiopia?"

Ikuko glanced up at her grandfather, shy and unsure what to do or say. Katsuo simply nodded his head and told her to answer. She stared back at Susheela the Ninth. "Yes," she said in a tiny voice. "I think so."

Sailor and I laughed and Katsuo welcomed us all into his home. Immediately I could smell wonderful scents and aromas emanating from the kitchen and closed my eyes to breathe them and taste them. Katsuo must have seen me. *"Takoyaki,"* he said. "Octopus dumplings and udon with ginger."

Sailor gave me a wink with his "ghost eye," which was still clear. I knew he loved octopus. In English, he whispered, "Heaven."

The meal was delicious. Katsuo and Ikuko shared everything with us, even though it was apparent they had been living a spare and harsh existence. Katsuo told us his only son, who was the father of Ikuko, was killed in combat and her mother had died during a bombing raid on Kobe. He said he had to close the family's puppet theater in 1942, and since then he and Ikuko had been living by their wits, scrounging what they could however they could. Luckily, Katsuo said, he knew many people and had many friends. He thought the entire war was a mistake from the beginning and Japan had been insane to attack the United States. He talked at length about the Emperor's speech, the surrender, and the vague future of Japan. Oddly, he never said a word about Hiroshima or Nagasaki. None of us mentioned the horrors we had witnessed in Nagasaki. Several times Katsuo said he wanted to reopen his theater, but admitted it would be extremely difficult for a variety of reasons, not the least of which was financing. "The people need the puppets," he said, "they need to lighten their hearts from all the losses they have suffered."

Soon after our meal, we were led to an unoccupied room with windows on three sides, and each of us was offered a tatami mat on which to sleep. Ikuko had already become fast friends with Susheela the Ninth and gave her some of her own clothes to wear, including a pair of shoes and clean pajamas. In return, Susheela the Ninth told Ikuko to call her "Sheela" and then gave her two ancient loop earrings made of ivory, gold, and lapis lazuli, which she had quickly shoved into her pajama pockets as we were leaving the Fleur-du-Mal's castle. Ikuko was barely able to speak. I think she wore them to bed that night, much to Katsuo's amusement. He told Sailor he hadn't seen her smile in over a year.

At last, the long and complicated day was coming to an end. I felt bone-tired and longed for sleep. I still had questions, but my curiosity was outweighed by my fatigue. As Sailor and I were stretching out on our tatami mats, Susheela the Ninth, without any inhibitions, began removing her black pajamas and putting on the clean pair given to her by Ikuko. Instinctively, I averted my eyes. Sailor saw me look away and asked, "What is the matter, Zianno? Have you never seen a girl naked? After all, she is only in the body of a child."

Before I could respond, Susheela the Ninth laughed and said, "A very old child, I might add."

I was embarrassed and tried to cover it up with a question. "Exactly how old are you, Sheela?"

" 'Sheela'?" Sailor interjected. "You address her as 'Sheela'?"

"Yes. I was told to do so."

"That is correct," she said, buttoning her pajama top and sitting down cross-legged on her mat. "I informed Z he should call me by my childhood name, and so should you . . . Umla-Meq." Sailor nodded once, but said nothing and Sheela turned to me. "I am older than the earrings, much older."

"The earrings?" I asked.

"Yes, the earrings I gave to Ikuko. They were presented to me three thousand two hundred eighty-eight years ago in Amarna by a handmaiden of Queen Nefertiti. By that year, I had experienced one thousand seven hundred eighteen birthdays, including my first eleven. This year, in your month of October, I will have my next."

At first, I was dumbfounded and blinked rapidly several times, trying to calculate the numbers in my mind. "That would mean you are going to be . . ."

With no trace of wonder or emotion, Susheela the Ninth said, "I will be five thousand and six years old on the day you Americans call 'Halloween.'"

I couldn't say a word. I couldn't even conceive of a life that long, particularly without the aid of the Stones. Sailor said calmly, "Trumoi-Meq and Zeru-Meq would be impressed."

"Would they?" she asked, looking directly at Sailor. Her voice had a slight edge of irony and melancholy. "It has not been easy, Umla-Meq . . . and it has been lonely."

I thought of Mama and Papa and their endless journeys, and I realized their travels and travails were nothing compared to what Susheela the Ninth must have seen and done in order to survive so long. I now had many more questions for her; however, I was simply too tired to ask them. Outside, a light rain began to fall. Sailor turned off the single lamp in the room and we all lay down on our mats to wait for sleep. For some reason, I recalled a poem Zeru-Meq had carved into a tree years earlier when we were searching for him in China. It was titled "The Quiet Rain" and went like this:

> In the back of our lives, steady and soft, a rain falls.
> We sleep through it, then wake at the sound of a distant train.
> Just in time to hear the quiet rain.
> Behind that, deep in darkness,
> The grinding crickets.

When I awoke in the morning I was alone in the room. After rubbing the sleep from my eyes, I found Sailor standing in the kitchen brewing tea. Katsuo, Ikuko, and Susheela the Ninth were not in the house.

Sailor had his back to me, but felt my presence. "I have a plan," he said.

"I don't want to hear it," I said quickly. "Not yet. I want you to tell me what happened in Nagasaki. How did you survive, and what about Zuriaa?"

Sailor sighed and poured tea for both of us, then turned to face me. "Very well, Zianno, though I have already told you it was sheer luck. Sit down and I shall give you the facts." I sat down and Sailor stirred his tea before beginning. "By the evening of August 8, after leaving you and Shutratek that morning, Sak and I had found the Fleur-du-Mal's *shiro* with little difficulty. The old castle was tucked away in a crowded neighborhood along the Nakashima River, not far from the harbor. The building itself was somewhat dilapidated and seemed abandoned. However, I knew this could be a ruse; the Fleur-du-Mal has used such deceptions in the past. Sak and I decided to wait and observe the castle through the night. No one entered or exited, nor did we see any signs of life within. By mid-morning of August 9, just as we were about to seek a way inside, Zuriaa suddenly appeared at the gate, paused a moment to look in every direction, and began walking briskly to the north. Sak turned to me and said, "I will follow her." There was no forethought or plan, Zianno. I could have said the same thing to him. I told Sak I would stay at the *shiro* and discover what was inside. I watched him walk away, keeping his distance behind Zuriaa. I never saw either of them again. Twenty-five minutes later, the bomb exploded."

"Where were you?"

"Three stories below ground. I assumed an earthquake had occurred. The entire structure shook violently. Within seconds my only exit had been blocked completely by fallen stone and I was left in total darkness in a subterranean dungeon. The dropping of an atomic bomb never crossed my mind." Sailor paused and took several sips of tea.

"What did you do next?" I asked.

"Once my eyes had adjusted as best they could, I explored the large space of the room. Even in darkness, it became apparent Zuriaa, or someone, had been living in these quarters. Eventually I located matches and an oil lamp. In the dim light, I saw countless sculptures, paintings, manuscripts, and maps strewn throughout the room. I expected another tremor at any moment and carefully examined the walls and ceiling of the structure itself. The *shiro* was old, indeed, but well constructed and I felt relatively safe. I then decided to investigate the various artifacts and wait for the earth to settle. Also, I knew instinctively Susheela the Ninth, or 'Sheela' as you call her, was nowhere to be found, although I did feel the residue of her presence."

"What do you mean by that?"

"This is difficult to explain. It is a phenomenon and I am still struggling with it." Sailor poured more tea for himself, took another sip, and continued. "Approximately two days later I emerged from the dungeon of the *shiro* only to be confronted by the total annihilation of everything around me. It was then I realized there had been no earthquake and something much more destructive and demonic had occurred—an atomic bomb."

"But how did you escape? I thought you said your exit was entirely blocked with fallen stone."

"Yes . . . it was," he said, then glanced at the pot of tea on the table in front of us. Without warning, the pot rose by itself into the air and sort of danced in a circle, then settled down gently on the table.

I looked at Sailor. I said nothing, but understood immediately. Sailor smiled faintly, rubbing his star sapphire with his thumb. The mystical and astonishing power of telekinesis! "Have I never told you how I came to wear this ring, Zianno?" Sailor asked, slipping the brilliant blue star sapphire from his finger and holding it to the light, staring, admiring the six separate shafts of color that shot in all directions from its heart.

I had always wondered and never asked. "No," I said. "You have not."

"It was a gift," Sailor whispered. "The last one . . . from Deza."

Just then I heard voices coming into the house. Susheela the Ninth was thanking Katsuo for showing her the family's theater and teaching her about Bunraku and its history. Sailor and I only had a few more moments alone. Quickly I asked him what he did once he was above ground. He said he ran out of the city as fast as Geaxi, following the Urakami River northward. For the next forty-eight hours he wandered the countryside, dazed from what he had seen in Nagasaki.

Katsuo and Ikuko were entering the kitchen, followed closely by Susheela the Ninth. Ikuko was laughing and talking and wearing her new earrings, which were older than Japan. In a whisper, I asked Sailor, "How did you know we were going to be at Urakami Station?"

Sailor leaned forward in his chair. His "ghost eye" was clear and focused. "I received instructions and directions," he whispered back.

"Instructions? From where . . . from whom?"

Sailor raised his head and nodded toward Susheela the Ninth, his eyes watching her every move. I had never seen him look at anyone in quite the same way. "From her," he said.

> You, my priceless locksmith,
> all milk and lace, all new and
> untraceable.

There are more mysteries in one heart and mind than can be counted. As Susheela the Ninth and Ikuko began peeling a few

scrawny carrots and washing some celery sticks, Sailor started
outlining his "plan" to Katsuo and me. I was listening, but thinking back to Norway and Askenfada when Sailor had first set eyes
on Susheela the Ninth. We were searching for the Fleur-du-
Mal and the Octopus. Sailor told me later her mind had spoken
to his mind in the voice of Deza, his one and only Ameq. I
didn't give it much credence at the time, or at least thought he
might have been exaggerating. Now I knew he had been telling
the absolute truth. Once Susheela the Ninth and I had escaped
the Fleur-du-Mal's castle, she must have been "communicating"
with Sailor, letting him know where she was and where to go. I
know I kept heading toward Urakami Station without realizing
why.

It had never happened before, but could it be so? Could a
Meq, could Sailor, have found his second Ameq?

"We are all aware of the dangers in traveling together," Sailor
was saying. "However, with Katsuo's consummate knowledge in
theater and skills of expression . . ." he went on. But I was thinking back. I recalled the moment at Caitlin's Ruby when Geaxi
and I were using "the Voice" to awaken Charles Lindbergh as he
flew across the Atlantic in the *Spirit of St. Louis*. We were joined
by someone else, someone Meq. Nova was present, yet the other
presence and voice did not belong to her or anyone else. It felt
strong and intoxicating. Geaxi referred to it later as male, but
whose voice was it? And from where had "he" come? I reminded
myself to discuss this with Opari when I saw her next. I wondered where she was. What if—

"Well, Zianno? Do you agree or disagree with this option?"

"I . . . I . . ."

"We shall be depending, of course, on an American sense of
guilt, as well as good-heartedness."

"I . . ."

Sailor's eyes glanced up at Susheela the Ninth, then settled back on me. "Hawaii is where we need to be, Zianno."

I had no idea what his "plan" was or what he'd said, but Hawaii sounded good to me. "Yes, I agree . . . Hawaii is where we need to be."

Later that night the three of us were in our room, lying in the dark on our tatami mats. The light rain of the previous evening had given way to a steamy, big-city heat. Our three windows were wide open. I confessed to Sailor I had been daydreaming as he elaborated his "plan," and I was completely ignorant of the whole thing. He assured me not to worry, I had plenty of time to hear it again. We would take no action until the Americans were in Japan and the occupation had begun. "Until then," Sailor reminded us, "we should stay close to Katsuo's home, only venturing outside at night to steal food or other necessities. For the sake of Katsuo and Ikuko, we must not be seen."

"Steal food? Did you say 'steal food'?" I asked.

"Yes," Sailor answered. "If stealing is required, then we shall steal. We have no reason to extend Katsuo's hospitality into providing sustenance for us." Sailor waited a moment. "I say we should extend and provide his sustenance instead, particularly by pilfering an odd bit or two from the few remaining decent restaurants in Osaka." He paused again. "This should be relatively easy for you, Zianno. I believe you were at one time a professional thief under Captain Woodget's tutelage, no?"

I laughed once in the dark. "I think the good captain referred to it as *smuggling*."

"Ah, yes, of course, I see my error," Sailor said with great sarcasm. "A much more honorable position and higher moral ground . . . no doubt, no doubt."

I laughed again and Susheela the Ninth, or Sheela, as even Sailor was calling her now, joined in the laughter. We continued talking and covered many subjects, including telekinesis, telepathy, and other phenomena. The talk was loose and open. Sailor did a lot of the speaking, but so did Sheela. Parts of a puzzle were revealed in reverse. She said when she beat us to the Octopus in Egypt, she knew Xanti and three others were also seeking it, but she assumed the others were working with Xanti, not against him. She had no idea one of the others was Umla-Meq. It wasn't until she was captured and taken to Norway that she learned the truth.

"How long have you known of the Fleur-du-Mal?" I asked her.

"For centuries," she answered. "I have always thought him to be a considerable nuisance."

"*Nuisance!* He is an assassin, a ruthless murderer and torturer!"

"Yes, I know, Z, and I do not mean to diminish his crimes or your abhorrence of them. However, in truth, Xanti is only a sad little boy. I do not think he can help himself."

"Zeru-Meq once thought the same way," I snapped back. Sheela said nothing. I took a deep breath and calmed down. "He has since changed his mind. If Xanti is a sad little boy, then he is the most dangerous one on earth." Despite their longevity, or perhaps because of it, I felt both Sailor and Sheela were being complacent concerning the Fleur-du-Mal. For me, it was personal. With my own eyes I had seen him slit the throat of Carolina's sister, Georgia, and that was no "little boy" who carved bloody roses into the backs of Mrs. Bennings and countless others. I decided to change the subject. "Sheela, why did you leave the papyrus in Salzburg, along with a note for Umla-Meq?"

Susheela the Ninth sat up suddenly. The lights of the city filtered through the windows and I could see her green eyes staring at me. "Papyrus! You know of the papyrus?"

I sat up. "Yes. I've seen it and read it."

"How is this possible?" she asked.

"A friend of mine, Ray Ytuarte, became good friends with Baroness Matilde von Steichen. She showed him your room, the portraits by Vermeer and Botticelli, and the papyrus. He brought it to us."

She turned to Sailor, who also sat up. "Umla-Meq, this is so? You have *read* the papyrus?"

"Yes," Sailor answered. "Or I should say, Zianno read it to me. I cannot read the old script."

"No one has ever been able to read the papyrus."

"Yes, well," Sailor said and paused, "Zianno Zezen can."

"*Ta ifi dite ifsaah!* Z, this 'ability,' is it true?"

"Yes," I answered, "but I have never thought of it as an 'ability.'"

"Oh, but it is, Z, it is . . . it is a magnificent 'ability,' and more fundamental and necessary to the Meq than either telekinesis or telepathy." She paused a moment and seemed to catch her breath. "You must tell me what the writing says."

"I will, and then we will discuss what it says and means, but first things first. Where did you get the papyrus, Sheela? Tell me its history."

She sighed deeply. "Ah, yes . . . yes." She waited another heartbeat. "After all this time . . ." she said, shaking her head and smiling. Her perfect, ancient teeth gleamed white in the faint light. It was late at night and the big port city was unusually dark and quiet. Even the crickets had surrendered.

I suppose I didn't realize it at the time, yet Susheela the Ninth must have understood intuitively that when I asked about the papyrus, I was really asking about her. She talked softly for two hours that night and two more the next, and then on and off for the next two nights. During these "talks" she not only revealed the history of the papyrus, but she also gave Sailor and me a brief history of her own long and extraordinary life.

We learned that she left the papyrus in Salzburg in order to pursue the Octopus and the possibility of possessing what it was supposed to contain. Her tribe had long known of the five Stones, but their only interest was in the mythical Sixth Stone. Its power was believed to answer all mysteries behind the Meq and our existence. It was also thought to answer the riddle of the Re-membering, an event they knew was coming, they just didn't know when or where. The papyrus and its cryptic inscription had been copied from another papyrus, which was also said to have been copied from something much older—a solid, polished stone ball. The original "copy" had been carried by another Meq, a mysterious loner who dealt in precious metals and was known simply as the "Black Sea boy," or sometimes as "the Thra-cian." He was thought to have perished, along with his papyrus, when the island of Thera, now referred to as Santorini, disinte-grated in a massive volcanic explosion. At that time, the second papyrus always traveled in the possession of Susheela the Ninth's much older cousin, Tereksaa. He was the one other member of her tribe still living. He had been born in western Africa before the Sahara became a desert, when it was still a lush savanna. It was from Tereksaa that Susheela the Ninth first learned there were other Meq in the world, including light-skinned tribes to the north and west, across a great sea, living in the mountains and along the coast of another land, a land now known as the Pyrenees. They were the ones, she was told, who carried the five Stones.

She said she and Tereksaa wandered the Near East and the eastern Mediterranean for centuries until a mad Assyrian king in the city-state of Urak managed to capture Tereksaa. The practice of child sacrifice to gain favor from the gods was the king's obsession, especially if the child happened to be one of the "Magic Children" he had heard the Phoenicians brag about. Just before Tereksaa was caught and beheaded, he transferred the papyrus to Susheela the Ninth with instructions to keep it safe until she could deliver it to one of the light-skinned Meq in the west—the one called Umla-Meq. And she kept it safe for century after century and a thousand tales of survival until late in 1921 when she first heard the rumor that the Octopus could exist and might be hidden in Tutankhamen's tomb. A man named Howard Carter was going to excavate in the Valley of the Kings to search for the tomb. The temptation was too great for her. Find the Octopus— find the Sixth Stone! She left the papyrus in Salzburg, always planning to return. She was on her way back when the Fleur-du-Mal captured her in Istanbul, and together with Raza, the three of them made their way to Askenfada in Norway. We knew the rest.

"Now the irony is complete," she said, lying back in the dark and laughing to herself.

"Irony?" I asked.

"I found the Octopus only to discover that it was empty, and after all my efforts at safeguarding, it seems the papyrus found its way to Umla-Meq quite easily . . . and without me."

I laughed once along with her and thought about Ray and his good fortune in finding the papyrus. Or did luck really have anything to do with it? Before I could answer myself, Susheela the Ninth said, "You must now tell me what the papyrus says, Z. I have pondered this mystery for too long."

I thought back to the first time I saw the papyrus on board the *Iona* in the Canary Islands. I understood its meaning now no more than I did then. "If my memory serves," I said, "it began with a title, *'Nine Steps of the Six,'* then nine lines followed in a spiral—'*The First One shall not know. The Second One shall not know. The Third One shall not know. The Fourth One shall not know. The Fifth One shall not know. The Living Change shall live within the Sixth One. The Five shall be drawn unto the Source Stone. The Living Change shall be Revealed. The Five shall be Extinguished.*'"

There was a moment of silence. Susheela the Ninth said, "Please repeat the last four lines, Zianno." I did. We were lying on our tatami mats as usual. I felt her lean toward Sailor in the darkness. She whispered, "Whatever the true meaning of these ancient words, a Sixth Stone exists. It must, Umla-Meq, . . . it must."

"I agree," Sailor said. "But we should ask ourselves if these words are instruction, direction, or a warning, perhaps? The last line, '*The Five shall be Extinguished,*' is both ominous and perplexing."

"Like moths to a flame, we are," Sheela said.

"What do you mean?" I asked.

"Just as '*The Five shall be drawn unto the Source Stone,*' the Meq are drawn unto the Remembering."

"Seventy-two years?" Sailor said.

"Seventy-two years?" I asked, then realized what he meant.

"Yes, Zianno, since the Time of Ice, those of us from the Pyrenees have believed we know the date of the Remembering, and it arrives in a mere seventy-two years. This amount of time will pass in the blink of an eye for us, yet still we chase the essential nature and purpose of the Remembering. Even its location continues to elude us."

The lights of Osaka glowed no brighter than starlight through the open windows. I could hear traffic sounds and horns in the distance, but not many. We talked until dawn about the papyrus, the Remembering, and the stone balls Geaxi and I had discovered, as well as the one from which the papyrus had been copied. Why could I read the entire script of the papyrus carried by

Susheela the Ninth and yet be unable to decipher no more than a single word on the stone ball Opari and I had seen in Cuba? There were many theories discussed, but no conclusions were reached. Two more weeks of late-night conversations and waiting followed. In the meantime, General Douglas MacArthur and his staff took up residence in Tokyo, while the U.S. Army gradually and peacefully occupied other parts of Japan. On September 15, Sailor finally thought the time was right to put his "plan" into action, though in reality it became more like performing an impromptu one-act play than executing a "plan."

The day was unusually hot and bright and without a hint of autumn in the air. Susheela the Ninth, Sailor, and I stood alongside Katsuo in the grass courtyard of the white-walled American Embassy in Tokyo. Ikuko was standing nearby, but she would wait for us outside. Katsuo wore the long, formal robes of a Shinto priest, and they were causing the big man to sweat profusely.

"This should not take long, Katsuo," Sailor said. He was staring up at the enormous American flag flying over the embassy. "Our story shall command the immediate attention of the Americans, and I would not be surprised if we were on our way to Hawaii within a day, two days at most."

"How can you be so certain?" I asked. I'd had my doubts ever since I first understood Sailor's "plan." "What if it goes differently, what then? What is our alternate 'plan'?"

Sailor smiled. "Zianno, please, you should know better," he said, motioning Katsuo forward. We all began walking toward the entrance to the embassy. Sailor looked over and gave me a quick wink of his "ghost eye," which was still perfectly clear.

Climbing the steps leading into the embassy, I felt the stares and heard the hushed comments from everyone coming or going.

Katsuo paid little attention and led us inside and directly up to an Army lieutenant sitting behind a long desk labeled "INFORMATION" in English and Japanese. The lieutenant seemed surprised by Katsuo's formal dress and height, but his eyes widened and his mouth dropped open when he saw us. Children with Western features, including one with black skin, were simply not supposed to be in Japan.

"What the hell . . . ?" the man said.

Katsuo ignored the comment. Bowing once with great dignity and speaking Japanese, he calmly asked to see whoever was in charge of "missing persons."

The lieutenant turned quickly to a Japanese man in civilian dress standing off to one side of the desk "Ichiro," he commanded, "tell this man . . . tell these children . . . to wait here. Just tell them to wait here. I'll be back shortly. Don't let them leave the embassy, Ichiro. Just tell them to wait a few minutes." The lieutenant rose from his seat and glanced once more at Sheela, Sailor, and me. He shook his head back and forth and walked away at a rapid pace. Ichiro and Katsuo had a short conversation. Katsuo feigned anger in response, dismissing Ichiro with a wave of his hand, but glancing at Sailor with a trace of a smile. Things were going well.

While we waited, Sailor unconsciously twirled an imaginary star sapphire around his forefinger. He had removed the real one, keeping it hidden inside his pants pocket. We both carried our Stones. In less than three minutes, the lieutenant returned and told Ichiro to instruct us we were all to follow him, and Ichiro was to accompany us. Katsuo grunted approval and we were led down a wide hall until we came to a door labeled "CAPTAIN BLAINE HARRINGTON."

The door was open, but the lieutenant stopped and knocked twice before entering. Captain Blaine Harrington sat behind his desk, which was spotless and almost bare, as was the rest of his office. He was leaning forward with his elbows resting on the desk and his hands folded together. He seemed young for a captain, maybe mid-twenties, and his unsmiling, stern demeanor did not match his boyish looks. His hair was cropped short in a military crew cut and he wore wire-rimmed glasses, which were too small for his large blue eyes. He motioned Katsuo to sit, then waved his hand in a circle, indicating for Katsuo to explain himself and tell his story.

Katsuo nodded and removed his formal headgear, but the long robes were still uncomfortable and beads of sweat gathered on his upper lip and forehead. He began recounting our tale to the captain, though he was speaking to Ichiro. He talked for twenty minutes in Japanese, enriching his speech with elaborate gestures and intermittent praises to the gods. And it was a tall tale indeed. Katsuo explained that Sailor and I had been Cuban born, while Susheela the Ninth was from Guyana. The three of us were the adopted children of a Brazilian industrialist and his wife, who were all traveling together through Japan during the late autumn of 1941. After a brief stay in Nagano, our touring car had crashed deep in the mountains, not far from Katsuo's village. The three of us survived the crash, escaping with only minor injuries, but our parents were killed. The date was December 6. Of course, as Katsuo emphasized, the next day changed everything. With war declared on America and the West, too many questions and problems might present themselves, for us as well as the village, should the priests turn us over to the authorities. Instead, they decided to hide and protect us until the war was over. Katsuo paused and took in a long breath, letting it out slowly, like a long overdue sigh. He looked once in our direction, then directly at the young captain. "Atara! The day has come," he said.

Captain Blaine Harrington made no response, but that was to

be expected. Katsuo had been speaking Japanese. The captain had
not moved or changed expression during the entire story. Instead,
he had been watching and studying Sheela, Sailor, and me with
cold, unblinking eyes that gave nothing away. I had no idea what
he thought of Katsuo's long-winded explanation, but Sailor was
convinced the details of our story would prove irrelevant. Sailor
believed the Americans would be compelled to help us leave
Japan out of sheer goodwill.

Katsuo turned to Ichiro and nodded once, as if giving him per-
mission to begin the translation. Ichiro said nothing. Several awkward seconds passed, yet Ichiro never started translating. There
was no need.

"You may speak directly to me, sir," the captain said suddenly
in perfect, measured Japanese. They were the first words he had
spoken and I knew immediately that Sailor's "plan" could be in
trouble. He waited a few more moments. Katsuo wiped a single
drop of sweat from his forehead and remained calm and com-
posed in his chair. "Katsuo," the captain said. "That is your name,
is it not, sir?"

Katsuo nodded slowly.

"You say you and the others in your village never had contact
with the authorities. Is that correct, sir?"

Katsuo nodded again.

"And no one came for the children or their parents. No one
inquired. Is that correct, sir?"

Katsuo nodded once more.

The captain looked in our direction, focusing on Sailor and
holding his gaze, but never changing expression. He looked
back at Katsuo and stood up, acting as if he were about to leave.
"Katsuo," he said, "what is the name of your village?"

Katsuo never hesitated and gave him the name Hakata.

"I see, and this village is near Nagano. Is that correct, sir?"

"Yes," Katsuo answered.

"Then why, sir, do you speak in the distinctive Osaka-ben dialect?"

Katsuo said nothing for a moment, then came up with a rambling explanation, saying he had been born physically in Osaka and spiritually in Hakata. I watched the captain and realized he wasn't buying Katsuo's story.

"I'm not at all sure who you are, sir, and I do not know who these children are or why they are in Japan, but whatever the truth, I believe this is a Japanese problem." The captain paused, then continued talking as he moved toward the door. He was still speaking Japanese. "The correct channels will be found and the matter shall be turned over to them. Come back tomorrow and see the lieutenant for the information. The children will receive proper care and attention and then you may return to whatever it is you do." He paused again and stared down at Katsuo with a thin smile. "Do I make myself clear, sir?" The captain didn't wait for an answer. He glanced once at us and reached for the door.

I have never known exactly why I said what I said next, but the "plan" had unraveled and we were out of time. The odds were long and it was a complete shot in the dark. I spoke in Spanish using the best Cuban accent I could remember, the one I had always heard spoken by Ciela. Just as the captain opened the door, I blurted out, "Where is Señor Jack Flowers?"

Captain Blaine Harrington froze in his tracks. He spun around and looked at me with a piercing stare. I could feel everyone in the room turn in my direction.

Speaking Spanish, the captain asked, "What did you say, son? Did you say 'Jack Flowers'?"

"*Sí* . . . Señor Jack Flowers."

"Solomon Jack Flowers?"

"*Sí, sí* . . . Señor Jack Flowers and Señora Carolina from

St. Louis, America. They save my brother and me as *ninos*. Señor Jack Flowers will help us."

The captain closed the door and paused, then took two steps in my direction. I was standing next to Sheela and Sailor off to the side of Katsuo. He stopped and studied me up and down, slowly taking in every detail. He bent over and leaned in closer. I could see his wire-rimmed glasses pressing into the skin of his temples and around his ears. His blue eyes were huge behind the lenses, and he smelled of American soap and shaving lotion. There was something slightly ominous about his total lack of expression or emotion. I felt like a butterfly being pinned into place and observed with cold and careful precision by its collector. *"Es verdad?"* he said.

"Es verdad," I answered.

The captain straightened up and let his eyes run over the three of us again. Finally, he told Katsuo we were to come back in two hours. The lieutenant would then bring us directly to the captain's office. "In two hours," he said, "this matter will definitely be sorted out." He waited another moment. "Am I clear?"

Katsuo nodded one last time. After reminding the lieutenant in English to please escort us out of the embassy, Captain Blaine Harrington turned and left the room. I glanced at Sailor and he shook his head back and forth with an expression that told me exactly what he was thinking. Sailor thought I had blown every legitimate chance we might have had. Now it would be a tricky affair for us to leave Japan.

We found Ikuko and quickly made our way back to the small room we had rented the previous evening. Katsuo removed his robes the moment we entered and sat down on his tatami mat, naked to the waist and barefoot. He crossed his legs and shut his eyes, taking in several long and deep breaths. Gradually his eyes opened and he looked at Sailor. "I believe I have failed you," he said. "You have my full apologies."

"No!" Sailor shot back. "No, Katsuo, not so. You have not failed, do you hear? We could not have anticipated the American captain understanding and speaking Japanese fluently. There was no failure, Katsuo. Your performance was a good one. It should have worked."

"He is correct, Katsuo," Sheela said. "Your actions were the only appropriate ones."

Ikuko was fanning her grandfather by waving a towel above his head. Outside, the traffic of Tokyo could be heard all around us. The minutes crept by and we said little. Finally, the two hours were nearly up and we got ready to return. Sailor told Katsuo the formal Shinto robes were no longer necessary, but Katsuo refused to step out of character and put on the heavy uncomfortable robes without complaint. He told Ikuko to stay in the room and kissed her on the forehead. Sailor and I said good-bye to Ikuko, and Sheela gave her an especially long embrace, then we set out for the embassy.

Once we crossed the courtyard and climbed the steps, we were met outside by the lieutenant, who seemed to be waiting for us. Without delay, he ushered us into the embassy and down the wide hallway toward the captain's office. As we neared the door, we passed a group of men standing off to one side, laughing and smoking cigarettes. They were all Americans, some civilians, some in uniform. One of the men said, "Well, well, would you look at that?" Sheela and I kept walking and staring straight ahead, but Sailor turned his head in the man's direction. At the same time, a flashbulb went off. Somewhere among them, a soldier had taken Sailor's picture. The lieutenant stopped and told the men there would be none of that, then commanded the soldier who snapped the picture to hand over the film. There was some protest from the man, but he was outranked and forced to comply. The lieutenant then asked all of the men to move along. By that time, the door had opened and Captain Blaine Harrington was standing in the doorway. He watched the man hand over the film, then said, "Inside, Lieutenant. Now." He turned to Katsuo with a false smile. "This way, sir," he said in Japanese.

As we walked inside, I noticed another man in the room. He was sitting casually in a chair next to the captain's desk. I tried not to seem shocked or surprised, but I'm not sure I succeeded. The man was dressed in civilian clothes, which were rumpled and slightly soiled, and he had at least three days' growth of beard. His eyes reflected a certain kind of maturity and experience that had not been there the last time I'd seen him. He was now thirty-nine years old and looked exactly like his father. It was Jack Flowers. I looked at Sailor and he raised one eyebrow, as if to say, "Let us see where this goes." We had expected to be quizzed about Jack, but we never expected to see him.

Before the captain and Katsuo had taken their seats, Jack said, "I'll be damned, Blaine, you were telling me the truth." He leaned forward, staring at me. In Spanish, he asked, "Is that you, Felipe?" Then he nodded in Sailor's direction. "And is that Hernando, as well?"

I paused, unsure what to do or say, then realized Jack had probably been briefed by the captain and had figured it out. Now he was leading me, telling me to play along. Whatever he was doing in Tokyo I could find out later. Captain Blaine Harrington sat down in the seat behind his desk. He was observing me carefully. "*Sí*, Señor Jack," I answered. "Felipe y Hernando."

Jack slapped his knee with one hand and laughed. The captain started to speak, but Jack cut him off and began a ten-minute fiction about Felipe and Hernando and a very bad Sunday in Pinar del Rio six years earlier. During mass, the roof of a church

had collapsed without warning and twenty-six of fifty-three people praying inside were killed instantly. Our parents were among
the dead. Jack and his mother, Carolina, personally found homes
for all the children who were orphaned from the accident. Obvi-
ously, the captain had told Jack everything I had said, including
the fact that Jack was supposed to have "saved" Sailor and me.
Jack was ready with a cover story and he was good at it. I almost
believed him myself. He ended by saying, "I'll tell you what,
Blaine . . . I mean, Captain Harrington, why don't you let me
take care of this? I know the perfect man. He's Japanese and he's
connected. He'll be able to find these kids a decent home."

The captain didn't respond immediately. He breathed in sharply
and glared at Jack, then at each of us until he let his eyes rest on
Katsuo. He raised his hand and pointed a finger at Katsuo's face.
"I do not believe one word this man has uttered." The captain
looked back at Jack.

Jack shrugged. "I'm sure it's harmless," he said. "The poor man
is most likely only trying to find something in it for himself. I don't
blame him. Anyway, nothing to worry about and my man in
Yokosuka will get to the bottom of it."

The captain removed his wire-rimmed glasses and wiped the
lenses clean. His eyes were still large, even without the glasses.
"The coincidence of all this is much too disproportionate." He
carefully refitted his glasses over his nose and back into the
grooves along his temples and around his ears. "How is this possible, Jack?"

Jack looked first at Sheela, then at Sailor and me. He laughed,
shaking his head back and forth. "Luck," he said. "Just pure dumb
luck." Jack leaned back in his chair. "What do you say? I'd really
get a kick out of helping those kids again, Blaine."

The captain gave Katsuo another piercing stare. "Well, all
right, Jack, but—"

Jack interrupted. "Listen, Captain, if I leave right now, I might be able to make Yokosuka by nightfall." Jack practically leaped out of his chair and opened the door to the hallway. "This way, everybody," he said in English, motioning Katsuo and the three of us out the door. "Andele! Andele!" Once we were in the hallway, he turned back to the captain. "I've got Sergeant Roper waiting for me. I'll send you a report from Yokosuka."

In two minutes we were out of the embassy, down the steps, and being hustled into a jeep. A red-haired man sat in the driver's seat. When he saw us, he said, "What the—"

"Never mind, Sergeant," Jack said. "Just step on it."

We took Katsuo back to the room where Ikuko was waiting for him. There was so much for which to thank him, but there was no time. Sailor said his farewells to Katsuo in Japanese, and Sheela bowed to him deeply three times. I said my good-bye and thanked him as best I could, then we were off on a hectic, rough ride to Yokosuka.

We arrived shortly after dark and made our way to the Japanese air base the U.S. Army now occupied. Jack told Sergeant Roper to drop us off at a small building squeezed between two enormous airplane hangars, saying he and the sergeant would be back soon. An hour later Jack, Sheela, Sailor, and I boarded a transport plane with no other passengers and little cargo. The plane took off, circled in a wide arc, and headed south. In less than ten minutes, I could no longer see Japan. Jack smiled and shouted over the noise of the engines, "Good to see you, Z."

I yelled, "You, too, Jack. Where are we going?"

"Midway," he shouted back. "Then we'll change planes and go on to Hawaii."

"You want to tell me what you were doing in Japan . . . and how you're able to do what you're doing? Are you in the Army?"

He laughed. "No, I'm not in the Army, Z. At least, not technically. I'll tell you all about it when we land." Jack dropped his smile and said, "It really was luck, Z . . . no doubt about it. I was supposed to go to Nagasaki the same day I heard from Blaine Harrington. I just happened to be in the right place at the right time."

"Why were you going to Nagasaki?"

"I was ordered to write a report about what I saw for a few people in Washington."

"Don't worry, Jack. I'll tell you all about it. People everywhere should know what that bomb did."

Jack shot me a look. "What? You saw it, Z?"

"Oh, yes, I saw it, all right. I saw the bomb drop and I saw Nagasaki . . . afterward . . . and it is in my mind forever."

"Tell me later," Jack shouted. "It's too damn loud in here."

I nodded my agreement and tried to get comfortable in the stiff makeshift seats. Jack tossed some blankets over to me. We were flying at several thousand feet and it was chilly inside the big plane. I turned to pass Sailor and Sheela a blanket and found them both asleep. She had her head on his shoulder and he was holding her hand. I put the blankets around them as gently as possible. For a moment they looked like two innocent children who had played all day and stayed up past their bedtime. I laughed to myself at the thought and closed my own eyes. I was on my way home. I couldn't believe it, it seemed too good to be true, and even though Sailor's "plan" had fallen through, he had been right about one thing—he said we would be on our way to Hawaii within a day, maybe two. And so we were, but not because of his or anybody's "plan." No, it was simpler than that. As Jack had said, it was nothing but pure dumb luck.

3

ORBAIN

(SCAR)

The event usually happens in an instant. The resulting injury is severe and traumatic. The healing is painful and slow. Time becomes the handmaiden, the nurse, and the clock that will gradually change, rearrange, and sometimes erase the event from memory. The mind plays tricks on itself, the body moves on, the soul calms and the spirit forgets, but the scar . . . the scar is permanent. The scar remembers.

"Pick it up, son. Pick up the baseball and give it to me," the voice behind the mask said. The sun was shining. I stood on the pitcher's mound and he was walking toward me. Who was he? Was he the umpire? I looked down and saw the baseball lying in the dirt. Instead of normal laces, the ball had been stitched together with jewels, and they reflected sunlight in every color and every direction. "Give it to me," the voice repeated. I was confused. Why should I give the baseball to him? Why?

"Wake up, Z! We're landing."

I was jarred awake just as the airplane's huge wheels hit the runway. I turned to Jack. "Where is this?"

"Hickam Field—but we won't be here long. I want to get the three of you to my place before anybody asks any questions." Jack looked over at Sailor and Sheela. He rubbed the stubble on his face and laughed once to himself. "You've got to tell me about her, Z. She's amazing . . . I had no idea . . ."

Jack didn't need to finish his sentence. I watched Sheela as we taxied to a full stop. I knew what he meant and he was right—she was amazing, and so was her story, but I knew I would only be able to tell Jack a portion of the truth about Susheela the Ninth. I could tell him she was the last of her kind among the Meq; I could tell him she had once known famous painters, princes, and queens; I could even tell him she possessed unique mental powers, but I could never tell him one thing—her true and actual age. He would never believe me. With the engines still running, Jack opened the door. The sound was deafening. He lowered the ladder, saluted the two pilots, and we stepped out of the plane and onto the ground. Jack waved us toward an empty hangar while the big transport turned around and taxied off to another runway. The last remnants of a storm were dissolving in the western sky and the sun was setting. Only a long, lone, horizontal sliver of bloodred light shone through the clouds. It looked like a scar between two worlds.

Jack had left his car parked inside the empty hangar. It was a 1939 Ford convertible, and the three of us piled into the backseat while Jack drove off the base. We put our heads down as he waved to the guards at the exit gates. One of them yelled, "Good to see you back, Jack!"

"Good to be back, boys," he shouted, then turned north onto the highway. About twenty minutes later we pulled into his house, a small bungalow on the north side of Pearl City. The house was only a few hundred yards from the beach and shielded from view by an overgrown hedge on two sides. We spent three days in Hawaii, mainly at Jack's place. During that time we talked often at the beach and learned about the obscure nature of his current "occupation" and some of what he had been doing during the war.

In 1940, well before the attack on Pearl Harbor, Jack was approached and asked to join a government covert intelligence unit, which later became known as the O.S.S. After agreeing to serve, he trained in Washington and later in England under British command. In July of 1942, he was ordered to set up his own network of agents in Lisbon, Madrid, and Marseille, along with direct connections to the French underground. His mission was simple and direct: by any means necessary he was to help certain people, primarily downed British and American pilots, escape through France and into Spain via the Pyrenees.

Absolute trust is absolutely necessary for any clandestine operation to work, particularly during wartime. I learned that fact from Captain Woodget and I have always found it to be true. Jack chose the first members of his organization from those he knew well—those few people who also happened to know of the Meq. He traveled to Caitlin's Ruby and enlisted the aid of Willie Croft and Koldo Txopitea. They both agreed on the spot to do whatever they could to help. The memories of Guernica and the German bombs killing most of his tribe, including his father, were still fresh in Koldo's mind. Arrosa even volunteered, but Jack told her to stay at Caitlin's Ruby, along with Star and Caine. He said he would need a place to plan operations when he was in England and the Ruby was perfect because it was remote and unattached to the British and the Americans. A year later, and against the protests of Star, Caine dropped out of college to join Jack in the field. Mitch Coates and Antoine Boutrain were also brought into the group. Jack found them in Marseille, along with Mercy, Emme, and Antoinette. They were all living together in one of

Antoine's homes. Mitch and Antoine became essential to Jack because almost everyone they knew was in the French resistance to some degree. Koldo recruited several of his Basque friends and relatives, and the whole operation was a success for the next two years.

Shortly after D-day in 1944, Jack was ordered to disband his group and transfer to Hawaii. Three months later he was assigned the task of training new recruits for covert intelligence missions in northern China and parts of Korea. Captain Blaine Harrington, then a first lieutenant just out of Princeton, was one of Jack's first trainees. After only one mission, Jack had to recommend that the young lieutenant be removed from the field and transferred to another position. Blaine Harrington's amazing facility with languages was a valuable asset, but his inability or unwillingness to improvise and act "outside the book" was a serious liability. Improvisation is a skill as necessary in the field as absolute trust. Blaine Harrington was soon promoted to captain and transferred to General MacArthur's staff. For the rest of the war, he held Jack responsible for steering his career into a long series of insignificant and boring assignments.

As soon as Japan surrendered, Jack was sent to Mukden, Manchuria, along with three other O.S.S. agents. They were there to take notes and snap pictures as evidence of Chinese peasants looting factories and Russian trains loading heavy equipment and machine tools to be shipped back to Russia. Ten days later the Russians ordered the O.S.S. agents out of the country without delay. Jack was then ordered to Japan to gather eyewitness observations of Hiroshima and Nagasaki. A few days after that we entered the American Embassy and I told my story to Blaine Harrington.

Jack looked at me. The four of us were sitting above the beach on a small outcropping of rock, facing Pearl Harbor to the south.

The sun was still high in the sky. "I saw something else when I was in Manchuria, Z."

"What was it?"

"A photograph—an *unexpected* photograph."

"Of what?"

"Not what—who!" Jack glanced at Sailor and Sheela, then turned back to me. "A Russian agent I only know as 'Valery' showed me a picture he had taken in China because he said the subjects were 'unusual.' They were standing in a crowd—there were three of them."

"Three of who?"

"Three of *you*—Nova, Ray, and Opari, I believe, though her face was turned away from the camera."

"*Ta ifi dite . . .*" Sheela whispered.

Sailor was looking at Jack without expression. "Tell me, Jack, for whom, exactly, do you work? Are you a spy, then?"

Jack laughed. "It's not that glamorous or romantic, Sailor. Right now I'm sort of a fact finder. The O.S.S. is dissolving and something else is evolving. The man I work for is in the middle of it."

"Who is he?" I asked.

Jack smiled. "Do you remember the man Owen Bramley told me about, the man who first helped us in Cuba, the one he called 'Cardinal'?"

"Of course. He helped us with the names on the 'List.'"

"Yes, well, we'll get to that, but he's the same man who recruited me. I work for Cardinal."

"What is this man's real name, Jack?" Sailor asked. "Who is he?"

Jack turned his head and gazed west, toward Japan. "Z, did you and Sailor ever find the family of Sangea Hiramura?"

I glanced at Sailor, remembering the faces of Sak and Shutratek.

"Yes, we found them . . . two of them. They are gone now. They were good people."

Jack seemed genuinely saddened by the news. "If you recall, there was one son who came to the World's Fair in 1904 with Sangea, but never returned to Japan."

"I remember," I said. "His name was Bikki."

"That's right. And sometime before the Fair began, Solomon had made a deal with Sangea to set aside a trust fund for educating Bikki in the United States. Bikki later changed his last name to Birnbaum and was sent to the very best schools, eventually becoming an ophthalmologist and surgeon among other things. He set up his practice in Washington, D.C., which was the perfect cover for his other job, the one he still practices." Jack paused a moment. "Dr. Bikki Birnbaum is Cardinal."

I shook my head and smiled. It had been over forty years since his death and my old friend Solomon was still surprising me.

"Is Dr. Birnbaum aware of the Meq?" Sailor asked.

Jack glanced once at all three of us. "Yes, he is. Solomon told Owen Bramley that Sangea Hiramura's entire family knew of the Meq long before they came to St. Louis."

"This is true," I said, remembering what we'd learned from Sak.

"True indeed," Sailor added.

Suddenly I recalled the brief incident on the way to Blaine Harrington's office. The lieutenant had confiscated the film containing the snapshot of Sailor, then handed it over to the captain. I told Jack about it.

"Damn! I wanted Blaine to forget you three as soon as possible."

"Why do you say that?" I asked. "Do you think he is a threat?"

"Possibly."

"How could he be a threat to us, Jack?" Sailor asked.

"Because he's like a ferret smelling a rat. He will gnaw and gnaw through anything until he finds that rat. He's obsessive and paranoid, but that's not what worries me most." Jack's eyes looked to the west again.

"Go on," Sailor said.

"I don't think Valery showing me the photograph of Ray and the others was coincidence. I think he suspects something. Exactly what he suspects, I'm not sure. The problem is that Valery is a double agent. He works for us and guess who his controller is?" Jack paused a moment. "Valery's controller is Captain Blaine Harrington."

"I have yet to see the threat in this, Jack," Sailor said. "A photograph or two from two distant countries should not lead anyone anywhere, even if they find our presence there 'unusual.' But more important, how many more in the military or government have knowledge of us?"

"None."

"How can you be so sure?"

"I can't, but Cardinal can. That is what he does, Sailor. He told me he is 'home base' in a plan Solomon had all along, a plan to prevent any government from ever learning about you . . . about the Meq. He called the plan his 'Diamond plan.' Basically, it was a vision of an independent intelligence organization with connections inside as many governments as possible. Solomon thought the world of men was not yet ready for the reality of the Meq. His assessment is, unfortunately, truer today than it ever was. The Russians, the Chinese, and especially the Americans would hunt you down like animals to gain your secrets and the power that's in the blood flowing through your veins. They would exploit all of you like lab rats to get access to that power. Cardinal says we must never let this happen, and I agree." Jack stopped and looked directly at me. "So does my mother."

For the first time in a long time my thoughts went to Carolina. She would be a much older woman now. My eyes drifted out across Pearl Harbor and followed a passing ship for a moment or two. "How is she, Jack? Is she well?"

Jack smiled wide. "My mother is the smartest, prettiest, feistiest seventy-five-year-old woman in St. Louis, Z. Yeah, she's doing just fine. She misses you. She told me if I ever saw you, I should tell you she wishes she was kicking leaves again, whatever that means."

I laughed to myself and remembered. I was twelve years old in actual years and Carolina was only slightly younger. We became lifelong friends that fall, kicking leaves as we walked through Forest Park. "Don't worry, Jack. I know what she means."

Jack rubbed the stubble on his chin. "You know, Z, she never has told me how you two met in the first place."

"I'll tell you on the way home, Jack."

"Is that where the three of you want to go? St. Louis?"

"Yes," I answered.

"No," Sailor interjected.

I turned to Sailor. I had made the assumption we were all going to the same destination. He saw the surprise in my eyes.

"I forgot to tell you, Zianno. While I was in the Fleur-du-Mal's *shiro,* I may have found evidence of another one or two of your 'stone spheres.' It is only a name, but I feel we should investigate." Sailor twirled the star sapphire on his forefinger and glanced once at Sheela. "You travel on to St. Louis, Z. It will be good for you. Wait there for word from Opari and the others. Should Jack be able to assist us, we are off to South America."

"No problem," Jack said. "That is, if you don't mind starting in Mexico City. I've got a man there right now who handles all of Latin America . . . and you can trust him completely, Sailor."

"Are you quite sure?"

"Maybe you should ask Z," Jack said, looking at me with a grin. "His name is Oliver 'Biscuit' Bookbinder."

Sailor turned to me and raised one eyebrow. "*Oliver 'Biscuit' Bookbinder?*"

"I know him well," I said, then paused. "Biscuit was the orphan boy who witnessed Unai's and Usoa's murders. Opari and I found him, but Carolina saved him, named him, and raised him in her home as one of her own. He was a good boy and I'm sure he is a good man."

"He is also a baseball legend throughout Latin America," Jack said. "It's the perfect cover for him. Biscuit is welcomed with open arms by everyone and given access to almost anything. He can get both of you into South America legally and without suspicion, but . . . uh . . . I wouldn't advise wearing that little blue beauty on your finger, Sailor."

Sailor laughed louder than I'd heard him laugh in weeks. He said, "Do not be alarmed, Jack. I shall keep it safely tucked away."

We flew out of Hawaii in two similar but separate directions. Jack and I left for San Francisco, while Sheela and Sailor left for Los Angeles, along with a Navy lieutenant assigned by Jack. Once there they would transfer aircraft and the lieutenant himself would fly them to Mexico City, where Biscuit would meet them and take care of everything, including proper paperwork and money.

Shortly before we took off, Sailor pulled me aside. "Be vigilant," he said. "The Remembering occurs in a mere seventy years, Zianno. We must not let the Giza detour us from being there." He paused, looking around the terminal at passing faces. "I believe Jack could be right in his assessment of this new age."

"What do you mean, 'new age'?"

"I mean the one we now inhabit since the Americans have invented and used that godforsaken bomb. I am not so worried of anyone discovering our existence as I am of the newfound ability of the Giza to annihilate each other and poison the entire planet in the process. Do you understand the implications?"

I watched Sailor carefully. He gave nothing away, as usual. I know the Meq, particularly the old ones, are often nonchalant about comings and goings, arrivals and departures, but Sailor and I had spent the last eight years traveling together every day and I would miss him. I smiled when Sailor asked if I understood the implications. After a moment or two, he smiled back. "I understand," I said.

His "ghost eye" was cloudless and bright. "*Egibizirik bilatu, Zianno*," he said, then turned and disappeared in the crowd with Sheela and the lieutenant.

Ten minutes after landing and gathering our gear, Jack and I made a spur-of-the-moment decision. We had planned on taking the train to St. Louis, but Jack came up with another idea.

"How quick do you want to get home, Z?"

"I don't know, Jack, what do you have in mind?"

"What if we drove?"

I laughed and said, "Why not?"

It took us half a day to find a vehicle Jack deemed appropriate for the journey. Eventually, he settled on a 1941 Ford Deluxe station wagon with wood paneling on the sides. The car was a beauty, and Jack paid cash for it. We headed east to Reno, then on through Nevada and Utah, crossing into Wyoming and Nebraska. It was wonderful to see, hear, smell, taste, and feel America again. I had missed it more than I thought. The weather was good the entire trip, and Jack drove at a leisurely pace. He talked most of

the way about the war and what he'd seen and learned while leading refugees, spies, British and American pilots, Jewish artists, and
others out of France and across the Pyrenees with Koldo and his
Basque compatriots. Most of it sounded like one long, grand adventure, only filled with very real threats and dangers. Jack had
been lucky to live on more than one occasion. Others had not
been so lucky. Somewhere in northwestern Missouri, Jack finally
got around to telling me about Emme Ya Ambala and Antoine
Boutrain. His eyes darkened and his voice cracked slightly as he
began. "It was a crazed act, Z . . . by a crazed Nazi . . . and completely unnecessary . . . the goddamn war was nearly over when it
happened."

As Jack told me the story, my heart felt pierced with every
word and sentence. On March 22, 1945, a Gestapo agent who
had been disgraced in Paris two years earlier in his pursuit of the
Russian revolutionary Voline was trying to escape Europe
through Marseille. His hatred and obsession with Voline had been
well known among the underground in occupied France. Purely
as a final, mad act of revenge, he decided to blow up the house
where Voline had once held court, the same address where
Antoine, Emme, and Antoinette now lived, along with Mitch
Coates and Mercy Whitney. It was the second day of spring and
the sky was a soft, light blue. Mitch and Mercy were out of town
visiting friends in Paris. Antoinette was in her last year of school
just a mile away. At ten after ten in the morning, she and each of
her classmates heard the explosion and ran to the window. For a
full thirty seconds, Antoinette and the other girls watched the
smoke and huge fireball rise into the air, wondering what or who
had blown up.

I closed my eyes and sat in silence. Jack drove the Ford on
through Missouri toward St. Louis. Inside my mind I said
farewells to Emme and Antoine by remembering every single sec-

ond I had spent with each of them, in the desert and at sea and in Paris. They were much more than friends to me and to the Meq. They were two of the best people I have ever known. Geaxi warned me once about becoming too attached to any Giza. She told me they would break my heart. "Your feelings for them cannot and shall not sustain them," she said. I disagreed with her then, but now I realized Geaxi was simply telling the truth. When I finally looked up, we were already in St. Louis, only one block from Carolina's house. Ancient oaks and maples shaded the streets. A few were just beginning to show leaves of red, yellow, and burnt orange. I could smell Forest Park in the distance. I looked over at Jack. "Where is Antoinette?"

He drove another block, then slowed and pulled into the long private driveway, coming to a stop under the stone archway just outside two massive oak doors that used to serve as the entrance to the best whorehouse in St. Louis. "Right here," Jack said with a grin. "Mitch and Mercy brought her back to the States with them and now they're all staying with Carolina." He turned off the engine and told me to be quiet. He grinned again. "We'll sneak in on them. They don't know we're coming."

Once we were inside the big house, we crept toward the kitchen. I could hear a man and woman talking, and a baseball game was on the radio. I had completely forgotten that the World Series was in progress. The Cubs were playing the Tigers. When Jack walked into the kitchen without a word, Mercy saw him first and broke into joyous laughter. She ran over to give him a hug and Mitch turned around in his chair. We locked eyes immediately.

"Well, I'll be damned," Mitch said. On the radio the broadcaster announced Hank Greenberg had just doubled for the Tigers.

"Who's winning?" I asked.

"Who cares?" Mitch said, pulling out a chair at the table and turning off the radio. "Come here and sit down, Z. You sure are a sight for sore eyes, man."

Mercy let go of Jack and bent over at the waist, giving me a warm embrace. There were multicolored specks of paint on her shirt and jeans and she smelled of turpentine. "You've been working," I said.

"Yes . . . finally."

I looked at both of them. Mercy was in her early forties and Mitch in his early fifties. They seemed well and healthy; however, the strain of living, fighting, and surviving in wartime France showed on their faces. I told Mitch how often I had thought of him and how much I had worried about everyone during the war years. Mitch asked if Jack had mentioned Emme and Antoine. I said yes, I had heard the whole bloody, idiotic mess, then Jack changed the subject, going into a long, vivid account of our journey east in his Ford Deluxe station wagon. He sounded like a teenager describing his first trip in his first automobile. Before he got us out of California, I leaned over and asked Mercy, "Where is Carolina?" She pointed through the window in the direction of the carriage house. I excused myself and headed out the door toward the "Honeycircle."

In the years since I'd been gone the honeysuckle, forsythia, and wisteria bushes had grown much taller and thicker. Everything inside the "Honeycircle" was completely hidden from view, but I could hear a woman singing an old Cole Porter song slightly off-key. I walked through the opening. She was kneeling in a small vegetable garden with her back to me, collecting a few puny tomatoes still left on the vines. She wore green slacks and a long plaid shirt with a sweater wrapped around her waist. She had her hair piled up and under a faded red baseball cap. I stayed silent and watched her work. Ten or fifteen seconds passed. Suddenly she

stopped singing. She seemed suspended, frozen like a statue holding the tomato she'd just picked. In a soft, distant voice, and
without turning around, she said, "It's you, isn't it, Z?"

Nicholas and Owen had said it time and time again, and they
were right—she was remarkable. I smiled to myself and waited
another heartbeat. "Those tomatoes," I said, "I think they might
be a lost cause."

Carolina dropped her arm and let the tomato fall away. She was
on her knees, but she turned slowly in a half circle until our eyes
met. Hers were wet with tears. She shook her head back and
forth once, then picked up the tomato and threw it at me.
I caught it easily in one hand. "I think *you* are the lost cause, Z!"
She wiped the tears from her eyes and shook her head again.
"Why did I not hear from you, not once, not one word, during
the entire war? I worried constantly about you, Z. There was no
way to know if you were alive or dead."

"It was difficult to correspond from Japan."

"Japan? What? Is that a joke, Z?"

"No."

Her face was lined and creased from seventy-five years, yet
beautiful, and inside her blue-gray eyes I could still see tiny flecks
of gold. She took off her baseball cap and let her hair fall free. It
was silver and just past shoulder length. Our eyes remained locked
on each other. "My God, Z," she said. "How . . . how did
you . . ."

"It's complicated," I said. "I'll tell you later."

"Come here, Z. Come over here now."

She stayed on her knees and opened her arms. I walked the few
steps between us and we embraced for several moments, never
saying a word. If someone had been watching, they might have
thought they were seeing a poignant reunion between a boy and
his grandmother, or great-grandmother. It was anything but that.

"You cannot do this to me again," she whispered. "I am too old, Z. Please, tell me you will be here for . . . for at least a while. If Opari calls, then I will understand."

"Has she?"

"No, I haven't heard from her."

"Have you heard anything from any of us?"

"Not a word, not even from Ray."

"Well, that's understandable. You know Ray."

Carolina smiled. "Yes, I know Ray," she said, then paused. "Z . . . will you stay?"

I smiled back. "Are you kidding? I wouldn't want to be anywhere else. Now, tell me about the current state of the Cardinals pitching staff."

She laughed and I laughed with her. I grabbed the basket of puny red tomatoes and Carolina stood up, then we walked out of the "Honeycircle" and toward the big house. It was October 7, 1945. The sun was just setting over St. Louis. "What's for dinner?" I asked.

"Whatever you want," she said.

I had been anxious to meet Antoinette, but she was nowhere to be seen. As Carolina and Mercy were preparing dinner, Jack asked about her absence. Carolina said Antoinette had entered Marquette University in Milwaukee, Wisconsin, and wouldn't be back to St. Louis until Christmas. A childhood girlfriend from Marseille was enrolled there and Antoinette wanted to be near her friend. She said it would be like old times, when they studied and played together before the war. As it turned out, Antoinette's absence allowed Carolina and me to spend hours and hours alone together, something we had not done in years. Everyone else was busy. Within days after arriving, Jack left for Washington, D.C., and elsewhere, promising Carolina he would be home for Christmas. Mitch was starting another new business downtown, and Mercy painted obsessively in her studio, which was really a converted bedroom in the carriage house. Every day, even as the temperature began to drop, Carolina and I went for endless wandering walks through and around Forest Park. She had arthritis in her hips and knees, yet she never complained or mentioned it. Once, on a cold and windy afternoon in late November, we were walking along one of our familiar trails. Suddenly, with silver hair flying and a heavy shawl wrapped around her thin shoulders, Carolina started running, laughing, and kicking wildly, scattering a pile of golden leaves in every direction. "Come on, Z," she yelled back. "Let's kick the leaves while we can!"

In the following days, I adopted the general look and attitude of a post-war American kid. It was easy. The look, which I liked, was simple—white T-shirt and blue jeans—and the attitude of the American twelve-year-old seemed to never change.

I silently hoped I would hear from one of the Meq, especially Opari. It didn't happen, although I did dream about her on five consecutive nights. They were all vivid dreams in faraway places, places I had never seen. Opari knew all the paths, trails, springs, valleys, caves, and beaches. In one of the dreams, under a broad bright night sky, she pointed out the stars and configurations of several new constellations. We held hands and whispered together, listening to the sound of the wind in the trees. Dreaming about Opari was one thing, but I also knew I could not let thoughts of her into my life on a daily basis. In my heart of hearts, I believed she was safe and would return to me eventually. The Itxaron, the Wait, deepens with the passing of time, and longing for your Ameq only makes it worse. Geaxi once told me there is an actual physical condition, a kind of paralyzing psychic ache, which the Meq can develop from excessive longing. The Wait is also a very real *weight* for the Meq, and it becomes heavier and heavier until we cross in the Zeharkatu. Above all, Opari and I were aware we must be present at the Remembering, wherever it was, and we must be there with our Stones. There was no option. Until that time, the Wait would continue.

Antoinette was expected to arrive by train on December 20. Carolina wanted to meet her at Union Station. She also wanted to wait for Antoinette before purchasing and decorating a Christmas tree. On the morning of the nineteenth, the temperature dropped rapidly and a cold front moved through St. Louis, bringing with it an inch or two of light snow. It wasn't much, but it was enough to change Carolina's mind about waiting to put up a Christmas tree. By midafternoon, Mitch and Mercy had found a suitably sized tree and by sunset the tree was decorated and lit with multicolored lights strung among the branches from top to bottom. After dinner, Carolina asked Mitch to turn on the phonograph and play some music, but not Christmas music. She said she wanted to dance and suggested a nice waltz by Strauss. Mitch picked out a few records and turned up the volume. Carolina looked at me. She removed her shoes so she could be closer to my height, then extended her hand for me to take. "I assume you know how to waltz, Z."

I had never waltzed in my life, but I wasn't about to admit it. "Of course," I said, and before I knew what was happening, we were gliding and spinning in wide circles around the big living room. Mitch and Mercy joined us, laughing loudly at my awkward attempts to be graceful. Carolina and I started laughing along with them. We were all dizzy with dancing and music and Christmas lights.

Then I saw her. She was standing ten feet from the Christmas tree staring at me with her mouth open. She wore a big Navy pea jacket with the collar turned up, dark slacks, a plaid muffler wrapped around her neck, and a red beret. She was taller than her mother, but she had her mother's eyes. And she was beautiful. She reminded me of the young American singer and actress Lena Horne.

I stopped dancing and stared back at her. I knew why she was staring; I had witnessed the same thing before on the faces of many Giza who had heard of the Meq all their lives, yet never actually seen one of us in the flesh. I took a step toward her. "Antoinette?"

She nodded her head a few times without speaking, then swallowed and said, "Yes, I am Antoinette." She spoke English with an American accent, and sounded just like Emme. "Are you . . . are you—"

"My name is Zianno," I said, walking over to her. I took hold of her hands. Her fingers were nearly twice as long as my own. I looked up into her eyes. I liked her immediately. "Call me Z," I said, squeezing her hands slightly. "I knew your mother and father well. We were great friends, and your mother saved my life on many occasions."

Finally, Antoinette seemed to relax. "I know," she said. "However, I have always heard it the other way around."

I smiled. "You are early. We expected you tomorrow."

"Yes, dear," Carolina said from behind me. "Is anything wrong? We wanted to meet you at the train station and welcome you back."

Antoinette gave Carolina a kiss on both cheeks. "A friend of mine was driving home today and going through St. Louis," she said, removing her beret, muffler, and pea jacket. "I asked if I could ride along. I wanted to surprise you and Uncle Mitch."

"And you did," Mitch said, coming over to Antoinette and hugging her tightly. "Welcome home, honey."

Antoinette turned to look at the Christmas tree, which blazed against the darkness outside the window. Suddenly tears welled up in her eyes. "I have never seen anything more wonderful in my life," she said. "It is . . ."

Carolina slipped her arm around Antoinette's waist and smiled. "Merry Christmas, my dear, Merry Christmas."

Jack never did make it back for the holidays. He sent a postcard from Panama apologizing and swore he would be home by base-ball season. Carolina was disappointed, but her spirits rose when she received a telegram on the twenty-second. Star and Caine and Willie Croft were setting sail for New York on January 1, then coming to St. Louis by train—a complete surprise to Carolina and she was ecstatic. I was excited by the news because I hadn't seen any of them in years. Antoinette mentioned that she had met Mr. Croft once, briefly, in Marseille. "He was a complete gentleman to a very young and silly girl. He gave me an enor-mous piece of the most delicious chocolate."

"That's Willie, all right," I said, then I had a curious thought. I asked Carolina, "How old is Caine now?"

"He's twenty-seven," she answered. "Why do you ask?"

I shrugged. "No reason."

On Christmas Day snow fell throughout the afternoon and Mitch played Scott Joplin tunes on the piano until late into the night. Mercy sat on the piano bench next to him, tapping her foot to the music. Carolina reminisced about the great musician, good friend, and humble human being he had been. Antoinette was familiar with ragtime music and wanted to know everything about him. I was amazed at how well Mitch could still play, and I loved hearing the music again. It reminded me of old St. Louis. I thought of Solomon laughing somewhere in the big living room when it was filled with expensive whores and the smell of cigars and the sound of poker chips and playing cards and silver dollars and all the time a piano in the background. I could hear him laughing and swearing when he lost, cheering when he won, leaning over and telling me with a wink, "Zis is good business, Z."

We awoke the next day to bright sunshine and a snow-covered city, though the streets were open and busy with traffic. Over breakfast Carolina said she wanted to go for a long walk in Forest Park. She wished Antoinette to see the sheer beauty of the place, especially after a decent snowfall. It was during this walk that a relatively minor incident provoked me into using the Stone. I hadn't needed to use it since before the war when Sailor and Sak and I slipped into northern Japan. The incident would also be the first time Antoinette witnessed the silent, mystical power of the Stone of Dreams.

Entering the park from Lindell Boulevard, we followed the few paths that were clear, making our way south with no particular destination in mind. The park was nearly empty, but the absence of people only made everything more beautiful and surreal. As we neared the southern boundary, we passed by the Jewel Box— a unique art-deco-style conservatory, made entirely of glass and steel, with stone at the base and concrete framing the entrance. Standing alone against the snow, the building glistened in the sunlight.

Just then, I caught a glimpse of two figures kneeling in the snow between two huge spruce trees. They were both aiming what looked to be rifles directly at the glass walls of the Jewel Box. Without hesitation, I reached in my pocket for the Stone and held it in my palm, then raised my arm. "Hear ye, hear ye, now, Giza," I said in a low, even drone. "*Lo geltitu, lo geltitu.* Go like lambs, now. You will forget. *Ahaztu!*"

The two figures rose slowly and turned around to go. They

both had blank, dull expressions on their faces. They were only boys, two boys about my size, and the rifles were only BB guns, which probably would not have had the power to penetrate the sturdy glass. Nevertheless, they were threatening to vandalize the Jewel Box, and I could not allow that. The boys dropped their guns in the snow and walked away without a word.

I glanced at Carolina and caught her trying to stifle a smile. I looked at Antoinette. Once again, her mouth hung open and she was staring at me. She mumbled something in French, then switched to English. "How . . . how did you . . . how is that possible?"

I glanced once more at Carolina, who had her eyebrows raised, waiting and wondering how I would answer. I decided the truth was the best and simplest reply. "I don't know, Antoinette." I took a step or two toward her. "There are only five of us who can do it. None of us know the secret. We never have." I paused and looked into her eyes, which reminded me so much of Emme. "Did your mother never mention this . . . this 'ability'?"

"Yes," she said softly. Her eyes looked away for a moment, as if she was embarrassed. "I . . . I must confess I never quite believed her."

"Believe her," Carolina interrupted. "Believe every word." She folded her arm inside Antoinette's arm and turned in the direction of Lindell Boulevard. "Come on, my dear, let's go home and build a big fire in the fireplace. I will tell you a few stories of my own, and I promise you, you can believe every one of them."

Later that night, long after dinner, Carolina caught me standing in the closet of Jack's bedroom. I was rubbing a thin coating of neat's-foot oil into Mama's glove. The old leather and stitching soaked it up. I pounded my fist in the pocket and thought of the last time I played catch with Papa. I was not aware Carolina was in the room and watching me.

"Your mama made that for you, didn't she, Z?"

I turned around, still wearing the glove on my hand. "Yes," I said. "It was the only one she ever made."

"What did you do for a baseball?"

"My papa made two."

"Do you still have them?"

"The first one was destroyed. The second served another purpose." I reached into my pants pocket and withdrew the Stone. "This was inside Papa's baseball."

Carolina looked hard at the pitted, egg-shaped black rock that is the Stone of Dreams. "Z . . . may I hold it? Is that allowed?"

I laughed and said, "There are no rules, Carolina. Of course, you may hold it." I gave her the Stone.

She held it gently in her hands and examined every detail. "It is heavier than I expected."

"Yes, and there used to be jewels embedded in the rock at four different points—a blue diamond on top, a star sapphire on the bottom, and lapis lazuli and pearl on the sides."

She continued to stare at the Stone. She seemed entranced, almost like a little girl. Her hands were thin, blue-veined, bony, freckled, and blotched, but her long fingers were graceful and beautiful to watch as she turned the Stone over and over. "What do you suppose it really is, Z?"

"I don't know. I truly don't know what it is or from where it came."

"It feels old," she added, handing it back to me.

"Yes," I said, then let my eyes settle on the Stone of Dreams and paused a moment, thinking of all the ones who had carried it before me. "Older than you can imagine."

Carolina stood silently as I placed Mama's glove in the shoe box where Jack, and later Caine, had always kept it. I put the shoe box back on the shelf and closed the closet door. In a soft voice, she asked, "Z, do you remember the day in Forest Park when you first told me you were . . . *different* than me? Do you remember what you did to prove it?"

I searched her eyes, but couldn't tell where she was going. "Yes," I said, hesitating. "I cut myself with a knife across the forearm. You were horrified and begged me to stop. I told you to wait and watch what happens."

She took hold of my hand and led me toward the hallway. She ran her fingers over my knuckles and wrist and up my arm to the elbow. "You healed in seconds, and in minutes your arm was smooth and unblemished. There was nothing—no red lines, no scars. And there are no scars still."

She let go of my hand and we turned to leave the bedroom. As I switched off the light, I said, "Oh, yes, there are. You just can't see them."

Antoinette surprised Carolina again by announcing she wanted to move back to St. Louis and transfer to Washington University and study literature, if they would accept her. Carolina was overjoyed and quickly made a few telephone calls to some old friends. Antoinette took a few tests, which she passed easily, and within days she was enrolled as a student in Washington University for the spring semester. Two weeks later, on a cold, blustery Saturday afternoon in the middle of January, the three of us were sitting in the kitchen discussing whether Antoinette should concentrate on English or French literature. Suddenly the back door to the kitchen burst open and Star and Willie stood in the doorway.

Star locked eyes with Carolina. Although they had exchanged letters throughout the war, they hadn't seen each other since it began. She was wearing a long wool coat with a fur collar turned up. She was forty-four years old and looked exactly like Carolina at that age. Her cheeks were flushed and her eyes were bright. The tiny gold flecks sparkled in the light. "Mama," she said, running over to Carolina and embracing her. Carolina nearly disappeared inside the coat, but I could hear her say quietly, "Oh, I missed you. Oh, how I have missed you."

Willie Croft looked remarkably well, and a little silly. On his head, with the earflaps pulled down and covering his ears, he wore a multicolored, cone-shaped, knitted wool cap. I couldn't help but laugh. Willie ambled over to me in his peculiar gait and smiled. "Peru," he said, then removed the cap and ran his hand through his hair, which had thinned and become more gray than red.

"Peru?" I asked. "What do you mean, Willie?"

"The cap, Z. The bloke who sold it to me told me it was Peruvian—from the mountains north of Cuzco. Quite handsome, don't you think?"

"Quite," I said. I laughed again and we shook hands vigorously. Willie looked me up and down. "It's good to see you, Z."

"It's good to see you, too, Willie . . . more than you think."

Star let go of Carolina and turned to give me a big hug. "I didn't know you would be here, Z. This is wonderful."

"Yes, it is, Star," I said, hugging her tightly. I saw Antoinette still sitting at the table and watching the homecoming with a wide smile. I asked Star if she had ever met Antoinette Boutrain.

"No," Star answered. She looked down at Antoinette and extended both hands. "But I've heard all about her from Jack."

Antoinette took hold of Star's hands and stood up. "And I've heard all about you," she said. "Since I was a little girl."

At that moment there was a loud banging on the kitchen door, then a man shouted, "Someone open the door! Hurry!"

"That would be Caine," Willie said, opening the door and letting in a rush of cold air.

I never saw the face of Caine's father, Jisil al-Sadi. He was already dead and facedown in the sand when I found him. But judging from Caine's face, Jisil must have been an extraordinarily handsome desert warlord. Caine stood in the doorway holding two large suitcases in his hands, another under his right arm, and a smaller one under his left. He smiled when he saw me and took a quick step forward, tripping and tumbling into the kitchen along with all the suitcases. He fell into me, knocking me back into Antoinette, and the three of us rolled together under the kitchen table in a heap of arms and legs.

I ended up on top of Antoinette with Caine sprawled across my feet. He raised his head a few inches and looked at me. "Sorry, Z. I suppose I tripped."

I laughed and said, "I suppose you did." Underneath me, Antoinette groaned and tried to wriggle free. I turned over and as I backed out from under the table, I saw Caine and Antoinette exchange a glance. It only lasted a moment, but it was an electric spark. No one else saw it. I smiled to myself because even though there was no way to know where it would end, there was no doubt something had begun.

The winter of 1946 passed quickly. In February, Mitch and Mercy purchased a house near the corner of Olive and Boyle. Carolina insisted on helping them furnish it, and a big house-warming party was held the next week.

Star and Willie had planned on staying at Carolina's a month or two, but decided in March to leave it open-ended. Willie said there was nothing to worry about concerning Caitlin's Ruby. Koldo and Arrosa ran the farm well and were completely accepted by the locals, which was not always the case in Cornwall, as Caitlin Fadle herself discovered four hundred years earlier. Star said Arrosa and Koldo now had twin boys, born during the war and named Kepa and Yaldi, after Koldo's grandfather and my papa. I felt honored and realized he still believed in the unique and ancient bond between our families. I promised myself I would visit our homeland in the Pyrenees, and I would do it with Koldo as my guide.

Caine had intended on returning to England in a few weeks, but to no one's surprise, by April he had changed his mind. He applied to Washington University as a professor in linguistics and by May he had been hired for the fall semester. It was not a shock he was accepted so rapidly. Caine possessed an advanced degree from Cambridge and his work in deciphering early Aegean languages and scripts was well known in academic circles. In a way, Caine and I shared the same "ability."

Carolina still had her box seats at Sportsman's Park and the two of us saw the majority of the Cardinals' home games. A young player named Stan Musial impressed me all season with his natural baseball instincts, and he was a terrific hitter. He batted .365 with 228 hits and was picked Most Valuable Player of the year in the National League. The Cardinals won the pennant and played the Boston Red Sox in the World Series. On October 13, just after the Cardinals had won game six, Carolina and I returned home to find Jack and another man sitting at the kitchen table drinking coffee. It was an unannounced and unexpected visit, and Carolina scolded him for it, then gave him a long, warm embrace. Jack winked at me and said, "Cards won—I know—we were listening."

I turned to look at the other man and he smiled at me. He was about sixty years old with a shock of white hair and a very distinctive face that I recognized immediately. For a moment I thought Sak had come back to life and aged twenty years. But it wasn't Sak, it was his oldest brother, Dr. Bikki Hiramura—Cardinal.

"I am Zianno Zezen."

"Yes," the man replied. "I have known your name for decades."
He extended his arm and we shook hands. "It is a pleasure to finally meet."

"Should I call you Doctor or Bikki?"

He laughed. "Bikki, please. And you, do you prefer Zianno
or Z?"

"Call me Z." I let a moment or two pass. He had dark brown
eyes, just like Sak. "Your brother was a fine man . . . a brave
man . . . and an excellent potter."

"Thank you. Those are kind words. We had different destinies,
but our beginnings were the same. I regret never having known
him as a man."

Just then a thought occurred to me. He had known about me
for decades. We could have met many times, anytime he wished,
but we did not. This visit was no coincidence. Quietly I said, "You
have come to tell me something. Should I hear it now or later?"

Bikki dropped his smile and glanced at Carolina and the
others. "Later," he said.

Over dinner, Carolina reminisced about the World's Fair
of 1904, the last time she had seen Bikki Hiramura or any of
the Ainu that Solomon had befriended before the Fair. After dinner and helping Antoinette clear the table, Bikki, Jack, and
I walked outside to the "Honeycircle" and began our talk. Bikki
stood next to Baju's sundial facing me. "First," he said, "I must ask
if you have noticed anyone following you, anyone at all, man or
woman?"

I didn't have to think about it. The Meq are instinctively cognizant of all Giza and their attention to us. It is a part of our basic
nature and necessary for survival. "No," I answered.

"Good. That is good. I feared they might find you before you
were aware of it."

"They? Who are 'they'?"

Jack answered my question. "We aren't sure, Z. We only know there is a new unit attached to the Army and they are running a covert program that might have something to do with the Meq."

"What sort of 'program'?"

Bikki looked once at Jack, then turned back to me. "It is still a mystery," he said. "I am working on it. There is someone I suspect is involved—"

Jack interrupted. "We think Blaine Harrington may be in on it."

"Nevertheless," Bikki continued, "I would recommend you pass this information on to the others, wherever they may be, until we get to the truth."

"Easier said than done, Bikki."

"What do you mean?"

"Never mind," I said. "I will keep an eye out for anything suspicious and report it to Jack immediately. And I . . . we . . . appreciate your vigilance on our behalf. Solomon would be quite proud of his *investment*."

Cardinal looked up at the night sky wheeling above the "Honeycircle" and laughed. I remembered Sak laughing the same way in the trough of a twenty-foot wave in the middle of the Bering Sea.

Jack and Bikki stayed long enough to see the Cardinals beat the Red Sox in game seven and win the World Series. In Carolina's kitchen, at Antoinette's request, we celebrated with champagne and hot dogs. The next day Jack kissed Carolina on the cheek and was in the middle of promising to come home for Christmas when she put a finger to his lips and said, "No promises, Jack. Just make it back if you can."

I took Bikki's warning to heart for the next two months. On every walk, especially in Forest Park, I used my hyper-hearing and kept my other senses at full alert. Nothing happened and I saw no one following me. Jack never made it back for Christmas, but he sent chocolates to Carolina from Switzerland. By that time I had relaxed my guard somewhat and by the spring of 1947, I rarely thought about it. What I did think about constantly was Opari. I longed for her presence, her voice . . . her touch. It didn't help to watch Caine and Antoinette falling deeper and deeper in love, although I couldn't have been happier for them. Still, every time I saw Caine whispering something to Antoinette and making her smile, I wanted to do the same to Opari.

Later that year, Willie Croft rediscovered his love of flying and bought a single-engine Cessna 170, which he kept at Lambert Field. Not long afterward, he sold the Cessna and bought a rare de Havilland twin-engine Mosquito, a British aircraft that had become famous during WWII for its versatility. The plane was light and fast, and Willie and Star would often fly to air races throughout the Midwest. Willie was an excellent pilot and always looked forward to flying, but in the spring of 1949 he had to fly for a purpose other than pleasure. Carolina received word that Ciela had passed away at Finca Maria due to complications from diabetes. Carolina was heartbroken at the news and wanted to be there for the funeral. Willie said he would charter a plane and take her to Cuba himself. I remained in St. Louis with Antoinette, but Carolina, Star, Caine, and Willie took off from Lambert Field the next day, circling once, then disappearing over the southeastern horizon.

Without Carolina and the others around, the old house suddenly seemed too big and too empty. Antoinette spent most of her mornings and afternoons on campus at Washington University, but we shared dinner and long conversations every evening in

Carolina's kitchen. I liked her candid and curious nature. We discussed anything and everything, including the Meq. One night she asked, "Do you get lonely, Z? I do not mean to pry, but it has been so long since you have seen any of your . . . any of your friends." I smiled inside because I had been thinking about Nova and Ray that afternoon. "I miss them all," I said. "And I worry about them. In matters of the heart, Antoinette, we are no different than you."

When Carolina returned two weeks later, she was visibly saddened and drained. She had known Ciela since they were both young women. They were more like sisters than friends, and Carolina took Ciela's death hard. Star said it had been difficult for everyone, and Willie said the weather hadn't helped, raining constantly for eight days in a row. It didn't take long, however, for Carolina's love of life to reappear. Antoinette graduated from Washington University in the spring of 1950 and Carolina held a small graduation party in the "Honeycircle." During the party, Antoinette and Caine announced their engagement along with their intention to marry in the fall. Carolina whooped and hollered as if she were cheering at Sportsman's Park, and the next day she and Star began making plans for the wedding.

A man's true secrets are more secret to himself than they are to others.
—PAUL VALERY

The summer passed quickly and on a golden Saturday afternoon in October, the wedding took place in Carolina's living room, then moved outside to the "Honeycircle" for the reception. Mitch gave the bride away and Jack arrived just in time to serve as Caine's best man. Mitch hired a few friends, all jazz musicians from St. Louis, to play at the reception. After kissing the bride

and congratulating the groom, Jack pulled me aside, saying he had
something extraordinary to tell me—now! I followed him up the
stairs of the carriage house and into Star's old bedroom. The colors of the constellations Nicholas had painted on the walls nearly
fifty years earlier were now dull and faded, but they were still
there, and they were still beautiful.

I looked at Jack. "What is so extraordinary?"

"Listen to this and tell me what you make of it," he said, beginning by telling me where he'd been and why. Since the end of
the war, Jack had been employed by the *Post-Dispatch* as an international sports columnist, a job that enabled him to travel the
world, and was also perfect cover for his other activities. His most
recent mission had been a rendezvous with "Valery," the Soviet
agent who also worked for Jack. Their meetings were often held
around major sporting events because they were public and usually crowded. This rendezvous took place in Belo Horizonte,
Brazil, during the 1950 World Cup soccer match between the
United States and England. Several of the players on the U.S.
team were from St. Louis and Jack knew two of them personally.
Jack said the game was terrific, with the U.S. pulling off a 1–0
victory, the biggest upset in international soccer history. After the
goal was scored, Jack said he was scanning the crowd with binoc-
ulars to watch the reactions of the crowd when he came across
something completely unexpected. Across the stadium, a boy
about my size was rising in his seat and turning to leave, and even
though Jack had never seen the boy before, he thought I might
know him. "His hair was tied back with a green ribbon," Jack
said, "and he wore ruby earrings."

"That *is* extraordinary," I said.

"And that's not all, Z. Two days later I was in a taxi on my way
to the train station, and I passed Sailor and Sheela walking down

the street. The traffic was too congested to have the taxi pull over, but there was no doubt, Z. It was them." Jack paused, then asked, "What do you think?"

I didn't know what to think. My first reaction was simply that I was glad to hear any of us were still alive. But what were Sailor and Sheela doing in Brazil? Were they tracking the Fleur-du-Mal? Was he tracking them? And where was everybody else . . . where was Opari? I couldn't answer Jack because I had nothing but questions myself.

"There's something else," Jack said.

"What is it?"

"We think Blaine Harrington has moved his unit and his operations to somewhere on the West Coast. We don't know the exact location—yet. It is a 'black' operation and 'Cardinal' has not been able to learn much about it. In the meantime, I would stay vigilant, Z. I don't trust the man in the least. Have you noticed any funny stuff, anybody following you or taking your picture?"

"No, nothing, Jack. Do you really think Blaine Harrington is after the Meq?"

"I don't know, Z, but one way or another, we're going to find out."

Below us, in the "Honeycircle," the band began playing something by Duke Ellington. I looked down through the louvered windows of the carriage house at Baju's sundial. There was just enough sunlight left for the gnomon to cast a shadow. It was late in the day and late in the year.

Carolina bought her first television set in 1951. It took two deliverymen to carry it inside, and she had to move a couch to make room for it. Mitch rigged an antenna on top of the house and after a few slight adjustments, the picture was sharp and clear. For a year or so, Carolina thought it was an interesting novelty to have in the home, but she soon changed her mind about television, worrying that people were going to forget how to entertain themselves. "Besides," she added, "I cannot stand the commercials."

In 1952 Willie Croft bought another airplane, a de Havilland Canada DHC-2 Beaver, and he and I embarked on a cross-country adventure through fifteen states. I kept in constant touch with Carolina and Star to see if there had been any word from any of the Meq. Each telephone call brought the same reply: "Sorry, Z. No word from anyone."

In 1953 the Cardinals had some good players, Stan Musial among them, but the team only had a so-so season. However, September 1 was a memorable day for two reasons: the Cardinals hit five home runs with the bases empty, tying a major league record, and Antoinette announced to everyone that she was pregnant and due in the early spring. Christmas brought nothing but baby gifts and by January Carolina had transformed Owen Bramley's sprawling bedroom into a nursery complete with everything Antoinette would need and more. Carolina was still active and in good health for a woman in her eighties, but on several occasions Willie and Caine had to keep her from doing the work herself. As the temperature dropped outside, the new life within Antoinette grew and the anticipation of a baby in the house grew with it. Except for dreams of Opari, I rarely even thought about the Meq. Then, during the last week of February, everything changed.

Carolina loved Walt Disney movies and on Monday, February 22, we had just returned home after seeing a matinee at the Fox Theatre. The animation in the film was excellent and the story one of Carolina's favorites. It was the classic by J. M. Barrie about a boy who never grew old—*Peter Pan*. She was making coffee and laughing at the irony when the telephone rang. On the second ring, she asked, "Z, would you get that?"

I picked up the receiver. "Hello."

"Well, hello right back at you," someone said. The voice sounded scratchy and distant. The connection was not a good one.

"Hello," I repeated. "Who is this? I can barely hear you."

"Someday, Z, you're gonna have to do somethin' about that hearing problem," the voice said, followed by a loud laugh I recognized instantly. My heart leaped. "Damn, Z, it's good to hear you," he said. "You're a pearl among pebbles, a peach among persimmons, a—"

I cut him off. "Enough! Enough! Where are you, Ray?"

"Mexico City, but not for long. I'm on my way to St. Louis. Nova is with me." Ray paused and the static in the background increased. "Listen, Z, I only got a minute. Somethin' strange is goin' on. I'll tell you when we get there, but I think—"

Suddenly the line filled with static and a few seconds later the connection was lost.

On Tuesday Carolina sorted through her mail and among the bills and letters was a ragged picture postcard addressed to her and postmarked ten days earlier. On one side was a picture of the old stone harbor in Cartagena, Venezuela, and on the other side there was a handwritten note, which read:

> *To he who it concerns—have found evidence of another sphere with*
> *MORE information—on our way with photographs*
> *—S and S*

On Wednesday there were no surprises, but on Thursday afternoon as I was helping Caine replace the hood on a bassinet, Carolina came upstairs to deliver a letter that Mercy had just given

STEVE CASH

her. It was still sealed and had been sent inside another letter that
Mercy received from Arrosa. Addressed to me, the letter was
written in Basque and read:

> I am aware Sailor is on his way to St. Louis and I know his pur-
> pose. You must tell him when he arrives that the prize is in Sochi
> and may be difficult to obtain. Zeru-Meq is in Istanbul. Mowsel
> and I are to rendezvous with him next week. We shall need your
> help, young Zezen. One more item—I am certain you remember
> the "Voice" that joined us when we awoke Lindbergh on his way
> to Paris. I have been "hearing" it again, but with a difference. Now
> I hear two of them! Perhaps you should ask Sailor what he thinks
> of this—Mowsel has no explanation, nor do I.
>
> *Geaxi*

Was this only coincidence? Why was this happening? Something
was in rapid motion and I had no idea what it was or what it
meant. After such a long period of silence, within four short days
I had heard from all of us, or at least all were accounted for . . . all
except one. I had to believe she was still alive. I had to believe she
was safe and well. I had to believe.

Friday passed without a word from anyone and I had trouble
sleeping that night. I dreamed of the umpire. He was walking
toward me and as he approached he removed his mask and let it
drop to the ground. Underneath his mask there was another mask
and he let it drop, then another, and another. He kept coming
closer. Sweat filled my eyes and his image blurred. My eyes
burned with sweat and I kept rubbing them to make it go away.
Then I woke up. All day Saturday I paced the house, looking out
the windows and never straying far from the telephone. No calls
came. Finally, I gave up waiting and went to bed around midnight.

Sunday was a different story entirely and events started early. During a hearty breakfast of buttermilk pancakes, fried eggs, and smoked bacon, a taxi pulled up under the stone archway and Ray Ytuarte and Nova Gastelu arrived unannounced at the kitchen door. Wearing a big smile and her usual black eyeliner, Nova came in first, along with a rush of cold air. Star cried out with surprise and pleasure, then rose from her seat to give Nova a warm embrace. They had always been close friends and hadn't seen each other in fifteen years. As Ray entered, he set down his tattered suitcase and took off Kepa's old red beret. He closed his eyes, tilted his head back, and sniffed the warm, bacon-maple-scented air of Carolina's kitchen. "Damn!" he said. "I do love pancakes."

Three hours later Caine, Willie, Ray, and I were still in the kitchen. Ray was sitting on the kitchen counter telling yet another bizarre story about Mexico City and some of the crazy American expatriates who were currently living there. Carolina, Star, Nova, and Antoinette had moved to the living room to talk about babies. Suddenly Ray stopped speaking in the middle of a sentence. I looked at him. We both felt it—the undeniable presence of Meq . . . old Meq. In a few moments, there was a knock on the door and Sailor and Susheela the Ninth entered the kitchen.

Sailor nodded to Ray and me without a word, then glanced at Willie and Caine, who was staring at Sheela. Caine had neither seen nor heard of her before, and it was easy to see how startled he was by her bearing, her beauty, and especially her color. Sailor introduced Sheela to Willie and Caine, then spoke to me. "The traffic in your country has become problematic, Zianno."

I laughed and Ray said, "I agree with you completely, Sailor. This country is goin' to the dogs."

Sailor looked at Ray with little expression, waiting for the punch line, but it never came. He shook his head back and forth once and said, "It is truly a joy to see you, Ray. Are you here alone?"

"No. Nova is with me."

"That is good." Sailor turned back to me with an expectant look on his face I'd seen before and I knew what it meant. He wanted to know when all of us could talk privately. He said one word. "When?"

"Later," I said. "After dinner."

Sailor nodded his approval. But we never got to dinner. Either from the excitement of everybody arriving or simply because it was time, Antoinette went into labor that afternoon. Willie, Star, Carolina, and Caine all left with her on the hectic drive to the hospital.

Not five minutes after they'd gone, Sailor asked Sheela to bring out the photographs of the stone sphere and lay them on the table. Ray and Nova gathered around and I showed Sailor the letter I'd received from Geaxi, which he read carefully. The black-and-white pictures were old and grainy, but the object being photographed was unmistakable. It was a stone ball exactly like the one we'd seen in Cuba with one important difference—there was twice as much script carved at the five broken intervals spaced around the ball. However, details were impossible to make out due to the poor quality of the photographs.

"Where did you get these?" I asked.

"Brazil," Sailor answered.

Sheela added, "From an art dealer with a questionable reputation. We have no idea where he obtained them. He said he 'found' them twenty years ago while on a trip to Europe."

Ray leaned over and examined each photograph. "Has that ball got somethin' to do with the Remembering?"

Sailor frowned and looked down at the pictures. "We do not

know. I think it must. These spheres are without question the oldest and rarest link to the Meq we have yet found. Perhaps Zianno will be able to decipher this one. It is imperative we locate it, if, indeed, it still exists." Sailor held Geaxi's letter in the air. "With this information we have a place to start." He paused and glanced at Sheela. "However, Sochi may prove difficult."

"Where exactly is Sochi?" Ray asked.

"Sochi is in the—"

At that moment a horn honked outside and a car pulled to a stop under the archway. Ten seconds later the door opened and Jack came rushing into the kitchen. He stopped in his tracks when he saw all of us staring back at him, then he smiled wide and said, "I don't know whether this is fate or coincidence. I was only expecting Z, but the timing of this surprise could not be better. I needed to get word to all of you, anyway."

He took off his coat and I asked, "What word, Jack?"

"We have recently discovered what Blaine Harrington is doing in California and it isn't good, Z."

"What is he doing?" Sailor asked.

Jack looked around the table at each of us. "He is looking for you . . . for all of you. He is looking for the Meq." Jack paused a moment. "He has already found one of you."

My mind went instantly to one thought and fear—Opari!

Jack went on. "And that's not all. The Soviets may be after you, too."

Sailor quickly gathered the photographs from the table and handed them to Sheela. He pulled a chair out from the table and said, "Sit down, Jack. Relax, have some coffee, and, please, you must tell us everything you know."

As Jack explained it, through an ally in Army Intelligence, Cardinal had discovered a top-secret file concerning a "black" operation code-named "SCAR," which was being run by Blaine

Harrington. Under the auspices of Army Intelligence he had converted a small ten-acre ranch outside San Diego into a kind of laboratory or prison where only one subject was being held and studied. The subject was a badly scarred female child who apparently had not aged, changed, spoken, or acknowledged anyone in nine years. They found her blood type did not make sense because it did not even exist in modern humans. They were studying the body chemistry of the girl to unlock the secret and potential power within such chemistry. Army Intelligence thought there might be strategic purposes for this knowledge, and they were going to make certain the United States had it first.

Jack talked for half an hour. I listened to every word, but as he spoke I kept feeling a strange sensation throughout my body, as if my legs and arms were waking up or anticipating something that was about to happen.

"Where did they capture this girl?" Sailor asked.

In a matter of seconds the sensations I'd been feeling increased tenfold. I felt a presence, almost a glow. My skin flushed and tingled.

Jack shook his head back and forth. "She wasn't captured, Sailor. She was found."

"Where?" I asked.

Jack said, "That's the crazy part, Z."

"Where, Jack?"

"Nagasaki. Three weeks after the bomb dropped, she was found wandering through the rubble like a ghost."

"Zuriaa!" Sailor and I said simultaneously. My heart was pounding, and I heard or felt someone behind me, silently slipping through the house from the front door to the dining room to the kitchen.

"*Zuriaa?*" Ray almost shouted, rising out of his chair. "You mean to tell me my sister is alive?"

I looked at Ray, but I could feel her behind me.

"No," she said from the shadows. Everyone turned at once toward the voice. "Zuriaa is dead, Ray, and I shall beg your forgiveness for as long as I live." She took two steps into the light of the kitchen. Her beautiful black eyes were staring directly at Ray. It was Opari. "Five days ago," she said, "I slit her throat from ear to ear."

The next day, March 1, 1954, on the Bikini Atoll in the Pacific Ocean, the United States conducted its second hydrogen bomb test. The fifteen-megaton blast was much bigger than anyone expected, erasing the atoll forever and leaving in its place a deep radioactive scar. In St. Louis a brand-new American and flawless seven-pound, eight-ounce baby girl, Georgia Caitlin Croft, was only a day old.

PART II

*People talk sometimes of bestial cruelty, but that's a great insult
to the beast, a beast can never be so cruel as a man, so
artistically cruel.*

—IVAN, *THE BROTHERS KARAMAZOV*

4

HEZUR

(BONE)

16,355 years BCE
Northern Caucasus Mountains

He used the late light of day to gather the sweetest scented wood and the only berries still available. He was now too weak to hunt for meat. It was the time of year when leaves fell from the trees and berries were rare. The task would take him far from the cave, but he would return in time to look out over the river and watch the sun setting in the west. He stood motionless at the entrance to the cave. He could feel the cold air coming down from the north. He knew it would be much colder in another two moons and snow would soon follow. Tonight, he thought, tonight will be a good night to die. He scanned the horizon once more, made the simple gesture for farewell, then turned and entered the cave. The others were waiting for him, huddled around the fire pit. They were too weak and sick to leave the cave. He didn't know how long they each had been alive, but he knew it was a long, long time. None of them had ever been sick. Their kind did not know sickness. He exchanged looks with each one. All agreed with him. They knew what he knew. They didn't have to speak. They used few words, yet their conversations were deep. As far as they knew, they were the last ones. The fire burned late into the night. In silence, they each positioned themselves into the special arrangement and closed their eyes. They found the Voice between them, and without a word, one by one, drifted away on the stream of the Long Dream.

In the end, there is nothing left. It all goes back, it all returns to nothing. Piece by piece, stage by stage, we disintegrate and disappear. Our

last breath is first to go, along with self, spirit, love, mind, all gone. Poof!
Then the body begins its inexorable degradation. The soft parts fade
quickly. Flesh, organs, muscle, sinew, all rot and decay. Only bone re-
mains. Bone is our last trace, our last message . . . our last echo.

When Opari appeared in Carolina's kitchen, she spoke for
nearly an hour. During her long story, she used several Meq
words and phrases I had never heard before. They were words
dating back to the Time of Ice and beyond. Opari and her sister,
Deza, learned the words from their mother as children. The
words describe certain actions, abilities, and states of mind common only to the Stone of Blood. Most have to do with practical
healing techniques, but two are quite different. The first ability is
called "Bihotzarin"—the Heartlight. Opari said the word matter-
of-factly in an even voice. It is a unique ability somewhat like
echolocation in bats, where Opari is able to find certain other
Meq who are in profound distress, except that she uses her own
heartbeat and the practice is more mystical than medicinal. The
second is an act, an extreme act, and Opari said the word in a
whisper with tears running down her cheeks. The ancient word
is "Kanporurrike." Loosely translated, it means "beyond compas-
sion," and it is the name for the act that killed Zuriaa.

During World War II, Opari was living in Hong Kong with
the current generation of an old and wealthy family named Liang.
They are a family of dealers and traders she has known and
trusted at various times for the last three hundred years. Most
of their businesses were and are legal, but a few of their interests
blur the line or erase it entirely. Zeru-Meq also knows this family
well. After the war, he managed to contact Opari through a
cousin living in Macao. Once together, and having no knowledge
of what had occurred in Japan, Opari and Zeru-Meq continued

their search for the Fleur-du-Mal. They spent the next eight years in a futile and frustrating effort, finding little or nothing and hearing less. Then, a brief encounter and a few overheard remarks by a member of the Liang family changed everything and suddenly made the search for the Fleur-du-Mal irrelevant.

David Liang Wen liked to call himself a "broker of information," but in truth he was a spy for hire. In January 1954 he was working in Hong Kong and Tokyo for the Soviets. In Tokyo, he went to a meeting with his contact, and the man was talking with another man as he approached. The men were speaking Russian and they must have assumed he didn't know the language because they finished their conversation before switching to Chinese. But David Liang Wen did speak Russian. He overheard his contact ask the other man, who he called Valery, "Is this true, have the Americans captured one of these strange children who do not age?" "Yes," Valery answered, "they are holding her now outside San Diego, California. I know the fool in charge. Do not worry." Valery smiled and changed to Chinese, introducing himself and saying something innocuous about the good food in Hong Kong. Then he excused himself and left.

Upon learning what David Liang Wen had overheard, Opari and Zeru-Meq made a rapid decision. Opari would travel to the United States to investigate and Zeru-Meq would leave for the Middle East, where he knew Geaxi and Mowsel were living. They would discuss the situation and try to reach the rest of us.

The Liang family supplied Opari with the proper forged papers and a chaperone to avoid suspicion. Together, they boarded a ship for the United States. Another cousin met her in San Francisco, then drove her down the coast to San Diego. From there, with Opari using the Heartlight for direction, they combed the hills and roads surrounding San Diego. After a frustrating week of searching, Opari finally picked up a heartbeat. It was weak but steady. They continued in a crisscross pattern along county roads until the exact location was pinpointed. The car slowed to a stop about nine miles northeast of the city. Across the road a locked, unmarked gate guarded a long, winding gravel driveway. At the end of the driveway was a Spanish hacienda and several outbuildings spread through a large grove of oak trees. The place looked idyllic. No cars or vehicles of any kind were visible; nor were there any dogs, at least not in the open. Opari decided to wait for darkness before entering the property.

At this moment in her story, Opari paused and the first tear appeared in the corner of her eye.

The night sky was clear and bright with stars. Opari told the Liang cousin, whose name was Sam, to wait for her with the motor running. She slipped over the fence and crept toward the grove of oak trees. Several lights shone from inside the hacienda and a few more from inside one of the outbuildings. She held the Stone of Blood in the palm of her hand and focused her mind on the heartbeat. It was coming from the outbuilding. Then she heard the sound of someone running through the trees and turned just in time to see three Doberman pinschers heading straight for her. Silent and deadly, they had their teeth bared, but they weren't barking. *"Lo geltitu, txakuri, lo geltitu,"* Opari whispered, holding the Stone of Blood in front of the dogs. All three of them acted as if they had been shot and fell to the ground instantly, staring into space and breathing heavily with their tongues hanging out. Opari continued on toward the heartbeat.

Two doors led into the outbuilding. Opari first tried the door on the southern end, but it was locked. The northern door was in full view of the hacienda and she made sure no one was watching before opening the door and stepping inside without a sound. She was standing in a long hallway. Light was coming from the open doors of two rooms at the far end. Opari didn't know what to expect yet she didn't hesitate. She walked in silence to the first door and stopped and listened. Inside, two men were in conversation. One of them called the other "Blaine." The air smelled slightly antiseptic. Holding the Stone, she stepped into the light.

The two men were standing on opposite sides of a girl lying back in what looked to be a dentist's chair. They each wore full-length white laboratory coats, and one of them was holding a scalpel in his hand. The girl's face and arms were so badly burned and scarred, she was unrecognizable. She was also the source of the heartbeat. She was Zuriaa.

Both men turned and stared at Opari.

"What the hell—" one man said.

"I knew it, I knew it," the man with the scalpel said. "I knew it was true."

"*Ahaztu!*" Opari said, holding the Stone in front of her. "*Lo geltitu, Giza, lo geltitu!* Go to sleep now, my lambs. You will forget."

Both men collapsed where they were, dropping to the floor and staring into space. The scalpel tumbled loose. Opari looked around the room, which had been converted from a ranch outbuilding into a small laboratory. There were vials, beakers, blood samples, skin samples, microscopes, and other assorted instruments, including syringes, needles, and scalpels. Not only had they been studying Zuriaa, they had been *experimenting* on her. Opari walked over and looked closely at Zuriaa lying back in the chair. Though it went against everything in her nature to do so, she knew in an instant what she must do. Zuriaa's heart was beating at a steady and even pace, but it was beating in a body that no longer cared, with a mind that was no longer there. Being Meq, she had somehow survived the nuclear blast, yet she had been burned and blown to a place from which she never came back. Zuriaa was most likely insane long before Nagasaki, and she had committed many heinous acts in her lifetime; however, Opari could not let her continue to exist as she was and be used and abused like a laboratory rat. Kanporurrike was the only answer. Opari bent down and picked up the scalpel from the floor. She whispered "Please forgive me" into Zuriaa's ear, then sliced her throat as quickly and cleanly as she could. She watched the blood pooling on the floor and held Zuriaa's hand until her heartbeat weakened and fell silent. Opari closed her eyes and kissed her once on the lips. She turned and stepped over the two men and walked out of the building. When she was clear of the oak trees, she broke into a run and within seconds was over the fence. Sam Liang was waiting with the engine running and they headed off in darkness toward San Diego and the train station. Early the next day, he was on his way back to San Francisco and Opari was on board a train bound for St. Louis.

When she finished her story, total silence filled the room. There was one fact that none of us could deny or avoid, and it was on everyone's mind. Zuriaa, with all her madness and misconduct, was still Ray's sister. Meq brothers and sisters are rare, and the bond between them is much stronger than the bond between Giza siblings, even if one of them has gone astray. I watched Ray carefully. He sat staring straight ahead without any expression, but I knew in his mind he was reliving those long-ago moments and events that only he and Zuriaa had shared. For a full minute no one said a word. Then Ray was the first to speak. He cleared his throat and said, "You did right, Opari. You did what needed to be done. I'd have done the same thing if I'd been there. I never heard of Kanporurrike, but I'd have done the same thing."

"Ray is correct," Sailor added. "Now you must let it go, Opari. There is no shame or guilt in your actions." Sailor turned to face Jack. "I am concerned about this Blaine Harrington."

Jack rubbed the back of his neck and said, "You should be

more concerned about Valery, Sailor. All of you should. He is much more dangerous than Blaine Harrington."

"In what respect?"

"He is smart, he is unpredictable, and he has a network of agents worldwide." Jack paused and looked at me. "This is an alarm bell, Z. I think all of you need to disappear for a while. Tell me how I can help and Cardinal and I will arrange it."

I glanced around the kitchen at each of the others, then Sailor said, "Get us to Istanbul, Jack. From there, we shall 'disappear.'"

One week later Jack called from Washington to say we'd hit the jackpot in lucky timing. A cultural exchange sponsored by the State Department and involving nearly a hundred children was leaving the United States for Turkey in less than three days. Jack said he could insert us into the group. Blending in with a hundred children would enable the six of us to travel together without arousing suspicion. And by coincidence, Cardinal was in Tel Aviv attending an international medical symposium, which also served as cover for his other activities. Cardinal could easily meet us in Istanbul and supply us with anything we might need. It was an excellent plan and we all agreed immediately.

"There ain't nothin' wrong with a little good luck," Ray said.

Carolina protested and complained about our leaving, especially mine, but I knew that would pass soon enough. She had a baby in the house again. Nothing had ever made her happier than the sound of babies and children in her home. This time, she could even think of her sister whenever she whispered the baby's beautiful name, "Georgia."

Willie Croft did us a big favor and volunteered to fly us to Washington, D.C., in his de Havilland, and we left St. Louis the next day. Jack was waiting for us at the airport. He escorted us to

New York by train, where we boarded our ship in plenty of time. Before wishing us farewell, Jack made all the proper arrangements and introductions, and that evening, accompanied by several loud blows of the horn, we set sail at 9:00 P.M. sharp.

Opari and I had not seen each other in eighteen years, yet during the voyage we spoke very little, although we were never outside each other's presence for more than a few minutes. When we were able to be on our own, we walked the decks of the ship, smelling the salty air, watching the ocean and the stars at night, oblivious to everything but the moment. I kissed her eyelids and she kissed the palms of my hands. I slept well, dreamed little, and woke each morning to find her next to me. My Ameq—my love, Opari.

On the morning of April 13, 1954, we entered the harbor of Istanbul, sailing slowly past the Hagia Sophia. High on the hill, surrounded by minarets and spires, and framed against a cloudless blue sky, it was majestic and magnificent, exactly as the Emperor Justinian wanted it to appear fourteen centuries earlier.

"There lies our letter box, with directions from Geaxi inside, no doubt," Sailor said.

"Letter box?" I asked.

"Designed and installed secretly for our use in 537 by Isidore of Miletus."

"Who was he?"

"A friend of ours, and also one of the two designers of the Hagia Sophia."

We disembarked along with all the children in the entourage, staying on the back edge of the group and keeping a close watch for Cardinal. He appeared almost at once. He was talking with a Turkish customs agent and showing him a clutch of papers in his hand. Now in his sixties, Cardinal wore a dark business suit, and his thick black hair was streaked with silver, but he still reminded me a great deal of his brother, Sak. Once he saw us approaching, he pointed to us, and within minutes we were separated from the others and led through the crowd by the customs agent. Cardinal looked at me as we were walking out. He winked and said, "Welcome to Istanbul, Zianno."

Waiting for us in his tour bus was Kerem, a gap-toothed man with deep creases in his face and large brown eyes that seemed to smile even when he wasn't smiling. Cardinal referred to him as "my man in the street." Kerem's tour bus was painted bright blue and gold outside and lined inside with multicolored fringe and tassels, tiny hanging brass bells and cymbals, and dozens of faded portraits of the founder of modern Turkey, Mustafa Kemal, better known as Ataturk.

We were driven through crowded and chaotic streets to a small hotel only a few blocks from the Tokapi Palace called the Empress Zoe. It was quiet and clean and easily within walking distance of the Hagia Sophia. Sailor decided to wait until the next day before checking on the "letter box." In the evening, Kerem took us to his favorite restaurant, where we ate a long and delicious meal and listened to his stories in broken English about the mysteries of Istanbul, and there were many. Cardinal said Kerem seemed to know everyone in the city, if not personally, then through a friend, a cousin, or an uncle. At one point, he suddenly stopped talking and stared hard into Ray's eyes. He looked concerned and slightly afraid. "Your eyes are much green," he said. "Do you possess the *nazar*?"

Ray glanced around the table at each of us. "I don't think so. What is it?"

"The evil eye," Kerem said. "In Turkey, green eyes are much dangerous for the *nazar*."

Ray told Kerem he had nothing to worry about and turned to me. He winked. "Did you hear that, Z? You better be on your best behavior or I just might zap you with the evil eye." Everyone laughed out loud, even Kerem, after he realized it was a joke. Finally, we returned to the hotel and our rooms. It felt good to lie down and spend the night in a comfortable bed curled up next to Opari.

Sailor woke me the next morning and the two of us left for the Hagia Sophia while the others waited at the hotel. He led the way through narrow, noisy alleys, past open windows and the smell of mutton and vinegar. I heard at least three different languages being spoken in the streets. Sailor never said a word, and we arrived at the southwestern entrance only minutes after they had opened the doors. Visitors and tourists were already spread throughout the cavernous old church and mosque. As we walked in, Sailor said, "The last time I was here, the air was filled with incense and smoke."

"When was that?" I asked.

"A thousand years ago," he said, glancing in all directions.

"Exactly a thousand?"

"Exactly."

Sailor said the letter box was in an upper enclosure, a central gallery called the "Loge of the Empress." It was where the Empress and her ladies of the court gathered to observe the proceedings below. The letter box was hidden in a wall directly behind where the Empress once stood. On the third step of the marble stairs leading up to the gallery, Sailor and I suddenly stopped and stared at each other. We both felt the same thing at once—the unmistakable presence of Meq.

Side by side, Sailor and I entered the upper gallery. The long, wide room was much larger than I had expected. At least twenty people were scattered throughout and it still seemed empty. We kept walking. In the central gallery, a few were peering over the balcony, staring into the vast space of the great dome. A round, green stone marked the position of the throne of the Empress.

Sailor saw them first. "Over there," he said, nodding to the right.

Forty feet away, directly behind the green stone, there appeared to be three children standing near the wall. Of course, they were anything but children, and they were waiting for us. It was Geaxi, Mowsel, and Zeru-Meq.

As we approached, I smiled to myself. For disguise, Mowsel and Zeru-Meq were dressed like any other kid in the streets of modern Istanbul and could blend in easily, but Geaxi defied all trends or fashions and didn't seem worried about any disguise. She was dressed as always—black leather leggings and a black vest held together with strips of leather attached to bone, a black beret, and ballet shoes. "There is only one Geaxi," I whispered. "Indeed," Sailor said.

Even though we hadn't seen the three of them in eighteen years, Sailor ignored traditional greetings and walked straight to Geaxi while acknowledging all three with a single nod. "Quite a surprise," he said. "I was anticipating finding only directions. I do not suppose this is a coincidence."

"The letter box is no longer in the wall," Geaxi said.

Sailor looked perplexed. "I do not understand. That is impossible. Where is it?"

"Gone."

Geaxi gracefully stepped to one side, letting Sailor see for himself. He reached out and touched the area in the wall where the letter box had been concealed. "The secret stones have been replaced!"

"Centuries ago, Umla-Meq. It is true," Mowsel said with a half smile, barely exposing the gap of his missing front tooth. He was standing next to Geaxi with his head leaning back, as if he was staring at the ceiling.

"We have been away too long, old one," Zeru-Meq added. His black hair was longer now, curling around his ears and over his collar. His green eyes flashed when he spoke.

"None of us have used this building since the Ottomans came to power," Geaxi said.

Sailor let the truth sink in for several moments. He seemed to be remembering or realizing something. He looked over his shoulder toward the balcony and the green stone marking the throne of the Empress. Then Sailor laughed, twice. He asked Geaxi, "How did you know we would be here today?"

"We felt your arrival yesterday. It was thunderous."

"Yes, Sailor," Zeru-Meq said. "Just how many are with you and Zianno?"

"Everyone," I answered. "That is, everyone except the Fleur-du-Mal."

"Zianno, my friend, it is good to see you," Zeru-Meq said, "but, if you please, let us leave him out of this."

Geaxi turned to me. "Hello, young Zezen. You look well," she said casually, as if she'd only been gone a week or two.

"So do you, Geaxi," I said, trying not to smile.

She went on. "We have much to discuss and this is not the place."

"Agreed," Sailor said. "We have rooms in a hotel not far from here, all provided by Cardinal. The others are there waiting."

"I will be glad to finally meet this 'Cardinal,'" Geaxi replied.

"He has been more than helpful. He is resourceful and reliable and truly wants to protect us."

"Is that so?" Geaxi said, raising her eyebrows slightly and glancing at me. We both knew Sailor rarely, if ever, praised a Giza.

Sailor motioned toward the marble stairs. "Shall we go?"

"Yes, yes, yes. Lead the way," Mowsel said, angling his head up and to the left. "I have been in here too long as it is. I abhor it."

Sailor walked over to Mowsel and gazed into his eyes. "What do you not like about being here, Trumoi-Meq?"

"I abhor the emptiness."

"But you cannot see."

"I can see the emptiness, old friend. I can see the emptiness."

We returned to the hotel just as the third call to prayer of the day echoed across the city. Zeru-Meq said he thought the calls themselves were one of the most beautiful aspects of Islam. Inside, the lobby of the Empress Zoe was nearly empty. The desk clerk and his assistant were playing dominoes and smoking cigarettes. The heavy, pungent aroma of Turkish tobacco swam through the air. Cardinal was the only other person in the lobby. He sat in a chair reading the newspaper. He stood up and his eyes widened as we approached. He had not expected to see three more Meq.

"This is quite a surprise, Zianno," he said, "but a pleasant one, a pleasant one." He looked at the three new faces. He seemed instantly enchanted by Geaxi and her attire, and he studied Mowsel for a few extra moments.

"Dr. Bikki Birnbaum," I said, "I would like you to meet Geaxi, Zeru-Meq, and Trumoi-Meq, also known as Mowsel."

"It is an honor and a great pleasure," Cardinal said, nodding to each one of them.

"The pleasure is ours," Geaxi replied, then added bluntly, "You are Ainu, no?"

Cardinal laughed. "Ainu-American," he said, "thanks to Solomon J. Birnbaum . . . and Owen Bramley."

Geaxi glanced away for a second, then put it together. "Ah!" she said, "you are the missing Hiramura brother."

Cardinal laughed again. "Guilty."

Sailor had been scanning the lobby. He turned to Cardinal. "Are you alone?"

"No," he answered, then looked over his shoulder and nodded toward an arch and a corridor leading off the lobby. Everyone's head turned except Mowsel's. Cardinal seemed to take notice. "They are in a small courtyard and flower garden waiting for you. I have a few errands, but I will return in time for dinner. I have information to share with all of you concerning Blaine Harrington, Valery, and the Russians."

"Good," Sailor replied. "We shall welcome it."

Sailor motioned for us to follow him. Cardinal watched the five of us as we walked by, especially Mowsel, who never hesitated or got closer than five feet from Geaxi, yet never missed a step. "Excuse me . . . excuse me, please," Cardinal said. Everyone stopped and turned. "Mowsel, if I may call you that, I have a personal question. I do not mean to pry or offend, and you do not have to answer."

"That is quite all right," Mowsel said, leaning toward Cardinal's voice. "Yes, you may call me Mowsel, and by all means, ask your question."

Cardinal paused a moment. "How long have you been blind?"

Mowsel stood motionless. Geaxi looked stunned. Mowsel's blindness was virtually undetectable to most Giza.

Sailor seemed amused. "Answer him, Trumoi-Meq."

"Since Guernica," Mowsel said, "1937. I was hit by flying debris when the bombs dropped."

"But there is no noticeable scarring," Cardinal said.

"All else . . . healed." Mowsel angled his head up slightly and grinned wide, fully revealing his gap. "Why do you ask, Doctor?"

"Have you ever heard of an ophthalmoscope?"

Geaxi broke in. "Yes, of course. I believe it is the instrument with a mirror centrally perforated for use in viewing the interior of the eye, especially the retina."

Cardinal smiled. "That's correct," he said. "Before dinner, I would like to examine your eyes, Mowsel. I may be able to help."

No one moved. Geaxi, Sailor, Zeru-Meq, and I all stared at Mowsel, awaiting his response. Being examined by a Giza, any Giza, for an old one like Trumoi-Meq was a difficult decision. For thousands of years old ones had only survived by never allowing such things to happen. Mowsel's grin faded, and even though he was blind he looked directly at us, one by one. In his mind, he knew exactly where we were standing. Then his grin began to return. He laughed suddenly and found Geaxi, winding his arm inside of hers. He looked in Cardinal's direction. "Hail, Hadrian!" Mowsel said and laughed again. "Why not, Doctor, why not?"

"Excellent," Cardinal said, picking up his newspaper and turning to go. "I will see you then."

After he left, we walked single file past the desk clerk and his assistant. They never looked up from their domino game. A blue haze of tobacco smoke surrounded them. To no one in particular, Geaxi said, "I think I like this 'Cardinal.'"

We entered the garden at the rear of the hotel by walking through an arched, bronze gate. Across the top, the gate was inscribed with a curious quotation—*Quis custodiet ipsos custodes?* Who will keep the keepers themselves? The space itself was open-aired and hidden from surrounding streets by an eight-foot wall on three sides. Tulips of every color, lilies, and crocuses encircled a small stone fountain and five stone benches. Opari and Nova sat on one bench, Sheela on another, and Ray stood by the fountain, twirling his old red beret on his forefinger. Zeru-Meq was the first to enter the garden, followed by Geaxi, Mowsel, and Sailor. For some reason, I hesitated and hung back, watching everyone as they greeted each other. I felt odd, separated, as if I was suddenly suspended in a dream. I looked up. The sky was a clear and brilliant blue. I could hear the drone of traffic beyond the walls, but it seemed miles away. Excluding the Fleur-du-Mal, I realized that all Meq, all of us who were still known to exist on earth, were gathered together in this one tiny garden in Istanbul. Without warning, I shuddered inside. I felt cold and lonely. Even with our powers, we were so few, so vulnerable. We were the last ones, I thought, the last of our kind . . . the last. Then I felt her fingers sliding gently between the fingers of my right hand. I blinked twice and looked into the beautiful black eyes of Opari. "This way, my love." She led me over to a place next to her on one of the stone benches. We sat down and she kissed the palms of my hands. She looked at me and smiled. So young, so old.

"First," I heard Sailor say from somewhere near the fountain, "we must discuss the Remembering. Then we must discuss our enemies."

Our meeting lasted three hours. It was serious in tone, almost solemn, and felt like a tribal council in the truest sense. From Nova, the youngest, to Susheela the Ninth, the oldest, everyone spoke, all with equal voice and import. Sailor began the "discussion," then deferred to Mowsel, who spoke at length, reiterating in great detail everything the Meq knew and did not know about the Gogorati, the Remembering. He recited a litany of names, places, ancient translations, insights, dreams, and mystical, elliptical riddles with multiple solutions. He spoke eloquently, often using old Meq phrases for emphasis. Because of the absolute truth and passion in his words, his blindness and the gap of his missing tooth were irrelevant. Trumoi-Meq had always been the historian and the recorder. He was the conscience of the Meq. He ended with one of his own poems. It was a short and strange poem, but its meaning was clear. *"Tie a knot in the air and pull tight. How does that feel? Ah, precious truth."* None of us, not even Mowsel, knew what to expect at the Remembering.

Sailor suggested that all pursuit of the "little wolf" be suspended. The "little wolf" was one of the Fleur-du-Mal's many nicknames. Everyone nodded in agreement. Zeru-Meq added, "Hear! Hear!" Sailor said our one objective must be to find the stone sphere we had seen in the photograph. "The writing on the sphere may be our last, best chance to discover a sign, instructions, directions, anything that might lead us to the exact location of the Egongela, the Living Room. Otherwise," he said, pausing and glancing at me, "we shall have to guess." He turned to Geaxi. "In your letter to Zianno, you said the prize was in Sochi, no? I assume you refer to the sphere."

"Yes," Geaxi answered. "According to a source we know well, someone who has seen it with his own eyes, the sphere is in a dacha once owned by the Minister of Culture under Stalin."

"Who is the source?" Sailor asked.

"A man I did not recognize initially. He is older now and his face and arms are badly scarred. I am sure you remember Giles Xuereb of Malta."

Sailor and I looked at each other in disbelief. Long ago, we both had assumed the Fleur-du-Mal had killed Giles Xuereb in revenge for lying to him, even while being tortured and carved one slice at a time. "I am glad to hear he is still alive," Sailor said. "He is the last of his line."

"Where is Sochi?" Nova asked.

"Sochi," Zeru-Meq said, "is a mere five or six hundred miles to the east, straight across the Black Sea."

"Is the dacha occupied?" Opari asked.

"At the moment, yes," Geaxi said, removing her beret.

"Sounds like all we need is a little 'breaking and entering,'" Ray said. "And that's right up my alley."

"Ray is correct," Sailor added. "Occupation should not present a problem."

"Normally, no. This time, yes . . . a slight one." Geaxi slipped her beret back on her head and adjusted it to the proper angle. She looked Sailor in the eye. "The current owner and occupant of the dacha, at least for the next month, is Nikita Khrushchev, the Premier of the Soviet Union."

A few moments passed. Sailor never changed expression, nor did Geaxi. "I suppose you have something in mind," he said, "for this 'slight' problem?"

"Yes, I do." Geaxi rose off the bench and began walking slowly toward me. "We are fortunate. However, we have only two days to prepare."

"We?" Sailor asked. "Geaxi, do you mean all of us?"

"No," she said, stopping about six feet from me. "We will likely have one chance to see the sphere, and it will be brief. I will need someone to help me make sense of what I see, and help me remember it." She took another step toward me. "Possibly even *read* it."

Everyone turned to look at me. Opari smiled. Ray was still twirling his beret on his finger. He winked. I didn't have to say I would do it; everybody knew I would do it. I looked at Geaxi. "I'm in, but tell me, why two days? What is happening in two days?"

"Nikita Khrushchev's birthday. A party is scheduled, along with entertainment. Through the generosity of Giles Xuereb, you and I, young Zezen, will be performing."

"Performing as what?" I asked.

Geaxi grabbed her beret, did a perfect standing back flip with a half twist, then spun in a gentle, graceful pirouette until she was facing me again. She flashed a smile and said, "Acrobats."

There was a moment of silence, followed by Ray howling with laughter. Opari had to cover her mouth to keep from laughing. Then Geaxi explained by recounting what had happened to Giles since we last saw him.

In 1923, after months of healing and rehabilitation, Giles Xuereb was released from the hospital on Malta. Though horribly scarred on his face, arms, chest, and back, his one thought and concern was the Fleur-du-Mal. He knew the Fleur-du-Mal would come back to kill him as soon as he realized Giles had lied to him. He knew he must leave Malta and disappear, quickly and completely. There was only one place where this might be possible. It would also be the safest.

Giorgi Zhordania was a name Giles had known most of his life. His father had told him as a boy that if Giles ever needed safe haven and protection, there was one man who would always provide it. The man and Giles's father were once the only survivors of a passenger ship that went down in a Mediterranean storm. Six days and nights they were alone together in the cold sea. They shared their life stories and each promised, should they survive their ordeal, to always welcome and offer sanctuary to the other and his family, no matter what, forever. It was a pact that Giles's father said was as true and sacred as any a man can make. Now Giles would find out for himself.

After an arduous journey to Sochi, Russia, he traveled into the Caucasus Mountains and found his way to the tiny town of Zuratumi. He asked and was given directions to a rambling old house and courtyard a few blocks away. As he approached, he heard shouts coming from behind the walls of the courtyard. The long gate was swung wide open. He walked inside. The first thing he saw was a boy in red tights flying through the air, turning three somersaults and landing squarely on the shoulders of a slightly older boy, who was standing on the shoulders of two other boys beneath him. Surrounding them in a loose circle, several more boys and five or six girls, some in their teens, shouted their approval. An older man, probably in his seventies, sat off to one side in a straight-backed chair. He was leaning forward on a cane and speaking softly in an ancient Romany dialect. "Again," he said, "you must do it again, Giorgi . . . again and again . . . until you do not doubt. I detected doubt. There must be no doubt and no fear."

Giles looked up at the boy on top of the human tower and the boy was staring back at him. The boy pointed at Giles, and all eyes turned to look, including the old man with the cane. Giles cleared his throat and spoke in Russian. "I am seeking a man named Giorgi Zhordania."

A squat, muscular man about forty years old with thick black hair and heavy eyebrows stepped out of the shadows. He motioned for the boy to climb down, then walked over to Giles, staring at the multiple scars on his face and neck. "I am Giorgi Zhordania," he said. "Who are you?"

Giles hesitated. "My name is Giles Xuereb."

The man looked Giles over once more. "Have we met before?"

"No. Never."

The man's eyes were coal black, and he stared at Giles without smiling. "What is your purpose? Why do you seek me out?"

The courtyard fell completely silent. Not one person moved or made a sound. Then the old man rose out of his chair and made his way over to Giles, tapping his cane on the ground along the way. He gazed up and into Giles's eyes, then smiled. "He does not seek you, Giorgi. He seeks me . . . and he needs no purpose for being here. He is welcome for any reason and for any length of time." The old man took hold of Giles's hand. "You are the son of Manoel Xuereb, no?"

"Yes," Giles said, covering the old man's hand with both of his. "Yes, I am, sir."

The Great Zhordanias, as they had been called for at least a hundred years, were an extended Rom family of acrobats and musicians well known throughout the Caucasus Mountains and southern Georgia. Because of the elder Giorgi's words, Giles was treated as an honored guest and accepted into their clan as much as any guest could be. He told Giorgi of the "evil one" who had scarred his face and body, and he warned Giorgi that the "evil one" might return to finish his handiwork. Giorgi told Giles there was no need for worry; the Zhordanias of this town and valley could sense when *mizhak,* or "evil," was near or in their company. Several years passed and Giles became a kind of booking agent for *The Great Zhordanias.* Then, in 1937, Stalin built a massive and secluded dacha in Sochi. For Stalin's birthday on December 18, the Minister of Culture staged a birthday party that included *The Great Zhordanias* as entertainment. Stalin loved their act, and they began a tradition of performing for him and his staff whenever he spent his birthday in Sochi. It was on one of these occasions that Giles was shown an unusual collection of bones and artifacts in a dacha owned by the Minister of Culture. Giles intuitively knew the stone sphere and its strange, carved script would be of interest to the Meq. Then Stalin died and the Minister of Culture "disappeared," though his dacha and its contents remained. Nikita Khrushchev became the Premier and new "owner" of the spacious villa. When told of Stalin's birthday parties in Sochi, Khrushchev decided to continue the tradition, and *The Great Zhordanias* were asked to perform on his birthday April 17. Using a long-standing mutual contact in Istanbul, Giles was able to find Geaxi and relay his information. Geaxi knew this could be an opportunity for the Meq to see the sphere, and sent word to us. Now it was April 14 and I had less than three days to become one of the leaping, flying *Great Zhordanias*. Geaxi didn't seem to think this was a problem. She said she would teach me everything I needed to know.

"Everything?" I asked.

"Well," she said, hesitating. "Most of it."

That same evening, Cardinal informed all of us about Blaine Harrington and his obsessions, one of which was his pursuit of a new weapon to use against the Soviets; a human weapon with superhuman powers. After his sadistic study of Zuriaa, then seeing Opari and witnessing a little of what she could do, he was now convinced the Meq and whatever is in our blood could be that weapon. Cardinal also told us what Valery looked like, but very little else. He said Valery had only been seen rarely since 1945, and with a network of agents who were equally invisible, he was impossible to track or predict. The CIA and Army Intelligence had not yet been able to "turn" anyone who had ever worked for him or with him. All Soviet agents denied his existence. When Cardinal finished his briefing, he asked if we needed anything. Geaxi asked if he might assist two of us in entering Russia secretly somewhere near the Sukhoy Kurdzhips River. He said it could be arranged through Kerem and his Black Sea contacts. Cardinal then told Mowsel he would examine him the next day and we ended the late night with Mowsel and Cardinal discussing various ocular trauma and the advances in modern ophthalmology.

It cost us $3500 plus the cost of fuel, but two nights later Geaxi and I were on board a Russian-built Mi-1 helicopter piloted by a Turkish smuggler named Babesh. We flew through the night, refueling twice along the north coast of Turkey, then making the long hop across open water at an altitude of no more than fifty feet, finally landing outside the small coastal town of Tuapse. Babesh never turned the engine off and left as soon as Geaxi and I were clear of the rotor blades. It was not a pleasant trip, yet dawn was breaking, we were safe, we were in Russia, and we were not far from Zuratumi.

Geaxi said, "Do you feel like a spy, young Zezen?"

"No. I feel more like a criminal."

"Even better," she said with a laugh.

The air was warm and humid, and we walked south at a quick pace for nearly three hours. Geaxi seemed to know exactly where she was going. She told me she had spent some time in the region two hundred years earlier and even though many of the roads were now paved, they were the same roads leading to the same places. By late morning we had reached an intersection about thirty miles north of Sochi. Geaxi paused and looked around. An old school bus was parked off to one side. It was painted in stripes of at least six different colors, which were all fading and chipped. On both sides in bold Russian letters were the words THE GREAT ZHORDANIAS. As we approached, the doors of the bus opened and a tall, badly scarred, white-haired man in his early seventies stepped out. It was Giles Xuereb. Speaking Maltese to Geaxi, he said, "I was beginning to worry."

Geaxi shrugged, then adjusted her beret and smiled. Also speaking Maltese, she replied, "Not to worry, old friend. After all, the show must go on."

Giles looked down at me. A moment or two passed.

"Hello, Giles," I said.

"Zianno . . . an unexpected pleasure. How long has it been?"

"Thirty-two years."

"Yes . . . yes," he said, pausing and glancing back at the school bus and the faces of a dozen Zhordanias staring out the windows.

"It is good to see you again, Giles. It is good to see you alive," I added, both of us knowing I was referring to the Fleur-du-Mal.

He put his index finger to his lips. "Shhh," he whispered, then laughed out loud. He turned and gazed down the road to the south. Traffic was sparse, as it had been all morning. "Come with us. You must be hungry following such a long journey. We will find something decent to eat in town. After that," he said, winking at both Geaxi and me, "we have a show to do."

On the drive into Sochi, Giles introduced Geaxi and me to the Zhordanias, one by one. The youngest among them was twelve years old, a wide-eyed boy named Noe, and the oldest was in his mid-forties. His name was Giorgi, and thirty-two years earlier he had been the boy Giles first saw tumbling through the air upon his arrival in Zuratumi. Now Giorgi was the leader of their troupe and the anchor of the flying four-tiered human pyramid, the highlight of their act and the feat for which they were famous. When Giorgi was told that I was American, he became very excited and insisted I sit next to him. "We will talk," he said, "and Giorgi will grow his English."

We stopped for a wonderful two-hour meal at a restaurant called the Black Magnolia. Giles ordered *osciotr* caviar, along with *zakuski,* which included pickled herrings, cucumbers, cabbages, and beets, then *ukha,* or clear fish soup with potato piroshki stuffed with wild mushrooms, then fried filets of salmon with dill sauce and cucumber, and finally pumpkin *oladi,* or pancakes, with honey from the Altai Mountains. "Normally, we drink good Russian vodka with all this," he said. "But not today. Today we shall drink good Russian tea." While we ate, Giles described for Geaxi and me the sphere and the room in which it was kept. He said we would have to devise a plan once we arrived, depending on where we were to perform and the amount of security around us. "Whatever you do, you must do it quickly," he warned. "If you are caught, all of us, including the Zhordanias, could be punished severely. We could even 'disappear.' It is not uncommon." Geaxi and I nodded our understanding. After the meal, full and in high spirits, we boarded the old school bus and continued on toward our destination. It was three o'clock in the afternoon and our show was scheduled to begin at six o'clock sharp. There was no time for doubt or worry. I had to trust that what Geaxi taught me in just two days about acrobatics would be enough.

Nikita Khrushchev's dacha was surrounded by a ten-foot stone and concrete wall with a heavy ironclad gate at the only entrance and exit. There were several outbuildings and two guesthouses, and the entire estate faced the shores of the Black Sea a half mile away to the west. To the east the snowy peaks of the Caucasus Mountains loomed in the distance. Fully armed and uniformed soldiers guarded the gate and patrolled the wall. After being told to stop, we were asked to step out of the bus while two of the soldiers, along with a large German shepherd, searched the interior thoroughly. Giles talked softly with the captain in charge, but none of the rest of us spoke and none of the other soldiers smiled or said a word. Twenty minutes later, we were allowed inside and directed to a service entrance at the rear of the huge dacha.

At least two dozen black Zil limousines lined the gravel driveway. Most of their drivers were gathered together smoking cigarettes, and as our noisy, multicolored school bus passed by, they all turned their heads to watch. At the service entrance, two men in dark suits were waiting for us. We were led through the kitchen and into a sparsely furnished, unused banquet hall, which was to

serve as our dressing room. I could hear music, loud voices, and
laughter coming from another big room not far from ours. One
of the men asked Giles if we needed anything. Giles answered no,
then changed his mind and said, "Perhaps some vodka . . . for
celebrations afterward." The man gave him a long, deliberate
look, then said he would see to it and both men turned and left
the room, locking the door behind them.

The costumes of *The Great Zhordanias* were each handmade
and combined the same rainbow of colors that were painted on
the school bus. Since the youngest of them, Noe, was about our
height and weight, Giles had brought two more costumes in
Noe's size for Geaxi and me. As everyone began changing their
clothes, Geaxi quietly asked Giles, "Where are we performing?"

"Judging from the music and voices, I would assume the great
ballroom. It is only one room away."

"Where is the room containing the sphere and the artifacts?"

Giles looked at both of us with concern. "Unfortunately, that
room is located at the other end of the dacha, all the way down
the long hall in the center."

"Will it be guarded?" I asked.

"From what we have seen so far, I would say so. I would not
be surprised if there were men stationed throughout the dacha.
The Soviets distrust their enemies *and* their friends."

Geaxi and I glanced at each other. We hadn't wanted to, but
now we knew we might have to use the Stones. "When will it be
best for us to slip away?" Geaxi asked.

"After the performance," Giles said. "I shall find a way to create a disturbance . . . a slight distraction," he added with a wink.
He looked around the room at the Zhordanias. Some were exer-
cising and stretching, some were doing cartwheels and back
handsprings with full twists. "Have you practiced what I told
you?" he asked Geaxi.

Just then the banquet-hall door opened and the two men in dark suits reappeared, along with a third man, also in a dark suit, carrying several bottles of vodka on a tray.

"Yes," Geaxi whispered to Giles, "we are ready, are we not, Zianno?"

I hesitated a moment, watching the three unsmiling Russians. "I hope so."

At ten minutes to six, the music stopped. At five minutes to six, we were led down the hall and through the double doors of the great ballroom. Inside, everything was brightly lit by two gigantic and elaborate chandeliers hanging forty feet over our heads. Dozens of people, including teenagers and children, sat at long tables facing the center of the room. They were all applauding as we walked into the light. After a few seconds, a middle-aged woman to our right stood and motioned for the applause to cease. She then spoke to us in a loud, strident voice. "Before the performance commences, the Premier of the Union of Soviet Socialist Republics would like to welcome each of you personally. Please come forward." This was unexpected. I glanced at Geaxi, then Giles, who was standing near the double doors. He shrugged his shoulders slightly, as if to say "nothing to worry about."

Nikita Khrushchev stood between two of his aides. He was smiling wide and almost giggling as we approached. With Giorgi leading, we walked by in single file. I was last in line. He shook the hand of everyone and nodded without speaking; that is, everyone except me. For some reason, he decided to ask me a question about being so young and still being a professional acrobat. I froze. I understood the question and I could speak some Russian, yet I knew if I did, it would be with an obvious Western accent. He repeated his question and I said nothing. The Premier's smile began to fade. My heart was pounding. Finally, I opened my mouth and just as I was about to speak, Geaxi stepped forward. In perfect Russian, she said, "I am sorry, sir, but my brother is mute." Nikita Khrushchev looked down at me with pity, patted my head, and I moved on to join the others with a sigh of relief.

The show went surprisingly well. Using a boost from two other Zhordanias, Noe led it off with a dramatic triple flip, landing like a feather on Giorgi's broad shoulders. Geaxi made all her moves with flawless precision, and I was adequate enough to not draw any attention or suspicion. During the final act, the famous four-tiered pyramid, Noe nearly scraped one of the chandeliers as he tumbled through the air, and the entire audience burst into spontaneous, wild applause. Waving to the crowd, we circled the great ballroom in a slow trot, then headed toward the double doors to make our exit.

Giles was waiting for us, whooping, hollering, and whistling louder than anyone else in the ballroom. Once Geaxi and I had reached the doors, he raised something in the air and turned, spilling and splashing the contents on the floor around him. It was one of the bottles of vodka that the man in the dark suit had delivered. Giles was feigning a state of drunkenness for all to witness. He took a sloppy sip and wiped his mouth with the sleeve of his jacket, then made a wobbly step toward Nikita Khrushchev's table. He held the vodka bottle above his head and yelled, "I propose a toast to our illustrious leader, Comrade Khrushchev, on the occasion of his glorious birthday!" He took another big gulp and seemed to *accidentally* drop the bottle. It fell to the hardwood floor with a loud crash, sending broken glass and vodka in every direction. Immediately, five men in dark suits, including two that were guarding the long hallway, rushed over to Giles, who had stumbled and fallen in a drunken heap. Geaxi grabbed my arm

and we seized the moment, running swiftly down the length of
the hall without anyone noticing. The whole event had taken less
than thirty seconds—a perfect "distraction."

The hallway was dimly lit, yet it was clear as we slowed to a
walk that the room we sought was unguarded. And not only was
the room unguarded, the door was unlocked and wide open.
"Unusual," Geaxi whispered. Both of us held our Stones at the
ready, fully expecting we would need to use them. Without making a sound, Geaxi crept into the room. I glanced once back
down the hallway, saw no one, and followed her inside.

Only a few lamps lit the cavernous room. One was near the
door, on a table by a refrigerator and a small stove. The other two
were in the far right corner, at either end of a large desk. The
room itself was just as Giles had described it—high ceilings, large
windows with iron bars on the outside, and cluttered throughout
with hundreds of artifacts from all over the world, representing
almost every culture and civilization. On first glance I saw an
Egyptian sarcophagus next to an ancient bronze Chinese funerary
urn with an African butterfly collection leaning against it. I saw
an assortment of Babylonian ceremonial swords, along with
Assyrian crossbows and an Aztec mask stacked up against a life-
size marble statue of Aphrodite. It was an amazing, eclectic array
of items and objects, all brought together in this one room without any apparent purpose or design. I looked around for Geaxi.
She was standing in the far right corner and staring at something
just beyond the desk with the lamps. "Here, young Zezen," she
said. "The prize is here."

I hurried over to where Geaxi was standing, and as I made my
way around the oversize desk, I noticed pages and pages of tracing paper spread across the desktop. They were each covered with
odd-shaped lines, dots, half-moons, circles, and combinations of
all four in multiple patterns. Several books on hieroglyphic lan-

guages, as well as books on codes and ciphers, were laid open on a bench next to the desk. Then I turned and saw the sphere. Perched like a circular egg on top of a wooden pedestal, the stone ball was perfectly round, and its polished black granite reflected the light of the two desk lamps. It was darker and slightly smaller than the one I'd seen in Cuba, but I could feel its silent power and mystery from where I stood. There were three bands of tiny markings etched into its surface, the same markings that someone had been copying onto the tracing paper. I knelt down and stared at the sphere in wonder.

"Beautiful, no?" Geaxi said.

"Yes . . . yes," I mumbled. "More than beautiful."

"Can you make anything of it, Zianno? Can you read it?"

"I . . . I don't know. I'm not sure. Give me a minute or two."

"Two is more than we can allow. You have one minute, then we must return."

"All right, then," I said. "One minute."

I began by taking a deep breath and letting it out slowly. I put my hands on the sphere and turned it, inch by inch, hoping to find a starting place in the bands of markings. But they were continuous, as if there was no beginning or end. I leaned in closer and examined each individual marking. Every single line, dot, circle, and half-moon was etched with the exact same precision, depth, and clarity. The sphere was a masterwork of stonecutting and stone polishing. Where had it been done? For what purpose, and most important, by whom? I had no answers, and the clock was ticking. Then, without thinking, I closed my eyes and let my fingertips dance lightly around the sphere, barely making contact with the markings, and something remarkable happened. Like a blind man reading braille, I suddenly understood one word— *West.* I read another word and then a phrase. It was the same phrase I had once discovered and deciphered in a cave in the middle of the Sahara Desert—*"Where Time is under Water, Where Water is under Time."* I opened my eyes and turned to tell Geaxi, but she was no longer beside me. She was standing by an exhibit ten feet away, holding something in one hand and gazing at it with her mouth hanging open. "Geaxi!" I said. "I can read the sphere!" She didn't respond or even blink. Her breathing was shallow and uneven. She seemed frozen, transfixed by what she was holding. I walked over to her and tapped her on the shoulder. Still, she didn't respond. I looked down and saw that she was holding a skull. The skull was human, yet not quite like modern humans. The browridges were raised and much more pronounced. Also, the forehead sloped and the jaw was different. And it was most likely a child's skull because it was too small to be that of an adult.

I turned to the exhibit, which was a collection of bones and a few tools. There were also photographs, a map, and a paper documenting the collection. The paper was written in Russian, but I was able to understand most of the context. It said the bones were that of a Neanderthal child, discovered along with five other children's skeletons, at Mezmaiskaya Cave on the banks of the Sukhoy Kurdzhips River in 1938. The paper also said the skeletons were all found together in an unusual arrangement resembling a circle, as if they had been holding hands at the time of death. Nearby the bones, but farther back in the cave, the black granite sphere had been unearthed. I looked up from the paper in shock. Geaxi was still mesmerized by the skull in her hand.

Just then, I heard voices down the long hallway, and they were coming toward us. I yanked the skull away from Geaxi and set it back with the other bones. Geaxi made a small whimpering sound, but she didn't move. Without hesitating, I slapped her hard across the chin. She blinked twice, then looked at me. "Young Zezen," she said. "Where are we?"

"About to be caught," I said, taking her hand and running across the room to the table next to the refrigerator by the door. The voices were close. I pulled Geaxi down and we ducked under the table just before two men entered the room.

They headed directly for the sphere, and as they passed by, I could only see them from the waist down. One wore brown trousers and plain brown shoes, old and scuffed on the toes and heels. The other wore black trousers and black Italian-style shoes, which looked almost brand-new. They were speaking in Russian. The man in the Italian shoes said, "I tell you, Arkady, I am at wit's end. I have exhausted everything I know. During the war I learned Chinese in three weeks, and now this damned stone and its code has had me completely baffled for six months. I want you to look at it and tell me what you think."

Brown shoes said, "If you haven't broken it, then I haven't much of a chance."

"Don't be modest, Arkady. You were once the best we had."

"A long time ago, my friend, perhaps too long."

"Still, I want you to see it before I send it off to Berlin."

"Berlin?" Brown shoes replied.

"Yes."

"The Beekeeper?"

"Yes, the Beekeeper. He is the only one. He will not fail to break it. I have done my best."

"He is a dangerous choice, Valery."

"I know, Arkady, but he is the only choice I have left."

When I heard the name Valery, I peeked out from underneath the table. The two men were standing beside the big desk, admiring and examining the sphere. I could see their faces clearly. I studied the taller of the two, the one wearing the expensive black shoes. His chin was narrow and pointed. His cheekbones were high and wide, but his eyes were small and close together on either side of his long, straight nose. His hair was a dark shade of burnt red, and he combed it back from his forehead, which was high and round. Cardinal had said Valery had vulpine features and resembled a fox in looks, attitude, and intelligence. The man standing by the sphere talking about codes and ciphers was, without a doubt, the reclusive, elusive Soviet agent known as Valery.

I glanced at Geaxi. She seemed to be herself again and was also paying keen attention to the two men. With my eyes, I indicated that it was time to leave. I held the Stone in my hand, but it was unnecessary. We sneaked out from under the table without a sound, then out the door and down the hallway until we reached the connecting hall that led to the kitchen and the banquet room. There were no guards anywhere. I could hear Giles arguing loudly with them in the kitchen, still creating a diversion. We walked into the banquet room, where the Zhordanias were quietly changing back into their street clothes. Everyone ignored our late entrance, except for Giorgi. He looked over and gave Geaxi and me a quick wink and a knowing smile. In another ten minutes, we were all back in the old school bus and on our way, including Giles. He had been dragged and carried out by two of the men in dark suits, who were more than glad to be rid of him and *The Great Zhordanias.*

Once we were clear of the dacha, I wanted to ask Geaxi about what had happened to her. I changed my mind, however, and decided to wait until we were alone.

Giles wasted no time in getting Geaxi and me safely out of the country. We made our way south for about fifty miles, crossing the Psou River and entering the Abkhazian city of Gagra. We made a brief stop at a sanatorium. It was one of many the Soviets had founded in the area. Giles said his "contact" worked in the sanatorium. While he was inside, Giorgi told me in his broken English that Giles had been to the sanatorium many times before, but for quite another reason. "He has a cancer of the bone," Giorgi said. "It eats him like a dark worm."

We drove on to the Pitsunda cape, a place Geaxi said she had visited in the late fifteenth century while in the company of Genoan and Venetian pirates. After being introduced to a man with an enormous black mustache and a booming, loud voice, we were ushered onto his fishing trawler and shown to a small cabin belowdecks. Giles informed us that the man could be trusted and that we would be leaving for Istanbul at first light.

There was little time for long farewells or proper thanks for everything that Giles had done for us. But he did ask one question. He asked if we had had enough time to determine if the stone sphere was indeed Meq. Geaxi turned to me, waiting for the answer. I glanced at Giles, but spoke to Geaxi. Judging from what I'd been able to "read" on the sphere and what I'd seen and read in the exhibit, I could hardly believe the answer myself. The implications were mind-boggling. "Yes," I said. "It is Meq."

Geaxi seemed startled and puzzled simultaneously. She looked away for a second, then looked at Giles and regained her composure. She smiled. "Perhaps we shall meet again soon, old friend."

Giles smiled back. He ran his hand through his white hair and leaned over, kissing Geaxi softly on the cheek. "Perhaps," he whispered. Then he turned to leave, ducking under the low door of the cabin and disappearing down the corridor toward the stairs. His footsteps barely made a sound.

5

ITZALPE
(SHADE)

In shade there is protection. There is shelter from heat and the glare of light. There is also obscurity, deception, darkness, and danger. In shade one may change, one may pass by imperceptible degrees into something else . . . someone else. Shade is crowded with ghosts. In shade there are countless dreams, schemes, hopes, triumphs, terrors, and fears that light will never see nor reveal. The truth seeker seeks not light. In truth, Truth is in shade.

It was a hot and windy afternoon on our third day at sea. Geaxi and I stood by the railing on the starboard side of the trawler, in the shade of the wheelhouse. We were watching the nets being pulled in for the last time before making port. Sea spray stung at our eyes, but felt good against our skin. Istanbul was on the horizon. We would be in the harbor and docked by sunset.

I wiped my eyes and asked Geaxi, "Where were you?"

"When?" she replied.

"When you were holding the skull . . . something happened . . . you, you went somewhere. Where were you?"

Geaxi turned to face me and turned her back against the sea spray. It jumped and danced around her head and shoulders like a halo of wet crystals and light. I looked in her eyes. She was clear and focused. She spoke softly, in a direct and even tone with little or no inflection. "I was in the past," she said. "I . . . *was* the past, and yet it felt like the future . . . like I was in the future. I was *inside* both, being both . . . dreaming both." She removed her beret and ran her hand over her face and through her hair. She stared down at the beret and turned it over in her hands. She sighed and rubbed her eyes, then smiled slightly, shaking her head back and forth. "You say this skull is Neanderthal, no?"

"Yes—Neanderthal, probably not an adult, and discovered along with five others in an unusual connecting design, in the same cave where they found the sphere."

"And you are able to read this sphere, Zianno?"

"I think so," I answered, hesitating. "I need to see the sphere again. I need time with it."

"But the sphere is Meq . . . there is no doubt the sphere is Meq?"

"Yes . . . the sphere is Meq."

Geaxi slipped her beret back on her head, adjusting the angle unconsciously. She looked over at the men pulling in the heavy, wet, tangled nets, most of them empty. Without a trace of irony, she said, "It seems we have a big new problem, do we not, young Zezen?"

I smiled but didn't laugh. "Yes, we do, Geaxi . . . yes, we do."

Before we disembarked, Geaxi made sure the captain of the trawler received several gold coins, which she handed over to him with privacy and discretion. Where she had been hiding them the whole time was a complete mystery and I didn't inquire. At first he refused the offer; however, Geaxi insisted he take the coins. The captain had been told he was reuniting an old family that had been displaced and separated, bringing two children back to the family. And he was. Geaxi spoke in Russian and I stayed silent. We shook hands and left the trawler just after dark. We sneaked into Istanbul and hurried through the loud and crowded streets to a small hotel called the Empress Zoe, where there was an ancient, aging family of children waiting for our return.

Geaxi and I entered through the lobby, which was quiet and nearly empty. We climbed the stairs to the second floor and saw a light coming from under the door to Sailor's room. There was a low murmur of voices inside. I knocked once and Geaxi spoke in Basque to announce our presence.

Moments later Mowsel opened the door, smiling wide and exposing his missing front tooth. *"Ongi etorri,"* he said, looking not at the ceiling or somewhere in space, but directly at me. His black eyes sparkled with intelligence and wit. Trumoi-Meq could see again.

Before I was able to respond, I heard Sailor's voice. "Well, did you find it . . . did you see it?"

Geaxi walked past me, giving Mowsel a warm embrace and staring into his eyes. "Good to see you, my friend," she said.

"That may be, Geaxi," Mowsel said, "but believe me, it is much better to see you."

They laughed and I walked inside, closing the door behind me. Ray, Nova, Sheela, and Zeru-Meq were also in the room. Only Opari was missing. I wanted to ask where she was and ask Mowsel about his eyesight, but Sailor wouldn't let me. He was sitting in a chair by the window.

"Were you able to see the sphere, Zianno? More important, were you able to read it?"

"Yes, and yes," I answered. "However, it's a little more complicated than that." I sat down on the edge of the bed. "Tell me, where is Cardinal? Is he still in Istanbul?"

"No," Sailor said. "He left shortly after operating on Trumoi-Meq."

"Operating?"

Mowsel interrupted, "You should have been there, Zianno. It was quite exciting. I remained conscious during the entire procedure. Cardinal employed an experimental technique to extract tiny fragments of shrapnel with microsurgery and a magnet. All this time they had been pressing in on my optic nerves, causing my blindness." Mowsel shook his head and laughed. "Just think of it, Zianno—a Giza repairing a Meq. The old ones are likely turning in their graves."

"It is remarkable, Mowsel, truly remarkable," I said.

"Yes, yes, yes," Sailor interjected. "Truly remarkable. Now, what did the sphere say, Zianno? Did it mention the Remembering?"

"I don't know. I didn't have time to read all of the text, if you can call it that."

"But you could read it, no?" Zeru-Meq asked.

"Yes, I can read this one. I need to see it again and spend more time with it." I looked back at Sailor. "Where did Cardinal go?"

"He is in Rome, as far as I know. Why do you seek him?"

"He may be able to help us find someone, someone called 'the Beekeeper.' "

"The Beekeeper?" Mowsel asked.

"Yes. It is probably a code name. The sphere will soon be in his possession, and if we can find him, then I can read more of the sphere." I paused and looked around the room at each of the others, including Geaxi. "But like I said, there are other . . . complications."

Ray said, "I'm gettin' lost, Z. Why don't you just start at the beginning and tell us all about it?"

And so I did. I recounted everything, even the close encounter with Nikita Khrushchev. I told them we had seen Valery, the Soviet agent, and I told them about the bones and the Neanderthal skull. Geaxi added a few details and mentioned her "frozen"

moments with the skull in her hands. Mowsel was especially interested in that and asked Geaxi several questions about the experience. Zeru-Meq wanted more information concerning the
exhibit, and I told him all I could remember, emphasizing the
peculiar arrangement of the skeletons, as they were found, and
the fact that each of them were Neanderthal children, not adults.
Sheela asked about the sphere itself, and I described it as best I
could, particularly the quality of the stonecutting and polishing.
While I was talking and answering questions, Sailor never said a
word and sat staring into the darkness outside the window. He
was wearing his star sapphire and he turned the ring round and
round his finger as I spoke. But he was listening, and listening
carefully.

"Sailor," I said, "do you have any questions? What do you
make of this coincidence? What do you think it means?"

Sailor stopped twirling his ring and looked around the room at
each of us, ending with me. "Assumption, Zianno, is the first step
on any and all roads leading to a wrong conclusion. Let us assume
nothing. What we must do, what *you* must do, is go to Berlin or
wherever this 'Beekeeper' is located. We must find this sphere and
you must read it. You must read it in its entirety. Only then may we
draw a conclusion from this unexpected and odd . . . coincidence."

"Sailor is correct," Mowsel added. "I will contact Cardinal tomorrow and ask for his assistance."

Everyone nodded in agreement.

"By the way," I said, "where is Opari?"

"In your room, Zianno," Nova answered. "She has been a little worried."

"Worried? About what, my ability to read the sphere?"

"No, Z," Ray said with a snicker. "Your ability as an acrobat."

Nova shoved Ray with a gentle push. "Z, that's not true. She
was just anxious for your safe return, and Geaxi's as well."

I wagged my finger in warning at Ray and we both laughed, then I turned and left the room. I hurried down the hall and the door to my room opened as I approached. Opari had felt me coming. She stood in the doorway with the dim light angling across her face. She was barefoot and wearing a simple cotton nightgown. I couldn't see her eyes but I could see her mouth. "Welcome back, my love," she whispered, then pressed her lips to mine.

That night, after telling Opari everything I had told the others, and falling asleep with her arm across my chest, I had a strange and unsettling dream. I was standing outside an enormous stadium, not a baseball stadium, but something else, something more dangerous. The stadium was circular and built with stone and brick. It was massive. All around the top of the walls, pennants and flags whipped in the wind. A crowd roared inside, rising and falling like waves. From somewhere in the shade by one of the entrances, I heard my name shouted three times in rapid succession, like gunshots. I ran or glided toward the arch of the entrance and walked through, into a glaring light and surrounded by dozens of snarling, growling lions, each one chained to a stake in the ground. I turned in a circle, looking for a way out. "Over here," someone yelled. "Over here," said another. Then one of the lions broke loose and began a slow walk my way. The walk became a trot, then a loping, full-out run until he leaped and opened his great jaws and hundreds, thousands of bumblebees came pouring out, buzzing, diving, and spinning around, never touching or stinging, almost taunting me, daring me to move a single muscle. Then I heard a voice, from somewhere I heard a voice that sounded familiar yet was unlike any voice I'd ever heard. High-pitched, strained, awkward, the voice seemed to be saying, "We are waiting for you."

I awoke from the dream and couldn't get back to sleep. Moon-

light shone through our open window and slanted across the bed
and onto Opari's cheek and neck. For the better part of an hour
I watched a tiny place on her throat where I could see her heartbeat rise and fall, over and over again.

Cardinal was attending a medical conference in Rome, and
Mowsel reached him by telephone, asking if he could "help us
find a friend." Cardinal replied that he would be glad to help and
suggested a meeting on May 1 in Montreux, Switzerland, where
he would be staying at the Grand Hotel Suisse-Majestic. After a
conference of our own, it was decided that Sailor, Sheela, Opari,
and I would make the trip to Montreux. The rest would travel to
Paris and wait somewhere for word from us. Mowsel suggested
San Sebastian, saying he might like to spend some time in Basque
country. "With my eyesight restored," he said, "there is no place
I would rather see than my homeland."

"I ain't ever been there, Mowsel," Ray said. "You mind if
Nova and I tag along?"

"Ray, it would be a pleasure. And I should warn you now, you
will never taste better food. If it still survives, I know a little inn
and restaurant where we shall begin and end our journey."

We left Istanbul over the span of a single weekend, traveling in
twos and threes, so as not to draw attention to ourselves. Old
trick, new century. We flew to Paris and Sailor, Sheela, Opari,
and I said farewell, promising to rendezvous in San Sebastian in
six months, or send word as soon as we had some answers.

Traveling by train, we gradually climbed out of France and into
Switzerland, stopping in Lausanne, then continuing on around
Lake Geneva until we arrived in the beautiful town on the northeast shore, Montreux. The sun had set an hour earlier, and the
lights of the town were shimmering on the water. The scene was

idyllic, almost magical. Sailor said, "I first passed through here on
the Roman road to Gaul through Besançon. I stayed that night and
four more. Even then, and by torchlight, it was equally beautiful."

Although Cardinal had yet to check in, rooms at the Grand
Hotel Suisse-Majestic had been reserved under his name for his
"nieces and nephews." With great respect and efficiency, we were
shown to our connecting rooms on the third floor overlooking
Lake Geneva. I walked out onto the balcony into the black diamond night and looked up and over the lake, which was dancing
with light. If you have to wait for someone, I thought, this is the
place to do it.

When Cardinal finally arrived the next day, he apologized and
blamed his tardiness on his surprise companion, a sports writer
who was in Switzerland to cover the upcoming FIFA World Cup
Soccer Championship in a series of articles for the *St. Louis Post-
Dispatch* and *The Washington Post*. The man, who was in his late
forties and just beginning to show a touch of gray, denied any
guilt whatsoever with a grin I'd seen since he was a kid. It was Jack.

"How's your mother?" I asked.

"She says you are already late."

"Late for what?"

"For not coming to see her."

"That sounds like Carolina. Well, maybe it won't be too long."
I paused and glanced at Cardinal. "I have seen Valery."

Jack and Cardinal exchanged looks of concern.

"Don't worry, he didn't see me. But he mentioned someone,
someone who might be in Berlin. He called him 'the Beekeeper.'
I . . . we . . . need to find this person. We were wondering if you
might have some information on him. He has something, or he
will soon, an object, a stone sphere, and I need to examine it."

Jack had never asked or involved himself in why the Meq did
certain things or how we did them. In our long relationship, he

had always left that part alone, and this time was no exception. "This is important, right, Z?"

"Yes."

"Then—"

"Then we will find the Beekeeper," Cardinal finished.

We only stayed in the big hotel one night. The next day, after checking out and renting a car, Jack drove us to a rambling array of connecting stone structures on the edge of a village called "La Tour-de-Peilz." Jack said it was a Catholic school named for the Renaissance priest, mathematician, astronomer, and philosopher Pierre Gassendi. It was built up against and along the north face of a sheer cliff. Because of the surrounding wall of rock, it had always been known to locals as *"école dans l'ombre,"* or "school in the shade." To me, it seemed more like a fortress than a school. However, the presence of several children, about our size and carrying a handful of books, confirmed its true identity. Jack pulled the car into a dark lane that was posted "PRIVATE ENTRANCE" and came to a stop in front of a two-story stone house, which was separate from but part of the complex of buildings. Jack told us they had been using the place as a safe house since the end of World War II. It was perfect because, except for the priests and nuns who ran the school, nobody knew it existed. Jack said with the many children coming and going, we would not be noticed. Sailor complimented Jack on his choice, Sheela commented on the beauty of the area, and within minutes we were settled in with our few belongings, waiting to hear from Cardinal.

We waited a week. During that time, we celebrated my birthday on the fourth. Sailor insisted on it, reminding me that birthdays for the Meq must be counted and celebrated. "Otherwise," Sailor said, "our hearts and minds would numb and we would simply be adrift in a meaningless sea of time with no beginning and no end." Opari actually baked a cake, a chocolate cake, and I blew out eighty-five candles in one breath.

The information Cardinal brought with him wasn't much. He said he had located a dossier on the Beekeeper that contained exactly one page, single-spaced. We were disappointed, but it was a start. "The Beekeeper," Cardinal said, "if he still exists, is an assassin for hire who was employed mainly by Stalin in the 1930s to eliminate several of Stalin's potential enemies living outside of the Soviet Union. However, on one occasion he is supposed to have worked for an American general in the Philippines, although the incident was never verified. According to a Soviet agent who defected, no one ever knew the true identity of the Beekeeper. His transactions were always done near a beehive, and he never removed the hat and net that concealed his face. He is said to have been a short man, and he spoke in English with a Cantonese accent. He is also believed to be a genius at code breaking and reading unreadable ciphers. But as far as we know, he and his services have not been used by anyone since World War II. Also, there seems to have been one other curious aspect to the Beekeeper. The Soviet defector said that often the agent who hired the assassin and conducted the transaction would disappear himself once the contract had been fulfilled."

"What about Berlin?" I asked. "Did you find any leads in Berlin?"

"Possibly. I am still working on it."

I glanced at Sailor and turned to Jack. "I need to go to Berlin."

Jack said, "No problem, Z. You can go with me while I do interviews with the West German soccer players. When do you want to go?"

"As soon as we can. Valery may be there at this very minute. If we can find him, we may find 'the Beekeeper.'"

"How about tomorrow?" Jack asked.

"Tomorrow is good."

As a sports writer, Jack had the perfect cover. He could travel at will almost anywhere and not draw attention. He was simply a journalist writing or researching a story, and I was his nephew. After leaving Opari, Sheela, and Sailor at the *école dans l'ombre,* Jack and I flew to Frankfurt, where the West German soccer team was based. From there, and over the next three weeks, we made several short trips to West Berlin. Each trip was unproductive and ineffective. The Beekeeper and Valery were ghosts, and Cardinal's clandestine network of sources came up with nothing. We returned to Montreux on June 16 so that Jack could cover the World Cup, which was played in various Swiss cities and concluded on July 4 in Bern. West Germany won its first title and defeated Hungary 3–2 in the final. It was an upset victory, and the game was labeled "The Miracle of Bern." Jack stayed on in Switzerland throughout the rest of the year, during which we made more trips to West Berlin, all with negative results. The rendezvous with the others in San Sebastian was postponed while we waited for a breakthrough. Jack paid an extended visit to St. Louis, but returned in three months. The whole year of 1955 passed without even a rumor of Valery or the Beekeeper, then in the spring of 1956, we heard a report that Valery may have been seen in Budapest. That report was never confirmed, but in October there was another, definite sighting of Valery in Budapest by one of Cardinal's agents. He was only seen crossing a street and was not followed, but he was no longer a ghost, and we knew where to look for him, and possibly "the Beekeeper."

"What about getting in and out?" I asked. "Hungary is a Communist country."

"It is for now," Jack replied. "Hungary is in transition. Nobody knows what's going to happen, but right now it's a volatile place. The AVH should be avoided."

"AVH?" Sailor asked.

"State Security Police. Very nasty." Jack was wearing a St. Louis Cardinals baseball cap. He tilted it back on his head with his thumb and forefinger. "But I can get you in, Z. In fact, this just might be a good time to interview the Hungarian soccer team about the 'Miracle in Bern.'"

"Jack," Sailor said, "I would like to go along. Do you think two of us would arouse the suspicion of this organization—the AVH?"

"No problem, Sailor. It might even be a better cover, more like a working vacation for me and my nephews, who both love soccer and think the Hungarian players are heroes."

"Good," Sailor said with a half smile, then added, "I shall learn all their names."

After clearing everything through the Hungarian Embassy in Geneva, we arrived by train in Budapest on the morning of October 23. There was already a November chill in the air, and I pulled my jacket collar up around my neck. Jack had the name of our contact memorized. Her name was Piroska Czibor. She was in her mid-thirties and was a professor at the Technical University. She was one of what Cardinal referred to as his "chaperones." They were various people throughout Eastern Europe whom he trusted implicitly but only used occasionally as agents. Every one had been recruited by Cardinal himself. Piroska Czibor had been approached because her father was Hungarian and her mother had been American. Cardinal thought it might make a difference in Piroska's decision. It did. She was hired just after the end of World War II, and Cardinal called on her at least once a year until

1951. That year, her husband was killed in an automobile accident and Piroska decided to end her work with Cardinal. He understood and wished her well. But she also possessed a rare ability, which she used to spot and verify her sighting of Valery— a photographic memory with total recall. Even though she had not seen a description of Valery since 1949, she recognized him the moment she saw him walking into a laboratory at the Technical University. Piroska debated a moment with herself, then contacted Cardinal immediately and asked if Valery was "still a person of interest." Cardinal told her "absolutely" and asked if she would assist us on our assignment, although she was under no obligation. After a few days Piroska made her decision and now we were looking for her outside the train station, where she was supposed to be waiting for us. Cardinal had said she would be wearing a large red and blue scarf around her neck.

"There she is," Jack said, nodding at a woman walking toward us. She was tall with dark hair, which she was trying to keep out of her face, and she was smiling. In a whisper, Jack added, "Cardinal never said she was beautiful."

Extending her hand, Piroska introduced herself to Jack. She was gracious and graceful, and Jack was right—she was beautiful. She only had a trace of an accent and her mother must have been from somewhere in the South because Piroska spoke English with a slight Southern drawl. She seemed a little surprised that Jack was with two boys, but she didn't ask why. Cardinal had trained her, and she knew when and where not to ask questions. Jack never mentioned it or explained our presence, calling us his "orphans of the month."

Piroska led us to her car, a tiny, ten-year-old Russian sedan, and we drove through the city to her apartment near the Technical University. The apartment was on the third floor and only had four rooms, but the ceilings were high and the windows wide and the long curve of the Danube was visible in the distance. Piroska brewed a pot of coffee, and Jack asked her to tell him about seeing Valery. Sailor and I sat on a bench by the kitchen window, playing cards and pretending not to listen. She glanced over at us and hesitated. Jack told her to ignore us and tell him everything.

Piroska said she had seen Valery entering the same building on three separate occasions, the last being just two days ago.

"What was the building?" Jack asked.

"The building contains the laboratory of Miklos Pazmany, the mathematician and physicist."

"What is Pazmany's claim to fame?"

"He has the only mainframe computer in Eastern Europe."

Jack was puzzled. "Was Valery alone?"

"Not the first time," Piroska replied. "The first time he was with someone, a much shorter man who wore an expensive Russian sable hat and a long muffler wrapped around his neck and half his face, covering his nose and mouth."

Sailor and I exchanged a quick glance and shared the same thought—the "Beekeeper."

Jack continued to ask Piroska questions, not only about Valery, but about Pazmany, about his computer, and about the building itself—how many entrances and exits, was there security in the building, and if so, how much and how many? Piroska answered every question and asked Jack a few in return. Jack answered as best he could. Of course, he couldn't tell her the real reason we were looking for Valery. Their conversation went on for most of the afternoon. Meanwhile, and unknown to us, there were students and demonstrators gathering by the thousands in the streets of Budapest to protest against the government and its Stalinist regime. Speeches were given and proclamations read at the Bem statue, where the crowd chanted the forbidden National Song with the refrain, "We vow, we vow, we will no longer remain

slaves." Later, they crossed the Danube and joined with other pro-
testers outside the Parliament Building. By early evening, the
crowd had enlarged to 200,000 people. The Hungarian Revolution had begun.

The next day Soviet tanks moved into Budapest, parking in
front of the Parliament Building while Soviet troops guarded important bridges and crossroads. Armed revolutionaries fought the
tanks with Molotov cocktails; the Hungarian resistance finally
forced a cease-fire on October 28, and a new but fragile government was in place. By October 30 the tanks had withdrawn from
Budapest to Soviet garrisons in the countryside. Many people in
the streets believed the Soviets had left Hungary for good. Jack
knew better and said he doubted they would ever do that.

During the first week of the revolution, fighting in the narrow
streets made it virtually impossible for any of us to watch for
Valery at the University. It wasn't until November 1 that Piroska
could show us where she had seen Valery enter Pazmany's laboratory. There were two entrances at opposite ends of the building.
Sailor and I set up a sort of stakeout at one of them, while Jack
and Piroska took the other. For three days we saw nothing but
students, teachers, and workers coming and going. Finally, early
on the morning of November 4, I caught a glimpse of a tall man
in Italian shoes and a tailored wool coat walking briskly across the
street toward the laboratory. He looked once over his shoulder
and hesitated.

Then we heard the tank fire followed by sporadic gunfire. It
came without warning, and it sounded as if it was coming from
every district in the city. The Soviets had returned, invading
Budapest in full force, including air strikes and artillery.

I looked at Sailor. "What should we do?"

"Stay out of the way as best we can," Sailor answered, but it
was too late. At that moment, three Soviet T-54 tanks turned the

corner and headed right for us. The lead tank was firing indiscriminately at buildings and civilians. One blast took out a corner of the building next to us, sending a shower of broken glass, bricks, and concrete into the street. I heard screaming and people started running in every direction.

One block away, Jack and Piroska were scrambling door to door, trying to make their way through the smoke and debris to Sailor and me. Jack shouted something, but I couldn't hear him over the sound of the tanks. Everything seemed to be happening in slow motion. I glanced at the entrance to the laboratory building. Valery was standing outside watching the carnage, and the moment I saw him, he saw me. Jack and Piroska were only fifty yards away and it looked like they were going to make it through the chaos. Just then, the lead tank came to a halt. The turret with its long cannon began to swivel and take aim directly at a small group of people that included Jack and Piroska.

Sailor did not hesitate. He walked calmly into the street and raised his arm, pointing his hand with palm out and fingers spread toward the tank. He mumbled something in Meq and closed his eyes, as if in a trance. Using his mind and his "ability" of telekinesis, in a split second he lifted the huge T-54 tank a foot off the ground and spun it in the air, just as the cannon fired. Sailor opened his eyes and smiled. The blast destroyed the tank directly behind it, and Jack and Piroska scrambled the last fifty yards to safety.

Jack grabbed Sailor by the shoulders and said, "I don't know what you did or how you did it, but thank God you did it, Sailor." Jack took hold of Piroska's hand and turned to me. "Let's get out of here, Z, and I mean out of here."

I looked across the street and found Valery's eyes. They were wide with awe and wonder. He took a step or two toward me. He had seen everything. We began to run and he yelled after us,

"Itxoin! Itxoin!" Jack and Piroska kept running, but Sailor and I stopped dead in our tracks.

"Who is that?" Sailor asked.

"That is Valery," I told him.

Valery had spoken in Basque and begged us to "Wait! Wait!" How, why, and what it meant would have to be answered later. We had to get off the streets and out of Hungary. Sailor and I caught up with Jack and within twenty minutes we were back at Piroska's apartment. As spontaneously as the revolution had begun, in three days it was cruelly and systematically crushed and stamped out. On November 10 we sneaked quietly out of the city and joined some refugees making their way to Austria. Jack tried to talk Piroska into leaving with us. She declined and stayed in Budapest, saying her work, her friends, her life was in Hungary, not Austria or anywhere else. Jack understood, but I could see the disappointment in his eyes.

We boarded a train in Gussing, then changed trains in Graz and took the longer, scenic route through the Alps on our way back to Montreux and the *"école dans l'ombre."* While Jack slept, Sailor and I stared out at the mountains and talked at length about what had happened in Budapest and what the consequences might be. I told Sailor I was surprised he had acted so quickly and with no fear of being exposed to the Giza. Sailor said, "There was no choice, Zianno, or more precisely, there was only one choice." As for the consequences, neither of us had an answer, but one thing was clear. The Soviet agent Valery seemed to know much more about us than we knew about him. And I still had not seen the sphere. I had to see the sphere again. In my heart and mind, I was becoming obsessed with reading the sphere. As we approached Montreux and the shores of Lake Geneva, which was shimmer-

ing in ten shades of blue, I was thinking only of the sphere and
the mystery carved into its stone.

We had telephoned Opari and Sheela from Graz and they met
us at the station in Montreux. Opari could see the distraction
and frustration in my face and she mentioned it. I told her I
would work it out, but I didn't. Over the next few months, we
heard nothing from any of Cardinal's resources. Valery (and the
Beekeeper) had vanished once again.

Jack went back to the States and to St. Louis for an extended
visit in March 1957. Sailor, Sheela, Opari, and I stayed on in
Switzerland. Cardinal communicated with us regularly from
Washington. We used the house at the *"école dans l'ombre"* as a
base of operations, and traveled throughout Europe exploring
our own means of obtaining information. At one point, in West
Berlin, we did uncover a rumored address for the Beekeeper.
It turned out to be just a rumor, and yet we kept returning to
West Berlin when we could, thinking every time we might get
lucky. Cardinal always provided one of his "chaperones" to ease
our way in and out of countries with tight security. Ray and Nova
came for a visit in late November and stayed through the New Year.
He said Geaxi, Mowsel, and Zeru-Meq were still living in the
vicinity of San Sebastian. He also said that everyone was feeling the
same frustration as I. Meanwhile, the clock was ticking and the
Remembering loomed in the distance. Opari told me, "Do not
worry, my love. I believe you were meant to read this sphere. And
you will."

There is no preparation for bad news, especially the worst kind of
bad news. It knocks you over with its suddenness, its sadness, and
its finality. On December 12 we received a telephone call from
Jack in St. Louis. He told me that Oliver "Biscuit" Bookbinder, the

orphan Carolina had saved, named, and raised as her own child, had been killed two days earlier in Las Villas Province in Cuba, somewhere in the Escambray Mountains. He had been fighting with Comandante Juan ("El Mejicano") Abrahantes and his revolutionary forces against the Cuban dictator Fulgencio Batista. He had also been working undercover for Cardinal and Jack. Jack said his last report contained some unexpected information that may have had something to do with his death. Biscuit had reported that he had seen Blaine Harrington twice, one time in the company of Comandante Abrahantes and another time in the company of Comandante Rolando Cubela. He said Harrington was carrying significant amounts of cash, guns, and ammunition. Biscuit also reported that "Colonel" Harrington, as he was being called, recognized him and asked him about several Latin baseball players. Biscuit reported that the conversation was innocent, but Blaine Harrington also knew that Biscuit worked for Jack. Biscuit said he was "concerned" about what "Colonel" Harrington might do with that knowledge and information. Exactly one day after Biscuit filed his report, he was found dead, shot twice in the back of the head. Jack was convinced it was no coincidence. I asked how long Blaine Harrington had been a colonel and Jack said, "Beats me, Z. The Army claims he doesn't exist. They've erased him from their records." Jack added that Carolina was deeply saddened and moved by Biscuit's death. He was worried about her and said a visit from me might help cheer her up.

I didn't even have to think about it. It was a good idea. I had been gone too long, and we were getting nowhere in our search for the sphere. I probably needed to see St. Louis and Carolina more than she needed to see me. I told Jack I would be there by Christmas if he could make the arrangements. He said that would not be a problem. I assumed Opari would go with me, but she decided she would stay in Europe, saying, "This visit should be yours, my love. At this time it is you Carolina needs to see, not me." Ray, on the other hand, practically begged to go along, saying, "Damn, Z! I got to admit it, I'm just plain homesick." Nova agreed with him and on December 14, the three of us left Switzerland for London, where we boarded a TWA Constellation and flew to New York, then changed planes and flew on to St. Louis and Lambert Field, arriving late in the day on December 18. Since the three of us were traveling on our own, the stewardess asked if we had family waiting for us. Ray spoke up. "You bet we do," he said, "we just don't call 'em that." The stewardess stared at Ray for a moment, then laughed, sort of, and we walked off the plane to meet Jack.

Jack was waiting for us in the baggage claim area and he was not alone. He stood next to a man with a full white beard wearing a bright red cap, red pants, and a big red coat with white fur trim around the collar and cuffs. A white belt held the coat together and wrapped around his enormous, inflated belly. "Damn!" Ray exclaimed. It was Santa Claus, only this Santa Claus was black. As we got closer, the man smiled and said, "Ho, ho, ho, Z! Welcome back, man."

The man was in his mid-sixties and I knew his smile and his smiling brown eyes well. He was my old friend Mitchell Ithaca Coates.

"Hello, Mitch," I said. "You probably make the best Santa Claus I've ever seen."

"Why, thank you, son. Maybe I'll let you sit on my knee and tell me if you've been good or bad."

Nova laughed out loud and the rest of us joined in, then we walked out of the terminal, causing a general stir all the way to the parking lot. We got into a long, pale yellow DeSoto sedan, and on the way to Carolina's house Mitch explained that he was in costume for a Christmas pageant he and Mercy had presented that afternoon for the kids in his neighborhood. He said they'd been doing it for three years, and he was proud to be the only black Santa Claus in St. Louis.

I asked Jack about the DeSoto. It was a beautiful car and looked and smelled brand-new. Jack was driving and he laughed and shook his head. He verified that it was new and told me the car was Carolina's idea. He said as soon as he told her I was coming back, her mood elevated and she insisted on purchasing a new automobile. When Jack asked her the reason why, she smiled and said Solomon had come to her in a dream and told her, "Zis is good business." I laughed to myself and remembered Carolina barreling through traffic behind the wheel of her first automobile, the huge, bright yellow Stanley Steamer. I stared out the window at the passing cars—so many more than before. I felt excited and anxious to see Carolina, see the gold flecks dancing in her blue-gray eyes and hear her laugh. I especially wanted to hear her laugh. That was all I wanted. She was now eighty-eight years old, and I couldn't wait to hear her laugh again.

Jack pulled into the long driveway of Carolina's house just after the sun had set. Every window in the big house was glowing with burning candles and a string of Christmas lights—blues, reds, greens, and golds—circled the doors and stretched across the roofline, finally fanning out and around the stone archway all the way to the ground. It looked like Fort Christmas.

"My, oh, my," Ray said.

Jack didn't wait for me to comment. He brought the DeSoto to a stop under the archway and said, "We sort of went crazy because of Georgie."

"Georgie?" Nova asked.

"*Georgie,* that's what we call her. Caine and Antoinette's little girl. She's only four years old and . . . well . . . what can I say? We went overboard."

I never said a word, but I did walk inside with a wide grin on my face. Santa Claus stepped out of the car and simply said, "Merrrrry Christmas!"

We entered through the kitchen door, as always, and were welcomed by Star, Mercy, Antoinette, and Caine. They were in the middle of preparing dinner, and the kitchen smelled like a dozen wonderful things. Star, now in her late fifties, looked radiant. She was dressed in a sweater and slacks and wore little makeup or jewelry—a touch of red lipstick and two small gold loop earrings. Her hair was a mix of strawberry blond and silver. It was cut short and brushed back from her face. Time had been good to Star. When she smiled, she was still the same eighteen-year-old I had escorted out of Africa. Mercy was also in her fifties. Her close-cropped, reddish-brown hair had turned mostly white. Nevertheless, she looked extremely healthy and happy. She was dressed in a sweatshirt and huge, puffed-out brown woolen pants, which were actually part of her costume from the Christmas pageant earlier that afternoon. She had played Rudolph the Red-Nosed Reindeer. I gave her a long embrace, and Star as well, then turned to Antoinette, who was making dinner rolls from scratch. Her hands were covered with dough and flour, so I leaned in and kissed her on both cheeks. She was a thirty-one-year-old mother now. Her dark hair hung down past her shoulders, and her dark eyes were shining. She was in the prime of her life. Caine sat at the kitchen table peeling potatoes. At forty years old, he was a tenured college professor at Washington University and looked the part. He'd grown a neatly trimmed beard and wore wire-rimmed glasses.

Mitch went to kiss Mercy, Jack poured a cup of coffee, and Nova sat down next to Caine. Ray jumped up and sat on the kitchen counter, letting his legs dangle while he closed his eyes and breathed in every one of the mingling scents and aromas. "Ah, home cookin'," he sighed, "there ain't nothin' like it."

I asked Star, "Where's Willie?"

"Rockford, Illinois," she answered. "He's meeting with some other men from Wisconsin. They're planning an air show for next summer with experimental and vintage aircraft. He should be back in a couple of days."

"Where's Carolina?" I asked. "And where's Georgia, or should I say Georgie?"

"She's in the living room with Gran-gran," Antoinette said. "She loves to play around the Christmas tree."

"Gran-gran?"

"That's what Georgie calls Carolina," Caine added. "It's her version of Great-grandma." He paused and smiled. "Why don't you go surprise her, Z? And I bet you a Budweiser beer you fall in love."

"A Budweiser?"

"Two!" Caine said with a laugh, waving me out of the room.

I turned and crept through the dining room into the long and wide living room. A fire crackled in the fireplace at the far end of the room. Candles burned on every table and in every window, and several pieces of Carolina's furniture had been removed to clear the way for a nine-foot Christmas tree, fully decorated and adorned with lights, ornaments, and tinsel. Gifts and presents of all sizes surrounded the tree. A few feet away, Carolina and a four-year-old girl sat on the floor playing. Carolina was wearing a turtleneck sweater and denim overalls, complete with shoulder straps. Her white hair was cut short and brushed back, like Star's. She was listening intently to Georgie, who also wore overalls. Georgie seemed to be instructing and slightly scolding Carolina about something. There was a big three-story dollhouse sitting between them; however, there were no dolls in the dollhouse. Instead, Georgie was filling the dollhouse with farm animals and she was making sure Carolina put the pig in his proper room. For a few seconds I watched them play without being seen, then Georgie looked up.

"Who are you?" she asked, but she didn't look surprised or confused, just . . . curious.

I looked down at her. She had the biggest, most beautiful brown eyes I'd ever seen, like milk chocolate, and they gazed right into mine. She was staring at me, waiting for me to answer. I glanced at Carolina and she winked.

"My name is Zianno," I said and paused, leaning over. "You, Georgie, may call me Z."

"Z, Z, Z," she repeated several times, saying it fast and slow, as if she was trying it out, getting used to it. Finally, she said, "That's a funny name."

"Yes, I suppose it is," I said, then whispered, "but it's my name."

"Will you play with us?"

"All right. Sure. Where should I sit?"

"There," she answered, pointing to my spot. "Sit there." As I was sitting down, she added, "You're a boy."

"Yes, yes I am," I said, trying to keep from laughing. I smiled at Carolina and glanced again at this little girl, and something happened. I looked into her eyes and saw all the faces of the people inside her, inside her blood, her genes, and it was amazing. I saw her mama and papa, Caine and Antoinette. I saw Antoine and Emme, and I saw PoPo, and I saw Captain Antoine Boutrain, the elder, and I saw the madness of Isabelle, Antoine's mother. I saw Star and the tragic Jisil al-Sadi, and I saw Nicholas and Carolina, and I saw Carolina's father, the "Whirling Dervish," Billy Covington. How did it happen? How did all those people find their way inside this little girl? I looked at Georgie and thought of the unlikely trail of time, circumstance, love, and dumb luck that it took. I thought of my own family and my own mama and papa. I still missed them. I thought of the Meq and the others and their families. I looked past Georgie at the Christmas tree and followed it up to its top, nine feet in the air. The great tree was crowned with a cone, and attached to the top of the cone was a bright red sphere, sparkling with glitter in the light. And I thought of the Gogorati, the Remembering, and I knew instinctively and with certainty that the sphere I was searching for had everything to do with the Remembering. There was no doubt—I had to find it and I had to read it, or there would be no Remembering for us.

"You are the sheep," a voice said.

I blinked. "What?"

It was Georgie who spoke. "Z, you are the sheep. Here," she said, handing me the sheep. "Gran-gran, you are the cow. Okay?" She handed Carolina the cow and glanced back and forth at both of us. "Well . . ." she said, annoyed that we were hesitating.

Carolina glanced at me and laughed. "Moo!" she said. "Moo!"

"Baa! Baa!" I said. I laughed and looked at Georgie and I knew immediately I owed Caine two Budweisers.

Inside Carolina's house, the holiday season of 1958 was nothing but joy. Every day was filled with feasting, drinking, laughing, singing, and sharing memories and stories, many of them told by Carolina, and they usually involved Solomon in one way or another. Her stories were always hilarious and somehow heroic. On Christmas Day, Carolina and Star cooked a dozen different Cuban dishes and Carolina blessed the meal with a silent prayer for Oliver "Biscuit" Bookbinder. And there were presents, too many presents, almost all of which were for Georgie. That Christmas, Georgie received everything she could ever want and more than she would ever need. Two weeks passed in a blur. The days were cold, but the nights were clear. Venus and Jupiter appeared close together in the southeastern sky, like a big sister and little brother carrying lanterns, lighting the way.

January began with Jack leaving for Washington, D.C., on New Year's Day after receiving a telephone call from Cardinal. Fidel Castro and his band of revolutionaries had run the dictator Batista out of Cuba. They were now in charge of the government and Cardinal wanted Jack in Washington. Carolina kissed Jack good-bye in the kitchen, cursing Batista and the revolutionaries.

During the next few weeks Carolina and I spent a great deal of time together. On fair days when it wasn't too cold, we took walks in Forest Park. The walks were not as long as in the old days, but in our hearts and minds they felt the same and were just as enjoyable. Carolina never once complained about her physical aches and pains or even mentioned them. I knew from Jack that she suffered from arthritis in her hips, and yet it made no difference. She always looked forward to our walks, which she began referring to as our "wanderings." On one of our walks we encountered a woman who also was in her eighties, a woman Carolina had known for years. The woman smiled when she saw us coming. Her name was Millie Westinghouse.

"Hello, Millie," Carolina said.

"How charming!" Millie replied. "What a gentleman you have there, Carolina. Who is this young man?"

Without hesitation or even a trace of irony, Carolina told the woman, "Why, this boy is my oldest friend, Millie . . . and he is not that young, by the way." As we walked on, I glanced back at Millie Westinghouse and winked. Her mouth dropped open and she looked completely blank. She was sure she had either heard or been part of a joke, and simultaneously, she knew she didn't get it.

Willie Croft took me flying on three occasions in January,

mainly because he now owned three airplanes, including his beloved de Havilland, and he wanted me to fly in each of them. Star went with us twice and the third flight I was alone with Willie, all the way to Kansas City and back in his red Beechcraft Bonanza. Willie was sixty-seven years old and most of his red hair had disappeared, except for a little above the ears and in the back, and that had turned gray. He had enough wrinkles and lines on his face and forehead to prove that he'd had his fair share of experience. But when he was flying, none of that mattered. I could see it in his eyes and in the grace of his movements. He wasn't just flying. He was out of Time.

Mitch Coates had opened yet another nightclub in a neighborhood now known as Gaslight Square. Gaslight Square covered the length of Olive Street from Pendleton to Whittier. Mitch owned two buildings, one on Olive and the other around the corner on Boyle. The nightclub was on the ground floor of the Olive Street building, along with the Mercy Whitney Art Gallery & Studio. They lived in a spacious apartment on the second floor of the building on Boyle. Mitch said there was good live jazz in his club, and he was anxious for Ray, Nova, and me to hear some of it. We all went together the first night and stayed close to Mitch. When somebody asked who we were, Mitch said we were his bartender's grandkids from New Orleans. However, the ruse wasn't necessary. Once the music started, no one paid attention to us anyway. Nova and I only went along a couple of nights. Ray went on a regular basis. He asked Mitch to take him to hear the rest of the music being played in St. Louis, especially rhythm and blues. One night Mitch drove Ray across the river to a club in East St. Louis, and after that Ray couldn't stop raving about a group called the Kings of Rhythm with Ike Turner, and a young girl Ike introduced as Tina belting out the vocals. Ray started listening to music on the radio and buying record albums. He listened to everything, but his new hero was a black, blind piano player, singer, and songwriter also named Ray—Ray Charles. "Genius," Ray said, "pure damn genius."

Nova began visiting Mercy in her studio and they quickly became fast friends and confidantes. Three or four times a week, Mercy held art classes for kindergarten-age kids in the neighborhood, kids who couldn't afford art supplies, and Nova never missed a class, acting as Mercy's assistant. I knew she loved it and she was a natural at working with young children, but she tried to shrug it off, grinning and saying, "I only do it because they're shorter than me."

On February 1 the weather turned bitterly cold and a razorlike wind blew in from the northwest. Everyone stayed inside and Georgie got lots of playtime and an abundance of playmates. We kept the fireplace going day and night. About ten o'clock in the morning of February 4, Ray was tending the fire, moving new logs in with the old. The radio was on in the background, tuned to KMOX. A song by The Rays called "Silhouettes" was playing. Just as they sang the line, *"a dim light cast two silhouettes on the shade,"* the disk jockey broke in with the news that Buddy Holly, the rock and roll star from Texas, was dead. He had been killed the night before when his chartered airplane, a red Beechcraft Bonanza, went down in Iowa at 1:50 A.M.

Ray turned to me and said, "That's the same airplane as Willie's, ain't it?"

"Yes. One of them."

"Same color, too, right?"

"Yeah . . . what are you thinking, Ray?"

"This is a bad omen, Z . . . a bad omen."

"In what way?"

Ray paused. "I don't know yet."

The next four days passed and the weather improved. By

February 9 it was warm enough for Carolina and me to embark on one of our "wanderings" through Forest Park. Antoinette and Georgie stayed outside all morning playing hide-and-seek in and around the "Honeycircle." Caine was out of town, lecturing at a seminar in Austin, Texas. Ray spent the day with Mitch, helping him build a new stage in the nightclub, and Nova and Mercy took their art class on the road, spending most of the day finger painting at St. John of the Cross Children's Home. Willie and Star had flown to Rockford, Illinois, and were due back in the early evening. Because of its speed, Willie had chosen his red Beechcraft Bonanza for the trip.

At four in the afternoon, while Carolina and I sat in the kitchen drinking coffee, Ray suddenly burst through the door, with Nova right behind him. "We got to get hold of Willie and Star!" Ray shouted. "They got to stay in Rockford. They can't fly home tonight."

I looked at Ray and he was dead serious. "What's going on, Ray?"

"I had one of my 'forecasts,' Z. Over at Mitch's place, clear as a tear, I saw it and I knew it."

"Knew what?"

"A 'big one' is comin', Z, and it's comin' soon. We gotta get hold of Willie."

I glanced across the table at Carolina. She was worried. She knew Ray, the "Weatherman," would not be mistaken. She had lost her sister the last time Ray had said a tornado was coming. Carolina rose from her seat and went directly to the telephone. Willie had left the number of their hotel and the number of the airport. She dialed the hotel and asked for Willie or Star. They had already checked out. She nervously dialed the next number, messing it up twice and having to start again. She got through to the airport and was put on hold for several minutes until she was finally con-

nected to the proper person. She found out Willie and Star had
taken off half an hour earlier. Carolina's face dropped, but she
didn't panic. She asked the man if she could get a message to
Willie now, while he was in the air. It was an emergency. The
man told her he thought they were still in range and asked what
she wanted to say. Carolina thought for a moment, then said,
"Tell him Z and the 'Weatherman' said to turn back, do not
come home. Repeat, do not come home."

Carolina hung up the phone, sat down at the kitchen table, and
waited twenty minutes before redialing the Rockford airport.
Ray paced the room. When she called back, she had to wait again
until the same man came on the line. She listened for a tense moment or two, then smiled and the blood came back into her face.
The freckles on her cheeks and across her nose all seemed to jump
out at once. "Thank God! And thank you, sir," Carolina said to
the man. "You have probably saved two lives." She hung up the
phone and told us Willie had received the message and was returning to Rockford.

"Yes!" Ray shouted. "Yes, yes, yes."

Carolina walked over and gave Ray a crushing hug for an
eighty-eight-year-old woman. "I am forever grateful, Ray," she
whispered.

Ray winked and whispered back, "We got lucky."

Nova glanced at me and I knew what she was thinking—there
could still be a tornado headed our way. "When is it coming,
Ray?" she asked.

Ray walked to the window and looked out at the sky and the
trees. The sky was cloudless and the trees were quiet. "Soon," he
said.

At six o'clock, we watched the local news on television, but
they only expected cloudy skies and the possibility of rain in the
forecast. Afterward, we played cards for a while, then watched *I've*

Got a Secret on TV and waited. Antoinette and Georgie said good night and slipped off to bed. Eight o'clock and nine o'clock came and passed. On the ten o'clock news, they continued to predict cloudy skies and the possibility of rain. Maybe Ray missed it this time, I thought. Following the news, Carolina retired, thanking Ray again and saying, "Wake me if necessary." Ray, Nova, and I stayed in the living room, watching TV. Eventually, Nova fell asleep on the couch and I fell asleep in my chair. Only Ray remained awake, turning off the television and sitting by the window, staring into darkness.

At 1:50 A.M., the same time as Buddy Holly's plane crash, Ray tapped my shoulder and woke me. "It's here," was all he said.

I blinked and stood up immediately. Outside, I could hear the wind roaring through the trees, and hailstones were hitting the windows. Just then, a tree limb cracked like a rifle shot in the front yard, waking Nova up. Thirty seconds later, Antoinette ran into the room with Georgie in her arms and a frightened look on her face. Carolina wasn't far behind, coming down the stairs in her nightgown and robe. "To the basement," she said, "everyone to the basement. Quickly."

One by one, we followed Carolina downstairs. We huddled together and waited. In ten minutes, everything was over. We walked back up into the kitchen. I got a flashlight and Ray and I opened the door and looked out. A light rain was falling, but the sky was quiet and the storm had passed. Tree branches and scattered debris covered the yard and driveway. We walked around the house to see if anything was broken or missing, then wandered into the "Honeycircle." In the beam of the flashlight we saw something that only a tornado can create. Impaled on the point of the bronze gnomon of Baju's Roman sundial was a street sign from the intersection of Manchester Road and Woodlawn. I looked at Ray and we shook our heads in disbelief at the power of such a storm. We both knew Manchester Road and Woodlawn was at least ten miles away to the southwest.

I looked up at the sky and whispered, "I'm glad Willie and Star are safe . . . but I think it's us who got lucky."

Ray was still staring at the street sign. "Ain't that the truth," he mumbled.

It wasn't until the morning newscast that we found out the extent of the damage in St. Louis County and the city of St. Louis. The storm path had missed us by less than a mile. The Channel 2 TV tower had been blown down, and many power and phone lines were down. There was heavy damage around Grand and Page, and entire apartment buildings had collapsed in several places, the worst being in the vicinity of Boyle and Olive. That was Gaslight Square and it was exactly where Mitch and Mercy lived.

All morning long we tried to reach them by telephone. We never got through and they never called. Willie and Star did call, and so did Caine from Austin and Jack from Washington. We assured them we were all right. Around noon, Antoinette drove Nova, Ray, and me near the neighborhood of Gaslight Square, but there was too much chaos to find anything out. Firemen and police had closed off several streets, including the area surrounding Boyle and Olive. We waited the rest of the day in Carolina's kitchen, hearing nothing. As the sun was setting, Willie and Star finally arrived home safely only to learn that Mitch and Mercy were missing. The local evening newscast estimated twenty-one people had been killed and more than three hundred injured, and the search through the debris of collapsed buildings continued. Carolina called every hospital in St. Louis looking for them and came up empty. No one said it aloud, but we feared the worst. Then, early the next morning, Carolina received a telephone call from the police. Mitchell Ithaca Coates, age sixty-six, and Mercy

Marie Whitney, age fifty-six, had been found dead, buried in the rubble and debris of their apartment building. The news was more than sad. It took the wind out of us. Carolina had known Mitch since he was twelve years old, as I had, and every one of us had been in love with the good and beautiful Mercy.

Jack came back on the first flight out of Washington, and Caine drove home from Austin. According to wishes stated in both their wills, Mitch and Mercy were cremated. We held our own service in Carolina's home, and instead of a preacher's words, Jack rounded up a few local jazz musicians, all of whom knew Mitch well, and they played some of his favorite tunes while everybody shared drinks, good food, and memories of Mitch and Mercy. All day long, I kept seeing the same image in my mind. It was Mitch as a twelve-year-old shoeshine boy in Union Station, snapping his shine rag with a loud clap, a big grin, and a wink of the eye. "Hey, Z, man," he'd say, "where you goin'?" I never had an answer for him, but he never stopped asking.

Long after everyone had either left or gone to bed, Jack, Ray, and I were still awake, sitting in the kitchen, talking and drinking the last of the coffee. Jack said he would take care of all the legal work concerning Mitch, Mercy, and their property. Ray pointed over to two brass urns sitting on a table near the door. They contained the ashes of Mitch and Mercy. "What are you gonna do with them?" he asked. Jack paused and the three of us stared at the urns.

Before Jack could answer, I said, "Paris."

Ray looked at me. "What do you mean, 'Paris'?"

"We're going to take their ashes to Paris and get on a boat and let them go, into the wind and over the water of the Seine, the heart of Paris. There's only one place where their ashes should be—the place where they fell in love."

Jack and Ray nodded in silent approval. We kept staring at the urns for another ten minutes, then turned out the lights and went to bed.

Instead of insisting that I stay, this time Carolina was urging me to leave. Once she heard my idea, she applauded it and suggested it should be carried out sooner rather than later. Jack made all the necessary arrangements and within two days, Jack, Ray, Nova, and I said our farewells, flew to New York, changed planes, and flew nonstop to Paris. On the flight over, I thought about the future. I didn't know when I'd return to St. Louis. The sphere had to be found and it had to be read.

In Paris, Jack leased an available *peniche,* or barge turned house-boat, for ten days. It was located on the Canal St. Martin and suited our purposes perfectly. Shortly after sunrise on the second day, with Jack as pilot, we made our way slowly out of the canal and scattered the ashes of Mitch and Mercy into the dark waters of the Seine. It was a quiet and solemn act and Jack ended it with a quiet sentence and prayer. He said simply, "God bless both of you, forever."

That afternoon I telephoned Opari in Montreux and told her where we were and why. The following day Opari, Sheela, and Sailor boarded a train and joined us in Paris. Just seeing Opari again lifted my spirits immediately. Sailor knew that Mitch and I had been close, and he gave me his condolences and sympathy, something rare for Sailor.

The *peniche* Jack had leased could accommodate up to a dozen people, so there was plenty of room, and living on the river and canals of a large and vibrant city like Paris suited all of us. At the end of the ten-day lease, Jack decided the barge would make an excellent base of operations and we agreed. He made a generous offer to buy it, which was accepted, and we became the new "river rats" of Paris. The name of our barge was the *Giselle* and in no time Opari, Nova, and Sheela had transformed her tiny galley into a floating gourmet's kitchen.

Jack's cover for remaining in Paris for an extended length of time was a series of articles published in the American magazine *Sports Illustrated*. Each article was written about different events in the upcoming 1960 Olympics in Rome. However, his real work was helping us search for any trace of Valery and the Beekeeper. For this, he used Cardinal's European network of agents and contacts. On several occasions during the summer and fall we thought we had a lead, but none of them ever became anything we could use.

Time passed. Sailor and I kept in touch with Mowsel and the others in San Sebastian, but mainly we stayed in Paris. We settled into a life living on the river. Every season was intensified and stood alone, and yet every season followed one into the other in a graceful, seamless parade. There is, without a doubt, something timeless about living on the river.

Finally, in the spring of 1963, an odd set of circumstances combined to create a breakthrough, although we didn't know it at the time. It came not from Cardinal's network, but from Ray and Opari and a conversation they observed quite by accident. Three years earlier Ray had discovered a new passion, photography, when he accompanied Jack to the 1960 Olympics and returned with stunning pictures he had taken of the sprinter Wilma Rudolph and Cassius Clay, winner of the light-heavyweight gold medal. He gradually acquired more and more cameras and lenses and began taking photographs all over Paris, often using Opari or Nova as models.

On May 15 Cardinal, who was now seventy-seven years old, came to Paris for a visit and to announce his retirement. That same morning Ray and Opari had gone to the Eiffel Tower to take pictures. Ray was experimenting with telephoto lenses and panoramic vistas. They had climbed to the upper observation deck with a full view of Paris spread out before them. At one point, while Ray searched through his equipment for more film, he handed his camera to Opari. To pass the time, she put the camera to her eye and scanned the crowd far below. To her shock and amazement, she recognized a man walking by, a man she could never forget. It was Blaine Harrington, the same man who had used and abused Zuriaa. He was walking with another man whom she had never seen before. Instinctively, she handed Ray the camera and told him to take a photograph of the two men. He quickly reloaded and focused, shooting a dozen snapshots of the two men before they disappeared in the distance.

Ray went directly from the Eiffel Tower to have the film developed and Opari returned to the *Giselle,* telling us of the encounter. While we waited for Ray, we speculated on what Blaine Harrington might be doing in Paris. Jack said the last rumor he'd heard of "Colonel" Harrington was that, through a third party, he'd purchased a vast and remote property in Mexico or possibly Texas. Cardinal added, "But no one I know in Washington knows for certain what he's up to."

Ray came back three hours later with a folder of eight-by-ten photographs. He laid them out across the kitchen counter and the table next to it. Every picture was clear with good resolution and detail. I studied the face of Blaine Harrington. He was older, of course, but underneath the creases and lines was the same hard and humorless expression. He still wore wire-rimmed glasses and his graying hair was short and cut exactly as it had been at the end of World War II.

"One thing is clear," Sailor said, staring back and forth at both men in the photos. "This is not a social conversation. These men are conducting business."

Cardinal put on his glasses and scanned the pictures, mumbling, "Well, well, well." When he was finished, he looked up and said, "I know the other man."

"Who is he?" Opari asked.

"His name is Sesine, but he is known by other names—'the Algerian' and 'the Broker' being among them. He is rich, he is ruthless, and Interpol would love to have these pictures, Ray. This man is a ghost. Whatever Blaine Harrington is buying, selling, or planning with Sesine, it will be exotic, illegal, dangerous, and expensive. Sesine has brokered everything from unattainable antiquities to international assassinations. He is also said to have been one of the few people who have successfully arranged an assassination by the Beekeeper and not been eliminated afterward." Cardinal paused and removed his glasses. He rubbed his eyes and said, "Well, I guess my retirement is postponed for a while. I'll get these pictures to all my contacts as soon as possible. Perhaps Sesine will surface again soon, and if he does, we will be watching."

We did not have to wait long. On June 26 Sesine was spotted in West Berlin, and once again it was quite by accident. One of Cardinal's agents, a Canadian woman working in Berlin for NATO, attended the speech given by President John F. Kennedy in Rudolph Wilde Platz near the Berlin Wall. She had brought her 8mm camera in order to record the event because she planned on sending the film back to her friends and family in Halifax. After the famous speech, as she was leaving, she happened to catch sight of Sesine and two others standing and talking at the edge of the thinning crowd. Without hesitating and without being seen, she moved in closer and began filming their conversation. She was only able to capture about thirty seconds before the three parted and walked away.

Two days later, the film was in Paris, where we watched it with shock and surprise. In the clip, Sesine is in conversation with a tall man wearing expensive tailored clothes and another man at least a foot and a half shorter. The tall man's face is visible and I recognized him immediately—Valery. The shorter man is turned slightly away from the camera, and he is carrying what looks to be a cane. He also wears dark glasses and a fishing cap with an elongated bill, which keeps his face in shade for the entire thirty seconds.

We watched the film over and over. Sailor could tell the men were speaking French, and after six or seven more screenings, he was able to read their lips. However, it was a broken conversation because people kept walking past and temporarily obscuring the faces of Sesine and Valery. As Sailor translated, this was the conversation:

> VALERY: *You have seen it?*
> SESINE: *Yes.*
> VALERY: *Is it what we seek?*
> SESINE: *Yes, but Cowboy wants to play at home* (INTERRUPTION) *the pawn is in place.*
> VALERY: *Then comes the prize?*
> SESINE: *Only* (INTERRUPTION) *order* (INTERRUPTION) *is arranged.*
> VALERY: *When?*
> SESINE: *In five* (INTERRUPTION) *on* (INTERRUPTION) *two.*

> *Both Sesine and Valery then turn to the short man. He says something and they nod, then all three leave in three separate directions. End of clip.*

The transcript of the conversation was studied by all of us. It was simultaneously enlightening and baffling, and our questions were endless. Why had they chosen that certain time and place for their meeting? What was Valery seeking? What was the "prize"? Who or what was the "pawn"? Who was "Cowboy"? Were they discussing a transaction, an assassination, or both? And most important, what was the exact date that Sesine mentioned at the end?

Ray filled in the blanks and concluded that Sesine had said, "In five weeks on August 2." It made sense, and Cardinal and Jack did the research to find out if the date held any significant conferences, speeches, or other events. There were many, too many to narrow it down to one person or one place. But August 2 came and went and there were no reports of anything out of the ordinary. I continued to study the film clip and transcript while we waited and watched. September passed without a clue, as did October. Then, on November 19, a break came from one of Cardinal's sources inside the NSA, or National Security Agency. They had picked up a message sent from Dallas, Texas, to East Berlin. In the message, the caller identified himself as "Cowboy" and referred to something called "Operation Checkmate," confirming to the other party that it was a "go." Because of the reference to chess, we assumed the caller had to be our "Cowboy." I thought back to Sesine's last remark in the clip, and finally it came to me. It was so simple. It was five *months*, not weeks, and the date was *twenty-two*, not two. He had said, "In five months on November twenty-two." That was now only three days away. I looked at the transcript again. Sesine had also said "Cowboy" wanted to play at home. Could home be Dallas, Texas?

I glanced at Cardinal and Jack. "Is anything happening in Dallas on the twenty-second?"

Cardinal thought for a moment. "I believe the President is in Texas this week. He could be in Dallas on the twenty-second."

"I think we better get on a plane tonight."

"Where we goin'?" Ray asked.

"Dallas, Texas."

We weren't able to book a flight until early the next morning, and not wanting to draw any extra attention to ourselves, only Sailor and I flew out of Paris with Cardinal and Jack. Ray was disappointed, but he understood. Also, Sailor and I carried the Stones, which Ray did not, and if a difficult situation arose, they might be needed. Even before landing, we learned that President Kennedy was, in fact, due in Dallas on the twenty-second. He and his wife were to arrive at Love Field, then ride along with the governor of Texas and his wife in an open motorcade right through the city. Jack said, "If it's going to happen, that's where it will happen—somewhere along that route."

Cardinal checked us into the Adolphus Hotel, an elegant old hotel he said he had first visited forty years earlier. We ordered a late dinner from room service and discussed our options. Cardinal made the critical decision to not pass our information on to the Secret Service. He knew they would doubt its veracity and he feared they might want to know more about where he obtained the information than its content. And they would definitely want to know more about Sailor and me, which we could not allow.

Early on Thursday, November 21, Jack rented a car and we spent the day driving back and forth along the route the motorcade would be taking. We were looking for vulnerable locations that a sniper might find attractive. There were too many to count, but one stood out above the others. It was the area around Dealey Plaza, where the motorcade would have to slow down consider-

ably in order to make a series of turns before exiting onto Elm
Street. We decided that was the area where we would patrol and
keep vigil the next day. Sailor said he felt somewhat like the
Basque shepherd, alone in a vast wilderness, watching for wolves.

That night I had several strange, convoluted dreams, each of
which woke me with a start and a gasp. In the morning I remembered none of them, but I felt exhausted, as if I'd been running or swimming all night long.

Around ten o'clock we separated and took our positions of
observation. Sailor wandered among the gathering crowd at the
entrance to Dealey Plaza. Cardinal stood near the steps of the
Texas School Book Depository, where the route turned onto Elm
Street. Jack was across the street next to the John Neely Bryan
concrete pergola. I was a few hundred feet to the south on the
triple underpass, a railroad bridge that crossed over Elm Street. It
was a clear day with very little wind, and the sun was already high
in the sky. We watched and we waited.

By noon the crowd had doubled. Many people carried cameras, but the majority simply lined the road hoping for a glimpse
of the President and the First Lady. I didn't see anything or anyone out of the ordinary. The minutes ticked by. At 12:30 a man
standing near me turned and asked if I had "cut school" to come
and see Kennedy. Before I could answer I felt a sudden chill and
prickly sensation on the skin of my arms and neck. Then the man
said, "Here they come." I looked north on Elm Street and the
motorcade was entering Dealey Plaza. The crowd shouted and
waved as the President's limousine turned onto Elm and passed
the Book Depository. Then a gunshot rang out, and then another. The President grabbed his throat. Then came the third and
fatal shot, but there was something extremely unusual about it
that only I could hear. Because of my "ability," I was able to pin-
point the source of the gunshots immediately—a window on the

sixth floor of the Book Depository. However, the third shot had actually been two shots at once, fired simultaneously so that they sounded like one shot. The other gun was fired from somewhere in the shade on a grassy knoll to my left. In an instant I looked that way to see a man leap behind a fence and vanish in a split second. His movements were as quick and graceful as Geaxi, and I was probably the only one who saw him. I had seen him before in a film clip. He was short. He wore a fishing cap with an elongated bill and he was carrying what looked to be a cane, only now I knew the cane was actually a unique and deadly sniper rifle. He was the Beekeeper, and he had just assassinated the President of the United States.

There is no way to adequately describe the shock, madness, and sadness that followed in the next few days. It is well known and documented that the events changed something in America and Americans forever. Perhaps it was the hard truth and unwanted knowledge that all dreams are assailable and anyone can be murdered.

As for us, Sailor and I made a brief visit to St. Louis with Jack. Then the three of us flew back to Paris via New York. Cardinal was devastated and horrified by what happened in Dallas. For days he kept repeating, "Why? Why?" None of us had the answer or any other concerning "Cowboy," the Beekeeper, and Valery. We came upon them too late and with too little. Now nothing could change it, and they had disappeared once again. Cardinal flew from Dallas to Washington, D.C., where he said he was going to stay. "I am too old for this," he said. "I'll send you anything that comes my way, but I'll be staying home." We understood and wished him well.

On the long flight to Paris, neither Sailor nor I could sleep, so we talked at length about all things Meq, including the Gogorati, the Remembering. What was it? Would it be a beginning, an end, or some kind of transition? Would we find out why we are the way we are? Would we learn the truth? I asked Sailor what he expected to happen. He laughed and said, "The unexpected."

"But what if we can't find the sphere?"

"Be patient, Zianno. It may take years, but we shall find this sphere and you shall read it."

"That is what Opari told me."

"She is correct, and she is your Ameq, Zianno. Believe her for your own sake."

Sailor was right, of course. Once we landed and made our way across the city to the Canal St. Martin and the *Giselle,* and I looked into Opari's eyes, those black and beautiful eyes, I didn't care how long it took to find the sphere. I, she, we . . . would wait.

But it is odd how things sometimes play out and turn around. Just under five months later, on April 16, Cardinal sent us a message. A sport-fishing yacht, a sixty-four-foot Bertram, was found drifting in the Gulf of Mexico, four miles off the coast of Matagorda Island in South Texas. On board, the Coast Guard discovered the bodies of two men who had been dead for several days. They had each been shot once in the back of the head, execution style, and their throats had been slashed ear to ear. No money, jewelry, or valuables of any kind were missing. The name of the yacht itself was *Cowboy's Dream,* and the name of one of the men, the owner of the yacht, was Blaine Harrington, Captain U.S. Army, retired.

Ten days later, on his birthday, April 26, Jack received a small package in the mail. The package had no return address, but was postmarked West Berlin. Jack tore open the brown paper wrapping to find a book titled *The Gashouse Gang: The St. Louis Cardinals of the 1930s* by Cappy Briant. That was Jack's favorite period of St. Louis Cardinals history. Whoever sent the package knew a great deal about Jack, intimate knowledge that he shared with very few others, which would imply that whoever it was also knew everything about Jack's family, including where they lived and what they did every day. It was a subtle message, yet it was there and meant to be noticed.

Stuck between the pages of the book was a handwritten note. It read:

Dear Jack,

Happy Birthday, Comrade. I hope you enjoy the book. I did. The American game of baseball is perhaps your best export. It has been a long time since Manchuria, has it not? You are an admirable adversary, Jack Flowers. You play a good game. On the back of this note are the instructions for the one called Zianno Zezen. I pray you follow them.

V.

The instructions were brief and simple. They told me to come alone to a certain intersection in West Berlin on a certain day at a certain time. The certain day happened to be May 4, my birthday, which sent another message that Valery knew much more than we suspected. But why had Valery surfaced now? And why me? Was it some sort of sacrifice, or trap, or exchange? Jack advised me not to go alone. However, that was the price and there was only one way to get the answers to my questions.

I waited the eight days, then boarded a plane in Paris and flew to Berlin, telling the stewardess and the woman sitting next to me I was on my way to spend the summer with my grandparents.

After landing and clearing customs, I took a taxi to the designated intersection, only a block from the Anhalter Bahnhof train station. I was forty minutes early. It was a warm and sunny day, so I rolled up my shirtsleeves and leaned against the street sign, waiting. In exactly forty minutes, a blue Volkswagen pulled up to the curb and the passenger side door opened. The driver, a man about seventy or seventy-five years old, waved me inside. I got in and without ever saying a word to me the man drove across West Berlin to a checkpoint into East Berlin. The border guard waved us through, never looking at me and barely glancing at the man, as if he knew him well. We drove on to the outskirts of East Berlin, where the man stopped in a parking lot and pointed toward a pickup truck parked twenty yards away. The driver of the pickup was a woman at least as old as the man with the Volkswagen. *"Danke,"* I said and walked over and got in the pickup. From there we drove northwest for about thirty miles. The woman spoke to me occasionally, but it was with a thick accent and I didn't understand a word. Finally, we turned off the highway onto a winding asphalt road that took us into a stretch of hills running along the east bank of the Elbe River. The hills were dotted with small farms and a few larger, older farms with landscaped terraces overlooking the river. After about five miles, the old woman slowed the pickup and turned into just such a farm. Two-hundred-year-old oaks and firs lined the driveway leading to and around the main farmhouse and a dozen other structures. All the structures had been built with stone sometime in the early 1700s and had been renovated many times since. She parked the pickup near a lavish flower garden. When we got out, she pointed west, past the flower garden and over a hill. Then she turned and walked away without a word.

I chose the central path through the enormous garden. The flowers were lush and well tended, especially the roses, which were in bloom, abundant, and all red—the fullest, richest red I'd ever seen. They looked beautiful in the bright glare of the sun. At the far end there was another path leading up the hill through a broad meadow full of wildflowers to a grove of oak trees. Beyond the trees the meadow sloped gently another fifty yards to a cliff overlooking a wide bend of the Elbe River. It was a stunning view, peaceful and magical.

As I came closer to the grove, I could see something moving in the dappled light between the trees. It was a man, or it looked to be a man. He wore a loose, baggy white suit, with oversize white gloves and a large white hat and veil, which completely covered his face and neck. He was tending to a long row of rectangular cedar boxes. I watched him lifting out panels or wooden frames from each box and scraping off a thick liquid, then returning the frames into the boxes. And then I saw the bees. They were swarming and buzzing around the man and the boxes. I got a sudden prickly feeling down my arms and legs. I reached in my pocket and took hold of the Stone. Was he the Beekeeper? I walked into the grove and the man kept working. He looked too tall to be the Beekeeper. Could he be Valery? I stopped twenty feet away and waited. The only sound was the buzzing of the bees. After he pulled and scraped one more frame, he took off his gloves and walked over to me. In my pocket I gripped the Stone a little tighter. He removed his hat and veil. He was not Valery. He was just a friendly old man, like the man in the Volkswagen and the woman in the pickup. He smiled and walked past me, making his way back up the hill through the meadow to the garden.

Then I turned and saw him. He was standing ten feet from the last wooden box in the row. I hadn't seen him before because he was standing in the shade, but he was no taller than I was. He wore a baggy white suit, gloves, and a big white hat and veil. His "cane" was at his side. The Beekeeper.

Neither of us moved. The bees quit buzzing. I could not help but think of the horror in Dallas. He started out of the shade toward me, taking off his gloves as he walked. I felt a strange sensation as he came closer, but it wasn't fear, it was something much more familiar. He stopped three feet in front of me. Slowly, deliberately, he raised his veil. I saw his green eyes, his ruby earrings, and his bright white teeth. I stared back at him.

"You!" I snarled.

"*Alles Gute zum Geburtstag,*" he said. "Happy Birthday, *mon petit.*"

PART III

A good traveler has no fixed plans, and is not intent on arriving.

—LAO-TZU

6

AMETSHARRI

(DREAMSTONE)

It took them twelve long winters before they finished. Twelve winters were nothing compared to what lay ahead. They would leave their work here. The work was now complete, polished and carved in the Language, with proper greetings, instructions, and directions. They were the only ones, they were sure of it. Soon they would sail to their new home and wait . . . and wait . . . and wait.

"You . . . you killed the President! You murdered the President of the United States!" I wasn't shouting, but I was close to it. "And with that!" I added, nodding back toward his "cane."

"Calm down, *mon petit*." The Fleur-du-Mal dropped his smile and looked away for a moment, through the oaks and down the steep slope to the Elbe River. "Regrettably, Zezen, your accusation is true, at least in a technical sense. The act was a necessary compromise, a necessary evil if you will."

"A *compromise*? What kind of compromise could condone such an act? And with whom, or what? The Soviet Union? Valery?"

"Valery? You are aware of Valery?"

"Yes. And Sesine."

"I am impressed. You and the others and your friend Jack Flowers have been busy."

"What about Blaine Harrington, or should I say 'Cowboy'? It was you who killed him, wasn't it?"

The Fleur-du-Mal didn't answer. He motioned me toward a small shed, where he climbed out of his beekeeper's suit. "You are upset and you must be hungry after your trip. Come with me and I shall have one of the Mannheims serve us lunch in the garden."

I started to say something else, then stopped myself. Instead, I followed him in silence along the path through the meadow.

The Fleur-du-Mal began talking as we walked. "I hope the Mannheims have treated you pleasantly," he said. "That was Eric you saw tending the bees. He is quite good with them. His brother and sister were your chauffeurs from Berlin to here. I have hired the entire family and it has worked out well. I find you cannot trust the young these days. Do you agree, Zezen?"

I ignored the question and kept walking. The Fleur-du-Mal laughed out loud, a long, bitter laugh, then continued talking about bees the rest of the way up the hill, describing in detail the different behavioral characteristics of *apis mellifera mellifera* and *apis mellifera ligustica*.

A portable table was set up in the garden with a full view of the surrounding countryside. Half an hour later, Bertholde, the oldest of the Mannheims, served us a light lunch of fresh trout with vegetables, and despite whom I was dining with, the meal was delicious. Afterward Bertholde delivered a chocolate cake to the table. It had twelve lit candles on top.

"Make a wish and blow them out, *mon petit*," the Fleur-du-Mal said. "This is your special day."

I paid no attention to the cake or the candles. Enough was enough. I looked the Fleur-du-Mal in the eye. "What do you want?" I asked. "Why am I here?"

He leaned over the cake and blew out all the candles. "You are here, my friend, because—"

"I am not your friend."

He paused and feigned a look of surprise. "You disappoint me, Zezen. I thought we were close, although in Japan you left without even saying good-bye," he said, smiling again. "Nevertheless, you are here because you, *monsieur,* are the Stone of Dreams, and though I hate to admit it, let alone say it, you may be able to help me."

"Help you? That is impossible. I wouldn't help you cross the street. We will never be friends and I will never help you do anything."

"Do not be so certain. I think you might change your mind when you learn the nature of the task. I happen to know you are familiar with the problem."

I looked away and tried to seem indifferent, but I wanted to hear more. "And what is the task?"

The Fleur-du-Mal's green eyes flashed and his smile returned. "Reading the stone spheres," he said.

I felt my heart beat a little faster. "Did you say 'spheres,' as in more than one?"

"Yes. I now have three of them in my possession."

"Three!"

"Oui, mon petit —trois."

I stared back at him and a half-dozen thoughts ran through my mind at once. I knew Valery had brought him the sphere found in the Caucasus, but what about the others? From where had they come, and how? Why would this "aberrant" assassin want them anyway? He had expressed his opinions about the Meq and the Remembering on several occasions, saying it meant little or nothing to him and we were wasting our time. So, why would he want to read the spheres? I knew one thing for sure. The Fleur-du-Mal never did anything that did not benefit himself. I asked him point-blank, "What's in this for you?"

"Why, Zezen, you disappoint me again. My motive is simple curiosity. I want to solve the puzzle, break the code, find the message. After all, I am Meq, and I have had a change of heart regarding the Remembering."

"You have a heart?"

"Oh, how clever! You are now a comedian as well as the Stone of Dreams. How do you do it?"

"Okay, then, why the change?"

The Fleur-du-Mal stood up and walked a few paces into his garden. He bent over a particularly beautiful red rose and examined it carefully, then snapped it off its stem and put it to his nose. He closed his eyes and inhaled deeply. "I have my reasons," he said, and dropped the rose on the ground. "The point is, *mon petit,* you and Sailor and the rest of you have no choice. If you want to see the spheres, you must deal with me. There is no option. Take it or leave it."

He was right and he knew I knew it. There was no way around it. "You got one of the spheres from Valery," I said. "Where did you get the other two?"

He nodded and said, "A fair question, and I suppose you have a right to know. I acquired the first one nearly eighteen hundred years ago on Cyprus from a man with whom I often traded various services for . . . well, things I desired. That day, I traded for an object that had once been the possession of a Meq known as 'the Thracian.' He was an old one and he had perished on Thera, now known as Santorini, when the island exploded." The Fleur-du-Mal paused. "Perhaps the Ethiopian told you about him. He was rather notorious."

"If you mean Susheela the Ninth, she mentioned him, but she never knew him."

"Yes, well, 'the Thracian' kept a hidden cache of properties on Cyprus. This cache was later discovered and passed down by the family of the man who sold it to me. The sphere itself was and is in a condition of deterioration, and many of the markings are worn away. It is without a doubt the oldest of the three. The second sphere, the one brought to me by Valery, is in a very good state, and in fact is quite beautiful."

"I agree."

The Fleur-du-Mal raised one eyebrow. "You have seen it?"

"Yes, but just briefly."

"Well, well, well, you must tell me the story, *mon petit.*"

"Maybe someday," I said. "What about the third one?"

"Ah, yes, the third one." He plucked another deep red rose from its stem and twirled it between his fingers, admiring each velvet petal. "The last sphere I acquired only recently. The craftsmanship is exquisite and sublime, and it is the most mysterious and complex of the three. It was uncovered six years ago in a cave near the Portuguese coastal town of Marinha Grande. From there, its history is a bit murky until it was brought to my attention through the man you know as Sesine. In order to obtain it, I was forced to perform an odious task for an objectionable man who was quite insane, but the disservice has since been rectified. He made the unfortunate mistake of believing he had, shall we say, 'won the chess match.'"

"Blaine Harrington?"

"Checkmate," the Fleur-du-Mal said with a smile. "Now, come with me and I will take you to the milk barn."

"To see the cows?"

Laughing, he threw the rose over his shoulder and said, "No, *mon petit.* To see the spheres."

• • •

The milk barn was anything but a barn and the only cow around
was in the leather that covered the furniture throughout. Every
chair and couch was designed in a distinctly western American
style, and the exposed cedar beams as well as the pine flooring
made it look and smell more like Montana than East Germany. The
vast space inside had been transformed into a combined studio,
laboratory, library, workshop, spa, and a few other areas for various arcane pursuits. I glanced around, but I couldn't take in
everything at once. It was obvious, although his flaws and crimes
were countless and beyond endurance, that the Fleur-du-Mal was
not lazy.

He flipped a switch on the wall and an area in the center of the
room was lit from all sides by a bank of lights. Three stainless-steel
cylinders about a foot in diameter and three feet tall stood in a
line. They were anchored to the floor and shining brightly in the
lights. Perched and resting atop each cylinder were the stone
spheres. "There they are, Zezen," he said. "Go closer."

I stepped toward them. I couldn't look away. I felt an instant
connection and sense of awe. I remembered something Star had
told me years earlier when she and Willie Croft were living in
Cornwall at Caitlin's Ruby. She said one weekend Willie drove
her to see Stonehenge and she had an experience unlike any she'd
ever had. Star said as she approached the megaliths, she became
almost intoxicated with a presence, an "intelligence," she called it.
She said it was undeniable, silent, and overwhelming, and it emanated directly from the stones. As I gazed at the three spheres, I
felt the same thing. The three of them together had a power that
was profound.

The Fleur-du-Mal flipped another switch and the steel cylinders began to rotate, so slowly it was barely perceptible, but just
enough to give the spheres another dimension. They seemed to
float or drift, and the markings seemed to swim as the stones

turned in the light. We both stood mesmerized by their beauty and mystery. Then he said, "You may not agree, *mon petit,* on how I procured them, particularly the last one, yet this is perhaps the lone true instance where the end does justify the means."

I didn't agree; however, I did feel a sense of guilt because I was so excited about seeing the spheres and I couldn't wait to study them.

The Fleur-du-Mal must have read my thoughts. "You need to lose your anemic, pathetic, obsolescent Giza morality, Zezen. Doing so would allow you to be much happier and probably do much better work. And while we are on the subject, I need to make one thing clear. I want you to tell Jack Flowers if he or any of his friends in Washington take any action whatsoever against Valery or me for the incident in Dallas, then they will sincerely regret it. I happen to have in my possession certain documents I removed from Blaine Harrington that clearly implicate several people in the Pentagon and other branches, people who could and would eliminate Jack and his entire family in one day. Jack is a smart man and I am sure he knows this to be true. But just re-mind him, *mon petit,* if you will."

With little or no expression I told him I would relay the mes-sage. I then asked him to turn off the rotation of the cylinders and leaned over and felt the oldest sphere with my hands. Wherever it had been found, the stone had suffered from countless thousands of years of exposure to the elements. It was also the largest of the three, and its markings, or what was left of them, were spaced far-ther apart than on the other two. I walked around the sphere from Portugal and marveled at its sheer perfection. It was the smallest one, and its granite surface was infused with a reddish hue and had been polished until it was nearly smooth as glass. It looked as if its creators had only finished yesterday. The carved script was complex and sublime in every way. I glanced at the sphere delivered by Valery and thought back to the exhibit and Geaxi's reaction to the Neanderthal bones.

"What do you make of the Neanderthal children's bones found with this one?" I asked, pointing to the Caucasus sphere.

"I have no opinion . . . yet. That is one of the subjects we must investigate. The stones may reveal the reason in time. But, tell me, Zezen—what makes you so certain they are the bones of children? Because they are small and immature?"

My answer was another question. "Have you had any breakthroughs with the markings?"

"A few. So far, they are random and inconsequential, but there was something odd about each breakthrough, or rather each *understanding*. Each one came to me after waking from a dream. I awoke and could not recall a single place, image, or conversation from the dream, yet I knew the meaning of a specific marking. It is a language beyond speech. It is a language with no vowels, no consonants, and ten thousand nuances of meaning and expression. It is a language of dreams, Zezen . . . a language of dreams." The Fleur-du-Mal walked over to the sphere found in Portugal. He ran his fingertips lightly over the markings, caressing the curve of the stone like a woman's cheek and neck. "I have a name for them," he said, letting his eyes roam from sphere to sphere.

"What is it?"

In a voice unusual for the Fleur-du-Mal, almost a whisper, he said, "Dreamstones."

Later that evening, over a dinner served by yet another gray-haired Mannheim sister, Ilsa, the Fleur-du-Mal and I came to a working arrangement. He was adamant the spheres would stay where they were, with him. I could not have them moved to Paris, Caitlin's Ruby, or anywhere else for study. However, I could have Opari come and live with me while I worked. I told him the others should have a chance to see the spheres, particularly his uncle, Zeru-Meq, who had a poet's mind, and because any one of us could have a sudden insight. We negotiated and the Fleur-du-Mal compromised, saying he would allow the others open-ended visits, but only one at a time.

We both realized working together might become difficult, so we devised a variable shift schedule for our time in the milk barn. I would work days and he would work nights. All notes and observations would be written down in a common log to which we both had access.

"What if I want to leave?" I asked.

"Then leave," he said. "You are not in prison, *mon petit,* except perhaps in your imagination. I will have the Mannheims assist you with any logistical concerns."

I stared down at the fruit pudding that Ilsa had brought out for dessert. It was made from red and black currants and was delicious. I looked across the table at the Fleur-du-Mal. He was sipping cognac and preparing to light a cigar. I thought, how did I get here? How did this happen and how would it play out? It was crazy yet somehow it made no difference. All that mattered to me now were the spheres. I didn't like it and I didn't want to admit it, but I was obsessed with them, and in almost the same way I had once been obsessed with killing the Fleur-du-Mal. I laughed out loud.

"Why do you laugh?" he asked, lighting the long Cuban cigar.

I shook my head back and forth. "Never ever did I expect to be in this . . . situation."

"Nor I," he said.

"Why do suppose we are doing this?"

"The answer is quite simple," the Fleur-du-Mal said. He inhaled slightly, then let the smoke out slowly in a single stream. "We are, you and I, more alike than you might think. We are obsessed with the truth, Zezen . . . the truth."

• • •

And thus began my long and strange alliance with the Fleur-du-Mal. The very next day I returned to West Berlin, then on to Paris by train to tell the others about this new, unlikely, and unexpected turn of events. Jack and I would also have to discuss Dallas and what the Fleur-du-Mal had said. I knew he was not lying or bluffing. Jack was no coward, but in this case I was hoping family would come first.

On the way to Paris, I stared out the window at the changing landscapes and couldn't quit thinking about the spheres. In every passing tree and rock face, I saw the delicate and beautiful script, the intricate connecting patterns and weaves, all separate and moving backward and forward together. I kept seeing the sphere from Portugal over and over. In my heart of hearts, I knew it was the heart of the mystery. It was the one that would lead us to the Remembering.

The train arrived at the Gard du Nord Station just after sunset, and it was completely dark by the time I reached the Canal St. Martin and stepped onto the dock adjacent to the *Giselle*. Sailor was sitting in a folding chair, facing my direction, as if he was waiting for me.

"Well?" he said.

I laughed and hopped onto the deck of the *Giselle*. "Come inside," I told him, smiling. "You won't believe it."

I gathered everyone around the long bench that served as a kitchen table and started talking. The true identity of the Beekeeper prompted groans, then comments of disgust in varying degrees. But when I mentioned the three spheres, it had the opposite effect. You couldn't even hear breathing. I told them the terms of the arrangement I had made with the Fleur-du-Mal, adding that I had had little or no choice.

After I stopped speaking, Opari asked the hardest question to answer. "Why would the Fleur-du-Mal have a 'change of heart' concerning the Remembering? He has never done so before concerning anything. Why this? Why now?"

"I don't know," I said, "but I think we're stuck with him."

One day later we took a train to San Sebastian and met with Geaxi, Zeru-Meq, and Mowsel. Zeru-Meq cursed loudly when he found out the truth about the Beekeeper. Mowsel asked at least a dozen questions about the spheres and their markings. Geaxi listened in silence to every detail, then stated her wish to be the first in the rotation of "guests" to study the spheres. No one had any objections, and we all agreed the study should begin as soon as possible.

The Fleur-du-Mal had given me a telephone number to call when I was ready to return. I made the call and identified myself to the woman who answered. In a thick German accent she told me to be at a specific intersection in West Berlin at a certain time on a certain date, just as I'd done on my first visit. It would become a pattern.

On May 13 Geaxi, Opari, and I stood on a corner only two blocks from the Brandenberg Gate in Berlin. It was 3:15 in the afternoon. An old black Mercedes sedan pulled to a stop and a door opened. The three of us climbed into the backseat. Our driver was about sixty years old with bushy salt-and-pepper hair and a grizzled two weeks' growth of beard. He introduced himself as Hans. As I was to learn later, he was the youngest of the Mannheims.

When we reached the farm an hour later, the Fleur-du-Mal was standing at the end of the long driveway, waiting to greet us. His black hair was neatly tied back with a green ribbon, and he wore his ruby earrings. His pressed pants and shirt were made of fine Egyptian linen. He was fully relishing the charade of playing the host. He bowed slightly to Opari, said hello to me, and seemed genuinely surprised to see Geaxi as the first "guest" Meq.

"Ah, Geaxi," he said with a wide smile. "How is Malta? I have always loved your little island."

Geaxi adjusted her beret and ignored the remark. In a flat voice she said, "I understand you have treasures."

"That I do, that I do." He turned and motioned for Hans. "First, let us get you settled in your cottage. Hans will show you the way. Dinner is served at six o'clock and afterward I shall take you to the milk barn."

"The milk barn?"

The Fleur-du-Mal was already walking away, toward the massive front door of his farmhouse. Over his shoulder, he said, "Tell her, Zezen," and kept walking.

Hans said, "Zis way, please."

Around nine o'clock we left the farmhouse and followed the Fleur-du-Mal down the path leading to the milk barn. It was a clear night and the moon had yet to rise. Venus was low and bright and looked as if it was hovering over the top of the barn. The Fleur-du-Mal laughed and said, "It seems we have a torch to light our way. Perhaps a good omen, no?"

He opened the door and flipped the switch. Geaxi was speechless when she finally saw the three spheres together, lit by the bank of lights and lined up on their stainless-steel cylinders. She walked in slow circles around each of them, pausing occasionally and reaching out to feel the markings. She touched the sphere from Portugal last and jumped back with a shout, as if she'd been shocked. "This stone is warm," she said.

"That is impossible," the Fleur-du-Mal replied. He rushed

over and laid his palm across the top of the sphere. He gave Geaxi
a quizzical look. "This sphere is cold as a tombstone."

I reached out and felt the stone. It was cold. I glanced at Geaxi,
trying to read her expression. She gave nothing away. She looked
back at me and I knew she was absolutely serious and telling the
truth. For whatever reason, the sphere from Portugal felt warm to
her touch. Before we even started our study of the spheres, another mystery had appeared.

We began in earnest the next morning. We had no set pattern
or routine. Each of us spent time alone with each sphere, and all
of us, including the Fleur-du-Mal, spent time together discussing
the problems. We studied and speculated, examined and medi-
tated, agreed and disagreed. Opari, Geaxi, and I spent our days
with the spheres while the Fleur-du-Mal spent his nights with
them. We truly expected a breakthrough right away. After all,
why not? The Fleur-du-Mal had previously deciphered a word or
two, although he didn't call them words. He referred to the markings as "dreamings." Opari and Geaxi had extraordinary facilities
with languages from every corner of the world. They could have
an insight at any time. And of course, everyone expected me to
have a complete breakthrough and be able to read the entirety of
the message, whatever it might be. I even expected it to happen.
In Russia I had "read" a phrase and a word in only a few minutes.
Now I had all the time I wanted, and I was obsessed with the
spheres. I could think of little else. "Today," I kept telling myself,
"today I will find the key and unlock the mystery." But it didn't
happen. Study became struggle and infatuation led to frustration.
Seasons passed in rapid succession, dressing and undressing the
landscape like a fashion show. The rotation of Meq "guests"
began and continued, with each one delivered and driven away by
the Mannheims. Some stayed longer than others and all returned

time after time. Still, nothing happened. Not a word was deciphered. Weeks became months, and months became years.
Throughout the turbulent sixties, while the rest of the world was
changing with abandon around us, we spent our time sneaking in
and out of East Germany, obsessed with solving a riddle carved
on three silent granite spheres, a riddle that refused to give up its
secret.

On occasion, Opari and I would return to Paris for a few days
or weeks, however long it took to revive our spirits, away from
the spheres and the dark umbrella of the Fleur-du-Mal. Twice on
these "holidays" we received sudden and sad news, the kind you
never want to hear and can never change. In September of 1965
Cardinal had been enjoying his retirement by going on a deep-sea
fishing vacation with several other men to a small resort on Great
Abaco Island in the Bahamas. During the night of September 6,
Hurricane Betsy, a storm that would later pummel Florida and
the Gulf Coast, roared across Great Abaco Island with winds
measured at 147 mph. They sheared the roof off the small resort
and demolished everything else for the next three hours. By
dawn, twelve people were dead and dozens had been injured.
Cardinal, Dr. Bikki Birnbaum, was among the dead. Jack flew to
the island and claimed his body, then buried him in a church
graveyard not far from his home overlooking the Potomac. Cardinal's death affected Jack deeply. Less than two years later, he decided to retire himself. He wanted to spend more time in St.
Louis with Carolina. The Vietnam War was, according to Jack,
"already beyond the point of no return." He said he'd been in the
spy business too long and added, "This war has nothing to do
with me, and I want nothing to do with it. I'm going to watch
baseball instead." Jack hired a man we could trust named Michel
to take care of the *Giselle* year-round, while we could come and
go as we pleased with no questions asked.

Opari and I arrived back in Paris on May 4, 1969, to celebrate my hundredth birthday. As we stepped on board the *Giselle,* Michel handed me a piece of paper with a telephone number on it. He said to call Jack at that number—it was urgent. I called the number and was connected to Barnes Hospital in St. Louis. I asked for Jack Flowers and was transferred to a private room. Jack answered after one ring. "It's Z," I said. "What's up?"

There was a long pause at the other end. Finally, Jack said, "Willie's dead."

"Oh, no . . . no."

"Yeah," Jack said in a whisper.

I closed my eyes and in a flash remembered nearly every moment I'd spent with Willie Croft. I missed him already. "Tell me what happened."

I learned from Jack that Willie had gone to the airport that same morning to take his beloved de Havilland out for a short flight. At seventy-eight years old he was still a pilot and flew at least once a month. Jack said Willie taxied to the end of the runway and waited to be cleared for takeoff. A short time later he was given clearance, but he never responded. As the de Havilland idled on the runway, Willie slumped over the controls. He had suffered a massive stroke. By the time help reached him, he had fallen into a deep coma. Jack said he was taken to Barnes Hospital, where he held on for a while, then passed away less than an hour before I called.

"How is Star?" I asked.

"She'll be all right . . . in time." Jack paused and let out a long breath. "He was a good man, Z."

"The best."

"I figure in a week or two, we'll take him back to Cornwall to be buried with his parents."

"I'll be there," I said, "just tell me when."

Jack and I talked for a few more minutes about Willie, then Jack said he would be in touch. I hung up the telephone with the heaviest heart I'd had in years. Sailor told me once that the Meq should celebrate every single birthday. Sometimes that is simply not possible. On May 4, 1969, there was nothing to celebrate.

On May 19 Geaxi, Sailor, and I traveled to the coast by train and took a ferry across the English Channel. Opari and Sheela and the others stayed behind in Paris and San Sebastian. Jack was to meet us in London, along with Koldo and Arrosa Txopitea. He said Willie had left Caitlin's Ruby and a large percentage of the Daphne Croft Foundation to Koldo and his family. They would be in London to finalize the papers. Afterward, we would drive back to Cornwall for the funeral. I looked forward to seeing Koldo and Arrosa. Too many years had passed since I'd seen them last. Their twin sons, Kepa and Yaldi, were now in their early thirties. The twins were the last of the tribe of Vardules, Protectors of the Stone of Dreams, and yet I had never met them. On the crossing, I thought about what Willie had done and smiled. "Good on you, Willie!" I shouted over the water. Then I wondered if ever before there had been an independently wealthy Basque landowner in Cornwall. I laughed out loud. Koldo Txopitea had to be the first.

Arrosa was waving to us when we stepped off the train in Victoria Railway Station. She looked as beautiful as I remembered, even with silver hair and a few lines on her face, which now crisscrossed their way through the tiny scar on her left cheek. Koldo shook our hands vigorously and Jack smiled, but it wasn't a happy smile, just a welcome one. We left the station and walked to a big Jaguar sedan parked a block away. They had concluded their busi-

ness earlier that morning, so we set out immediately on the long
drive to Cornwall, with Jack and Koldo taking turns at the wheel.

I asked Koldo, "What would your grandfather think of this
car?"

Koldo grinned. "If he were here, I would not have this car."

Even Sailor laughed at that, having known Kepa well.

The next three days were quiet, relaxed, easygoing, and sometimes awkward, almost like Willie himself. The funeral was simple and solemn, and Star was gracious and patient, personally
thanking every person who came, and there were many. The
Crofts had been generous contributors to the whole community
for generations. Koldo and Arrosa had become an integral part of
the community years ago, and they, too, accepted condolences.
The twins, Kepa and Yaldi, were not there, nor were they at
Caitlin's Ruby. I learned on the drive to Cornwall that both were
professional musicians and both were currently on tour. Kepa was
a classical pianist and Yaldi was a rock guitarist, and yet Koldo said
they were very much alike. I looked forward to meeting them,
but it would have to be another time.

Carolina had stayed in St. Louis, saying the trip would be too
long and difficult. However, she did send a short letter, which
Star handed to me as soon as I arrived. In the letter she said it was
past time I came home, if not for good, at least for a visit. She reminded me that she was approaching three digits in age. With typ-
ical Carolina good humor, the letter ended, "A girl can only wait
so long." I folded the letter carefully and slipped it in my back
pocket. I felt guilty because I wanted to go, and probably should
go, but I knew I couldn't. Not now, not yet. I owed it to the
others to solve the mystery of the spheres. They would never say

it aloud or display it in any obvious manner, yet each and every Meq, including Opari, believed that I was the only one who could truly do it. I had to return to East Germany and the spheres. The awkward moments came when Star asked when I would be coming back to St. Louis. I had to tell her I didn't know, but I couldn't tell her why. Star leaned over and whispered in my ear. "ZeeZee," she said, using a name she hadn't called me since she was three years old. "Mama needs to see you. I don't know how much time we have left with her. She's strong now, but . . ."

Star was now sixty-eight years old herself. I knew she was telling the truth. "I'll be there soon, Star," I said, then added, "I promise," hoping that I was telling the truth.

Jack and Star left Caitlin's Ruby for home on the morning of May 25. I made the same promise to Jack as I'd made to Star, and we said our farewells. Before we left the next day, Geaxi, Sailor, and I took a long walk along one of the six paths that Caitlin had cleared centuries earlier. It made no difference which path we chose because they all led to the same place. It was a wild and desolate, nearly barren hill on the western corner of the property, an ancient station from a distant past known as Lullyon Coit or, as Geaxi called it, "the slabs." It was here in 1918 that Sailor took down the huge stone structures that had stood upright for millennia. In a fit of bitter rage, which he never fully explained, and using only his mind and his "ability" of telekinesis, he shook the tons of granite and the ground beneath them until the sacred stones collapsed and fell like dominoes in just a few seconds.

Now several rugged wildflowers poked their way up between and around the giant, scattered "slabs." The wind was down, and Geaxi spread a blanket across one of the stones. I brought cheese and bread and a basket of fresh strawberries. Sailor brought a bottle of wine and three tin cups, perfect for a picnic on a bright and clear day in Cornwall. Four miles away, along the horizon to the south and west, the open sea was visible, which was rare at Caitlin's Ruby.

Sailor uncorked the wine and filled our cups. He stood and looked as far to the west as he could, to where the sky and sea became one. "We have time, Zianno," he said. "Or should I say we still have *enough* time?"

"Enough time?"

"Yes. Do not pressure yourself in your study of the spheres. We have forty-eight years to answer their riddles, forty-eight years before the Remembering is upon us."

"You're probably right." I was facing west, the same as Sailor, then for some reason turned and faced north, looking out and over the windswept, empty landscape. Geaxi was facing the same way. She held her beret in one hand and seemed transfixed on an invisible point in the distance. For a moment or two I watched Geaxi watching nothing. "The answer we seek, Sailor, is not in *time*. The answer we seek is . . . somewhere else."

We returned to Paris by air from London, with Koldo acting as our grandfather and purchasing our tickets, then seeing us onto the plane.

"Perhaps Kepa or Yaldi will be performing in Paris one day," he said. "If so, you should pay them a visit. They will know who you are."

I told him I would do just that if the opportunity arose and I thanked him for his generous hospitality. Koldo reminded me he was Aita of the tribe of Vardules and it was unnecessary to thank him. We embraced and he said, "Our grandfathers would be pleased, no?"

I turned to board the plane. "Yes, they would, Koldo, and so would their grandfathers and their grandfathers' grandfathers." Then we both smiled and I waved good-bye.

• • •

Later that summer the American astronauts Neil Armstrong and Buzz Aldrin walked on the moon. Practically the whole world stopped to watch. Inside the milk barn, I barely noticed. I was back in my routine of studying the spheres. It was Nova's turn in the rotation of Meq "guests" and I was optimistic. Nova carried the Stone of Silence, and I had always felt that if any of us who carried the Stones were going to have a sudden breakthrough, it would be the one who carried the Stone of Silence, not the Stone of Dreams. Nova had also been prone to "visions" in the past. Perhaps she would "see" a breakthrough. But, once again, nothing happened. Nova sat for hours with the spheres, hours without moving or speaking . . . listening, waiting . . . listening. She did this for weeks and months, staying at the farm longer than ever before. Seasons came and went, and so did the other Meq, one by one, studying the spheres in vain. The Fleur-du-Mal tended his bees and we drank their honey with our tea. Two of the Mannheims died and Opari and I attended the funerals. We got back to Paris less and less. I even became somewhat fluent in German, though Geaxi labeled my accent "deplorable and pathetically American."

Late in 1973 the Fleur-du-Mal casually mentioned that Valery had passed away at his villa on Lake Como in northern Italy. I had always been curious about the true nature of the relationship between them, so I asked. The Fleur-du-Mal took his time before answering. He sipped his cognac and swallowed slowly. "There was no mystery, *mon petit*. Valery helped me and I helped him. Let us say he was . . . my Jack Flowers."

To counter the constant frustration and failure, I always had Opari. Never once did she allow me to doubt or despair. We became closer than ever, and many times, usually in the spring and often late at night, we went for long walks among the fields over-looking the Elbe. We talked about anything and everything, in-cluding the Remembering and the Zeharkatu. The only two Meq I had known who had "crossed" in the Zeharkatu were Unai and Usoa. Unfortunately, I never got to talk with them about the rit-ual. Opari and Susheela the Ninth, the oldest among us, possessed only the vaguest idea of what "crossing" actually meant or how it was accomplished. This was experiential knowledge. We would have to learn for ourselves, if and when the time came.

On April 15, 1974, Ray Ytuarte arrived at the farm for his turn in the rotation. He was in a black Mercedes limousine and Hans Mannheim was with him, but Ray was driving. He could barely see over the wheel and he was laughing like crazy all the way until he came to a stop.

Ray hopped out with a big smile and his beret in his hand. I said, "When did you start driving?"

"Just as soon as we crossed into East Berlin," he said, laughing again. "Happy New Year, Z. It's been a while. Good to see you," he said, winding up and throwing me an invisible baseball, which I pretended to catch.

"Good to see you, too, Ray."

Even the Fleur-du-Mal enjoyed Ray's visits, although Ray al-ways insulted him whenever he got the chance. That night, the Mannheims served a wonderful meal, which was arranged in Ray's honor. After we finished and Ray had eaten everything on his plate with great gusto, the Fleur-du-Mal asked Ray if the meal had been satisfactory. Ray smiled and wiped his mouth carefully, almost daintily with his napkin, and said, "A bit salty . . . a bit salty." The Fleur-du-Mal laughed and poured more wine into Ray's glass.

Later, when Ray and I were alone, he told me he had a mes-sage from Jack.

"What is it?" I asked.

"Jack said, and these are his exact words, 'Tell Z if he's ever coming back, he should come back now.'"

"Is it Carolina?"

Ray's expression turned serious. "He didn't say, Z."

This time, I didn't hesitate and Opari agreed with my decision. The next morning Hans Mannheim drove me into East Berlin, then through a checkpoint into West Berlin, where he booked a flight for me to New York with a connecting flight to St. Louis. I took my seat on the plane, closed my eyes, and thought about Carolina the entire trip.

As we approached St. Louis, it was just after sunrise, and the Gateway Arch, which had only been constructed six years earlier, stood tall on the West Bank of the Mississippi. It gleamed and sparkled in the sunshine. This was the first time I'd seen the monument and it was magnificent.

After landing, instead of calling Jack, I took a taxi to Carolina's house. I wanted to surprise her, but it didn't work. I walked in the kitchen door and she and Star were sitting at the big table in the center of the room, drinking coffee. She looked smaller and much older. Her freckled white skin was wrinkled and blotched, and the veins in her thin hands crisscrossed and stood out like a map of blue creeks and streams. Still, her eyes were as bright and clear as ever. The tiny gold flecks danced in the light. Carolina was one hundred and four years old.

She looked up at me without a trace of surprise, as if she'd been expecting me. "You're late," she said.

I wanted to laugh. "It's complicated," I replied with a slight smile.

"You always say that."

I walked over and kissed her on both cheeks and did the same to Star. "What's for breakfast?"

Finally, Carolina smiled and reached out for my hand. Star laughed and said, "Anything you want, Z . . . as always."

Jack joined us for breakfast, dressed in his pajamas and a St. Louis Cardinals baseball cap. He gave me a quick wink when he entered the room, and mouthed the words "Thanks for coming." Even though Jack was sixty-eight years old, Carolina made him remove his cap at the kitchen table. Some things never changed. He told me he was writing a book about "Dizzy" Dean and his brother Paul "Daffy" Dean, the fantastic pitchers and personalities for the Cardinals of the 1930s. He said the book was going to be titled *Me an' Paul,* after the famous bragging quote by "Dizzy" that "me an' Paul are gonna win forty-five games in one year"—and they did.

I asked about Caine, Antoinette, and Georgie, and was told by Star they were all out of town. Antoinette was with Caine in Chicago, where he was researching his own book and giving a series of lectures at Northwestern University. Georgie was away at college, where she was now in her third year, studying anthropology at the University of California in Berkeley. Star showed me a recent photograph of Georgie and I was astounded. She was beautiful. Carolina assured me she was smarter than she was beautiful. Jack added, "She is a remarkable girl, Z." I had no doubt it was true. Everyone in her bloodline was remarkable.

That first day back was golden. We spent the whole day talking and laughing. Carolina seemed full of energy. After dinner, she suggested the two of us take a stroll to the "Honeycircle." She held my arm and we walked through the twilight at a slow but steady pace. The forsythia was in full bloom and the honeysuckle would not be far behind. We stopped next to Baju's sundial and Carolina raised her eyes to the sky. We watched the sky darken

from blue to purple to black. Venus was already bright in the
south. Mars had yet to rise.

"I have expressed my wishes to Jack," Carolina said and paused.
"Now I will tell you, Z. I want my ashes to be buried right
here . . . where I'm standing . . . next to Baju's sundial, inside the
'Honeycircle.' "

Her voice was firm and clear. There was nothing fragile or
pitiful in it. "It's a little early for that, isn't it?" I said.

"No, Z . . . it is not. When you age physically as long as I have,
you know your body well. I say these things because they need to
be said and said now. Do not be sad; do not grieve. I have lived a
long, wonderful life." Carolina paused and I could see her smile in
the darkness. "It's all right, Z. I'm ready to go."

I said not a word. It was the most pure, honest, and peaceful
statement I'd ever heard.

For the next week Carolina and I spent nearly every waking hour
together. She was no longer able to walk on our aimless, wandering journeys through Forest Park, so Jack bought a wheelchair
and I pushed her along the paths and through the bright bloom-
ing dogwoods and redbuds. We talked about Solomon, Mrs. Bennings, her sister Georgia, Owen Bramley, and Nicholas, but often
we walked in silence, especially in the mornings. Forest Park had
always been a special, magical place for us. It was somewhere
deep in Forest Park where I first revealed to her that I was Meq,
slashing my forearm with a penknife and making her watch the
wound bleed, then heal within minutes. One day Carolina turned
her head in the wheelchair and looked up at me. She was smiling.
"All our secrets are here, aren't they, Z?"

I smiled back and said, "Yes, they are, Carolina. Yes, they are."

Caine and Antoinette returned from Chicago on Thursday,

and on Friday, April 26, we decided to celebrate Jack's birthday at the ballpark. Carolina insisted on going, and she stayed for the entire game, only to see the Cardinals lose 4–3 to the powerful Cincinnati Reds.

Caine was impressed with his grandmother's stamina and the next day he suggested we all go to an outdoor concert being held at Washington University. I asked who was playing and he named several artists and bands unknown to me, but one name got my attention and drew a small shout of recognition from Carolina. The blues singer and guitar player Walter "Furry" Lewis from Memphis, Tennessee, was among the musicians who were going to appear. Decades earlier, in the 1920s, Carolina had befriended him and even put him up in her home when he played St. Louis. Now he had been rediscovered and was finding newfound popularity in his early eighties. "I must go and see Walter," Carolina said. "Not going would be an insult."

It was a warm, sunny day and Caine found a spot in the shade, off to the side of the main crowd, where he set up folding chairs for all of us. Several solo acts started the concert, including John Hammond, Jr., and Captain Beefheart. Next came a new band from Missouri called the Ozark Mountain Daredevils. Carolina seemed to be enjoying herself and when the band ended their set, I asked her what she thought of them. Smiling slightly, she said one word, "Quaint." When "Furry" Lewis played, Carolina stood and cheered, holding on to Jack's arm, and clapped as hard as she could when he finished. Caine asked her if she wanted to go backstage and talk with him, but she declined, saying she was "feeling a little tired."

Once we were back at the house, Antoinette began preparing dinner, a routine that usually included Carolina, but she excused herself, telling Star she might like to "lie down for just a bit." Star and I helped her to her room and into her bed. Star arranged two or three pillows under her head so that she was almost sitting up. Star kissed Carolina on the cheek and said, "Why don't you and Z talk for a while, Mama?" As she left, Star touched my shoulder. "I'll be in the kitchen if you need me."

"Star—" Carolina said.

"Yes, Mama?"

"I love you."

Star was standing in the doorway. She turned to leave and there was a tremble in her voice. "I love you, too, Mama."

For several minutes after Star left the room, Carolina and I said nothing. Her eyes were half-closed and I thought she might have fallen asleep. I listened to her breathing. It was steady, but with tiny, shallow little breaths.

"Carolina?" I whispered. "Are you awake?"

"Yes, oh yes, Z. I'm awake." She opened her eyes wide and looked at me. Her eyes were shining and seemed to be smiling. "I was daydreaming, Z, remembering those days when Georgia was still alive, when we were still together right here."

"You mean, when you two were running the most expensive and exclusive whorehouse in St. Louis?"

Carolina laughed out loud and so did I. "Yes, oh yes," she said. "Those were wonderful times, Z. Do you remember all the characters who came and went?"

"I can't remember them all, but there were many."

We laughed some more and then started talking. We talked about things at random, back and forth—shared adventures, shared embarrassments. At one point Carolina had me retrieve a box of photographs from her desk. We spread them out across her bed and traveled back in time through the images and faces in the pictures. Solomon, Georgia, and Nicholas appeared over and over. Carolina kissed the photograph of her and Nicholas holding hands under the table on the same night they fell in love. I even showed up in a few pictures. Carolina shuffled through them and stopped at one in which Caine and I had just finished playing catch. He was about ten years old and we were standing in front of the "Honeycircle." We were about the same height. Caine was holding his baseball glove and the baseball. I was holding Mama's glove.

"My, oh my," Carolina said. "I haven't seen that glove in years."

I thought for a moment and realized I hadn't seen it either. I was sitting on the edge of the bed and stood up. "Is it in the same place?" I asked.

Carolina looked at me with a faint smile. "I believe it is, Z."

"I'll be right back," I said, heading for the door. I knew Mama's glove was in a shoe box on a shelf in Caine's old bedroom.

Before I got out the door, Carolina said, "Wait, Z." I turned and she was sitting up, leaning forward. Her silver hair shimmered in the light from the lamp. Her eyes were moist and they focused directly on mine. "I love you, Z," she said in a clear, even voice. "I always have and always will."

Without hesitation, I said, "I love you, too, Carolina—always have, always will."

I shut the door and walked down the hall. I found Caine's old room and switched on the light in the closet. The shoe box was under a sweater on the middle shelf. I opened it and there was Mama's glove. It looked exactly as I remembered. The stitching was still good and the leather hadn't cracked. I put it on my hand and pounded the pocket. It felt the same and there was nothing like that feeling. "Thank you, Mama," I said. I stood there for a few seconds, admiring her work and remembering her touch. I thought about her and I thought about Papa. It was so long ago and it seemed like yesterday. Then I remembered Carolina. I switched off the light and walked quickly back to her room and opened the door.

She had fallen sideways from a sitting position and was sprawled across the photographs with her head hanging over the edge of the bed. I ran to her, lifting her head and straightening her body, resting her head on Mama's glove. I put my ear to her chest and listened for a heartbeat. I heard something, but it sounded too faint to make a difference. Her eyes were barely open. She was looking at me. I leaned down close to her mouth to see if she was breathing. Then she tried to speak. "What . . . were the words, Z? *Egibizirik* . . ."

Then there were no more words. Carolina's heart stopped, her breathing stopped, and her eyes stared into space. I closed her eyelids and answered her question with my finger on her lips. *"Bilatu,"* I said, *"egibizirik bilatu,* the long-living truth, well searched for."

I have no explanation for what I did next. Maybe in some way I wanted to help Carolina leave, or maybe I wanted to keep her from leaving. I don't know or care. I do know I have never regretted it. I turned Carolina on her side and lay down next to her with my arms wrapped around hers. I wanted to cry, but I didn't. She had told me not to grieve, yet that, too, was impossible. Instead, I talked to her. I held her close and simply talked to her, as if we were on a plane or a train, or just kicking leaves in Forest Park. I held her close to me and talked until every last degree of warmth had left her body and she was far, far away.

I only said a few words when I finally entered the kitchen. Star and Jack, Caine and Antoinette, were expecting what I had to tell them. Antoinette said a prayer in French and Jack called an ambulance. I held Star's hand while the tears ran down her cheeks and each of us sat in silence, remembering the most amazing woman any of us had ever known.

• • •

Because of the numerous local organizations and charities to which Carolina had contributed throughout her long life in St. Louis, Jack, Star, and Caine held a small service at First Unitarian Church, only a few blocks from Carolina's house. Many representatives of those organizations attended; however, there were no close friends. Carolina had outlived them all.

At sunset on May 1, 1974, inside the "Honeycircle" and next to Baju's sundial, we buried the urn containing Carolina's ashes. Antoinette said another prayer in French, while Jack and Caine and I shoveled the dirt. Star sang a beautiful and simple lullaby, one that Carolina said she had sung to Star as a baby. Jack smoothed out the surface and said his own prayer. "I love you, Mama. Be at peace now."

Jack and I stayed up late that night, talking and drinking coffee in the kitchen. It was well after midnight when we finally said good night and I walked upstairs and went to bed. The big house felt empty without Carolina's presence. I lay in bed and thought about her until I eventually drifted off and fell into a deep sleep.

The dream begins with me on the pitching mound in old Sportsman's Park. It is midday and the sky is a clear bright blue. The grandstands are empty except for my mama and papa, who are sitting twenty rows up, directly behind home plate. I have Mama's glove on one hand and Papa's baseball in the other. There are no other players on the field and no one is at bat. Somewhere in the distance a dog is barking. A figure walks up out of the dugout and steps onto the field. It is the Umpire. He is dressed completely in black. Even his chest protector and mask are black. He starts toward me and I walk to meet him. He is only an inch or two taller than I am. He stops. He reaches up and slowly removes his mask, then runs his other hand through his strawberry blond hair and smiles. He is a she. The Umpire is Carolina. She is about twelve years old and the freckles spread across her cheeks and the tiny flecks in both her blue-gray eyes sparkle like gold dust. She takes hold of my hand. "Come with me," she says. "I have found something for you."

She leads me down the steps of the dugout and into a tunnel that narrows, then widens and changes into an underground passage through a cave lit by torches burning animal fat. The stone walls are cold to the touch and I can see my breath. Carolina seems unaffected by the drop in temperature. We pass by a long panel of spectacular paintings in black charcoal and red and yellow ochre, depicting herds of mammoths, reindeer, rhinoceroses, aurochs, and horses. We turn left, then right. "Where are we going?" I ask. "Shhh," she says, and walks through the ashes of a still-burning campfire in the passage, scattering coals and sparks all around. I am right behind her. We come to a set of brass double doors. She pushes her way through and we are standing in a massive empty space with marble floors and a great vaulted ceiling. I recognize it. We are in the Grand Hall of Union Station. Carolina points to something shining and spinning in the middle of the huge room. It is a carousel, but instead of painted ponies going up and down, I see all the markings on the sphere from Portugal. I hear strange music and look to my left. In the shadows, Scott Joplin is playing ragtime on a calliope. He waves at me.

Carolina leads me closer to the carousel. It is lit from within and seems to glow. The markings are life-size, as tall as I am. They are floating in something, spinning and bobbing up and down. The something is neither here nor there. It has no appearance whatsoever, no top, no bottom, yet it floats, it moves, it supports the markings. It is the "water" of Time. Carolina squeezes my hand and we walk through the "water" into and onto the carousel and step around the markings while they spin round and round, up and down, and the calliope is playing its endless, jangling melody in perfect time with the bouncing, circling, floating markings. And

I know I know how to navigate; how to shepherd; how to listen, learn, teach, dream, and travel my way through. They are each one as common and familiar and known to me as the toys in a child's bath. I think back to the first Meq phrase I found inside the cave in the Sahara Desert. The phrase was in the form of a cross or an X with the word "is" as an axis. It read: "Where Time is under Water—Where Water is under Time." And now I am there. Carolina lets go of my hand and kisses me on the lips. I taste honey and rose water. She turns and walks in the direction of Scott Joplin and the calliope, then vanishes into the shadows. In my heart and mind, I hear an echo. It is Carolina. She says, "Farewell, Z . . . my only Z."

I awoke to the sounds of a cardinal and her chirping hungry chicks nesting in the big tree outside my window. The sun was just rising. My first thought was of a milk barn in East Germany and what was inside. My second thought was, "How fast can I get there?" That same morning I told Jack my intentions and he said he would take me himself. He said he needed to get away from St. Louis, and he could check on the *Giselle* in Paris. As soon as Star was told of our plans, she asked to go along and Jack said, "Good idea. Let's go tonight." Star said, "Okay," and that's what we did. Caine and Antoinette drove us to Lambert Field and after saying good-bye, we left on the last flight out to New York. From there, we flew to Paris, where Jack and Star remained, and I continued on to West Berlin alone.

Before we parted, I said to Jack, "Tell Sailor I may have found it."

"And he'll know what that means?"

"He'll know."

• • •

A light rain was falling when Hans Mannheim turned into the long driveway of the farm and finally brought the big Mercedes to a stop. I leaped out the door. I had called ahead, and standing under a wide umbrella, Opari and Ray were there to greet me. The Fleur-du-Mal was nowhere in sight. I ducked under the umbrella.

Ray said, "Are you all right, Z? You look kinda odd."

I gave Opari an embrace and told Ray I was fine. I also said I had the worst of news and the best of news. Briefly, I told them about Carolina's passing and the burying of her ashes next to Baju's sundial. Both of them were saddened, especially Ray, who had known Carolina well, and he promised to give a toast in her honor after dinner. Then I told them I had experienced a special and unique dream unlike any other. I asked Ray, "Where is he, where is the Fleur-du-Mal?"

"He's in the milk barn," Ray answered. "He's always in the milk barn."

I kissed Opari and ran out from under the umbrella. "Follow me."

Without knocking, I opened the door of the milk barn. The Fleur-du-Mal turned his head and looked up as I entered, with Opari and Ray close behind. He was sitting at his desk near the cylinders and spheres. There were stacks of books and charts around him, and to his right stood a large, portable chalkboard filled with theories, notations, and scribbles. "Ah, *mon petit!* You have returned."

"Yes . . . I have," I said, ignoring him and walking over to the spheres. All the lights were turned on. I watched as each sphere turned in a slow rotation on top of its gleaming steel cylinder. In my mind, I saw the image of the carousel, lit from within and turning. Carved exquisitely in granite, the familiar markings floated by. "You were right," I said, glancing at the Fleur-du-Mal and reaching out to gently touch the sphere from Portugal. "They truly are 'Dreamstones.'"

Twenty minutes later I had "read" every marking on the sphere. It was as simple and clear as if I were reading an invitation to a party, which, in a way, I was. In its "dream language," the message carved on the sphere began with the salutation "Welcome, Traveler."

7

BIDAITARI
(TRAVELER)

All our journeys are singular. We travel within ourselves, no matter where we go, alone among others we learn a traveler's language, a code of recognition and respect. The longer the journey, the deeper the dream, the more we become one. We never forget. We remember everything and everyone. We survive. We are travelers.

No one said a word while I was "reading" the sphere, and if they had I would not have heard them. The experience was trancelike. As the markings and their meanings came to me, it was much more like being in a dream state than the conscious act of translating or decoding. It was an intuitive understanding, but I also realized that once learned, the ability could be taught to others. The markings were there not just for me; they were there for all of us.

I turned to look at Opari. She had a nervous, excited expression on her face. "Are you able to read the sphere, my love?"

At first, I said nothing. Then for some reason, I laughed. "Yes . . . yes, I am."

The Fleur-du-Mal had walked out from behind his desk and was standing near Ray. "Is it a message? What does it say, *mon petit?*"

"It's not really a message. It's more of an . . . *invitation.*"

"An invitation to what?" Ray asked.

"I'm not sure what, but I know where. These markings are directions—elaborate, specific directions to a specific place on Earth. It is a system and a language that is not words, not symbols, but an intuitive, collective set of instructions, understood by the heart as much as the mind."

"Damn!"

"The Remembering is never mentioned?" Opari asked.

"No," I answered, then smiled. "But the Sixth Stone is, and the Egongela, the Living Room, although the markings are closer to meaning the 'Shelter.'"

I walked over to the sphere from the Caucasus and studied it briefly, then circled the oldest sphere of the three, the one found among the possessions of "the Thracian." Each sphere was a set of instructions and directions, with the one from Portugal being the most complex, ornate, and precise, as if the "dream language" had evolved or added layers. There was one marking that did not change and appeared exactly the same on all three spheres. "The nearest equivalent in English is the word 'West,' but in the 'dream language,' the meaning is animate. It is a *living* 'West.'"

"Where is this 'place on Earth'?" the Fleur-du-Mal asked.

"Nearer than you might think." I looked around me, into the shadows of the spacious room. "Do you have a globe somewhere in the milk barn?"

"Yes, of course. Come with me."

We walked between the desk and the chalkboard to another crowded area in the rear of the room. The Fleur-du-Mal switched on a floor lamp and pointed to a beautiful freestanding globe two feet in diameter. "There," he said.

I turned the globe until I found the location, then put my finger on it.

"The south coast of Wales?" Opari said, a little surprised.

"Yes. Near Swansea."

"That ain't far from Caitlin's Ruby," Ray replied.

"About a hundred miles."

The Fleur-du-Mal said nothing for several moments, staring at the globe and frowning. "Can you teach me to read the markings, *mon petit?*"

"Yes, I think so," I said, realizing suddenly that I finally had some leverage with the Fleur-du-Mal. "However, I will not do it here. I want you to move the spheres to Caitlin's Ruby. It may be difficult to get them out of East Germany, but I know you can find a way. And I will teach everyone to read the spheres, not just you. This *invitation* is for all of us."

The Fleur-du-Mal stood motionless for a few seconds, still frowning, then reached out and spun the globe with one hand. "Agreed," he said with a bitter smile.

Opari, Ray, and I left for Paris the following day. The Fleur-du-Mal assured me it should take no longer than a month to arrange delivery of the spheres. I asked him how he planned to do it and he told me to mind my own business. He also demanded his own private quarters at Caitlin's Ruby, saying it was nothing personal, just habit. I said I would look into it and reminded him that Koldo and Arrosa Txopitea were the owners of Caitlin's Ruby; we were merely their guests.

Once we were back on the *Giselle,* things went very quickly. After Sailor heard about the breakthrough, he seemed happier and more gregarious than I'd seen him in years. When I told him I could teach him to "read" the spheres, he became almost ecstatic and couldn't wait to begin. Sheela said, "Well done, Z." I told her it wasn't me, it was Carolina, and Sheela and Sailor exchanged puzzled looks.

The next day we sent word to Geaxi, Mowsel, and Zeru-Meq to meet us at Caitlin's Ruby within the week. Jack and Star acted as our "chaperones" entering England, and we all boarded a train in London for the trip west to Cornwall. Along the way, the weather was perfect, and the passing farms and fields were green and lush and in full flower.

Koldo and Arrosa greeted us in Plymouth and drove us in separate cars the rest of the way to Caitlin's Ruby. I was told by Arrosa that once again we had missed seeing Kepa and Yaldi. They were both touring in North America. I told her more of us were on the way, and she said there was plenty of room and we should not worry about it. I brought up the Fleur-du-Mal's request and she had the solution. He could stay in the garage, which she had recently refurbished and converted to a studio with a small apartment and a full kitchen. I asked if Tillman Fadle's old cottage was occupied, and when Arrosa said no, I knew it was the ideal place to house the spheres, once they arrived, and teach the others how to "read" the "dream language." As we pulled into the long gravel driveway and approached the main house, almost all the cats of Caitlin's Ruby were there to greet us. They lined the low stone walls and every window ledge.

"Is this an omen?" I asked Arrosa.

"Oh, yes, Z! A good one," she said.

Jack and Star returned to London two days later, only hours before Geaxi, Mowsel, and Zeru-Meq arrived. The trip to Paris had worked its magic and lifted their spirits, and they were both anxious to get back to St. Louis. As we were saying good-bye, I told Jack something important was about to happen for the Meq, but I couldn't tell him what it was. I also said I didn't know when I would be in St. Louis again and apologized for being so mysterious about it. Jack laughed and told me no apology was necessary; it never had been and never would be. He said, "Mama explained to me when I was a kid that you and your ways should never be doubted or questioned. She was right, Z. Just knowing that you and the others *exist* in this world has made my life a rich one." We embraced and he added, "Be well, Z, and we will see you when we see you." I hugged and kissed Star, then Koldo drove them away, with Star waving out the back window until they were completely out of sight.

It felt good to have everyone in one place again. We settled easily into Caitlin's Ruby and our routines, which included a great amount of walking and talking. We didn't hear a word from the Fleur-du-Mal, and we expected to wait at least three to four weeks before we did. However, just ten days into our stay, we were surprised to see two identical white vans driving up to the main house and entrance and coming to a stop. In bold black print on the sides of the vans were the words, "MINISTRY OF AGRICULTURE, FISHERIES & FOOD." The two drivers and two other men stepped out. They each wore white coveralls with the letters MAFF printed on their backs. The side doors of the vans were opened and inside were three large crates, two in one van and one in the other. "FRAGILE" was stamped in red on the crates.

Koldo looked at the men. "May I help you?"

One of the drivers said, "Where would you like us to put them?"

"I'm sorry," Koldo replied. "Put what?"

"The beehives, the Czechoslovakian HFN2 beehives. We took good care of them. Nothing to worry about there, sir. Now, if you please, we have a long drive back, so where would you like us to put them, sir?"

Koldo gave me a blank look. "How about down by Tillman Fadle's cottage?" I said, nodding my head up and down.

"Yes, yes," he told the men. "Of course, that's right—Tillman Fadle's cottage. I will show you the way."

After the vans and the men had gone, we opened the three crates with a crowbar and a hammer. Then we opened the beehives themselves, and inside sat the three spheres. To get them into the old cottage, it took the efforts of Koldo and four of us. Koldo had no idea what they were or what their purpose was, and he didn't ask. With a slight smile and a wink, he only said, "Strange-looking bees, no?"

An hour later a cream-colored Rolls-Royce convertible drove through the gate and slowly made its way down the long driveway to the main house. Arrosa walked outside to greet the visitor. A chauffeur got out from behind the wheel and opened the rear door. A boy wearing an expensive short-sleeved silk shirt and linen slacks stepped out. He had his black hair combed, pulled back, and tied with a green ribbon. His red ruby earrings sparkled and so did his false smile. "I am Xanti Otso," he said, glancing around at the beauty of Caitlin's Ruby. He took hold of Arrosa's seventy-year-old hands and kissed the backs of both of them. She smiled. "And you must be the lovely Arrosa," he said.

Ray and I were standing on the front porch of the cottage watching the arrival. Ray slipped off his beret and scratched his head. "He's a genuine, certified piece of work, ain't he, Z?"

"That . . . and a few other things."

A doctor must be a traveler, . . . Knowledge is experience.
—PARACELSUS

Teaching everyone to "read" the spheres began the next morning. They were all familiar with written and oral languages from around the world, but I told each of them that "reading" the

spheres required an approach that was more unconscious than
conscious, and more collective than individual. That was the reason why it was necessary for every single one of us to "understand" the *invitation* before we answered it. I assumed the oldest
one among us would be able to do this much easier than the
youngest one. However, it was not Susheela the Ninth, it was
Nova, the youngest Meq, who was first to break through and surrender to the meanings behind the markings. She smiled and
touched a sphere with her fingertips. "Oh, yes," she whispered.
"Oh, yes." Perhaps it was Nova's long history of having "visions"
that did it. I don't know, but she was the first to "read" the
spheres. Ray and Geaxi were next. Then it was the Fleur-du-Mal,
who had an expression on his face that I had never seen before. It
was a cross between profound wonder and absolute humility.
Sailor was humble himself when he made the unconscious connection to the markings and their meanings within meanings
within meanings. Zeru-Meq, Trumoi-Meq, and Opari followed
Sailor, and finally the eyes of Susheela the Ninth watered and tears
ran down her cheeks. She reached out with both hands and, one
by one, we made a chain of hands, a circle around the spheres,
and breathed the air around us as one body, one mind, ready to
travel, ready to answer the *invitation*.

On June 3, a cold, wet, blustery day, not unusual for any time of
the year in Cornwall, we prepared to drive out of Caitlin's Ruby
and head north. Koldo had purchased a full-size tour bus with
great, wide windows all around. The ten of us, including the
Fleur-du-Mal, boarded the bus, and Koldo kissed Arrosa good-
bye, saying he would be back as soon as possible.

We took the A38 from Bodmin to Bristol, and the rough

weather seemed to make the West Country even more wild and beautiful. From Bristol, we traveled on the A403 to Severn Bridge and crossed into Wales just as the skies to the west began to clear. We drove on to the outskirts of Swansea and stopped for the night at a small hotel and restaurant along the coast of Swansea Bay called the "Crab and Cockles Inn," a place Koldo knew well from visits in the past.

The next morning little was said over breakfast, yet there was a glint of excitement in everyone's eyes. We were calm and anxious simultaneously. On this day something was going to happen, something fundamental to all of us, and none of us knew what it might be. Ray likened it to the feeling you have at the carnival, just after being strapped in and you're about to enter the fun-house.

Once we were in the tour bus and on our way, no one had to consult a map to know our direction. We even took turns telling Koldo where to turn because inside ourselves our destination was like a beacon in a fog—we merely followed the beam, the path, the compass . . . the "Voice." Under a cloudless blue sky, we traveled west along the southern coast of the Gower peninsula. At the far end of the peninsula we came upon the small village of Rhossili and each of us knew we were very close. We drove slowly north, beyond Rhossili Down and along a winding narrow road that followed the contours of the heather- and bracken-covered slopes. Two-hundred-fifty-foot cliffs overlooking the sea loomed only a half mile away. We traveled on another twelve miles until, finally, I told Koldo to pull over and stop. Nothing was around to suggest we were there, only an open gate and a paved country lane that disappeared around a ridge to the west, but each of us knew we had arrived.

Sailor opened the door of the tour bus and stepped out. The

others were close behind. I turned to Koldo and paused. He spoke first. "Don't worry, Z. I will remain here and wait for your return. Now, go," he said. "*Onzorion!* Good luck!"

"Thanks, Koldo." I practically leaped out of the bus and hurried through the gate to join the rest. We walked in silence along the asphalt lane for a quarter of a mile, then rounded the ridge and saw our destination. Facing the sea and nestled against the rock outcroppings on the western side of the ridge was an ancient, fortified manor house of timber and stone. It was a composite of architectural styles and was likely built over the span of several centuries. There was also an unmistakable presence that we all felt at once. It was strange, exotic, and powerful, yet familiar.

I glanced around at us. Almost everyone would have fit into any crowd of twelve-year-old children anywhere in Britain. Even the Fleur-du-Mal had dressed simply and left his hair hanging loose and untied. Only his ruby earrings separated him from the others. Geaxi, however, wore her finest black leather leggings and black vest, which was held together with strips of leather attached to bone. She had adjusted her black beret to the perfect angle, and for shoes she wore her favorite ballet slippers. In full view and dangling on a leather necklace was the Stone of Will. Opari also wore the Stone of Blood around her neck, but inside her shirt, as did Sailor the Stone of Memory and Nova the Stone of Silence. The Stone of Dreams I kept in my pants pocket.

"Do you feel that, young Zezen?" Geaxi asked.

"Yes. Yes, I do, Geaxi." I took hold of Opari's hand and we continued on, climbing the wide steps and approaching the massive oak door that served as entrance to the manor house.

I raised my hand to knock and the door swung open. A tall, elderly man, probably well into his eighties, stood in the entryway. He had ruddy cheeks and pale blue eyes, and except for a few long silver wisps that were left uncombed, most of his hair was gone. He was dressed in formal attire, although everything was slightly ill fitting and a little wrinkled. For ten or fifteen seconds, he stared back and didn't say a word, gazing at each of us with a kind of childlike wonder. Finally, he said, "Please, come in. We've been waiting for you."

Is it possible to have your whole life and everything you've known and taken for granted change completely and forever simply by walking from one room to another? The answer is yes and the next ten minutes would prove to be the most extraordinary ten minutes in the history of the Meq.

We were led through a sitting room crowded with furniture accrued over generations to a much larger room with twenty-foot-high ceilings and wide windows on the south and west sides, which let in a flood of sunlight. Two immense Persian rugs covered the floor and at the far end of the room a fire was burning in the fireplace, even though it wasn't needed for warmth. Facing away from us toward the fireplace there was a long couch and two chairs, and though we couldn't see who it was, someone was sitting in one of the chairs playing the cello, and playing it with passion. The low, slow, sonorous tones lifted and filled the big room. The old man turned to leave while the ten of us stood motionless, listening. Then Geaxi, who was on my left, leaned in close to my ear and whispered, "Concerto in D Major by Arthur Sullivan." A moment or two later, the playing stopped.

"That is correct," the cellist said. The voice was male, but high-pitched and raspy, and the accent was educated British. From behind the chair, he asked, "When did you last hear the piece?"

We all turned to Geaxi. Without hesitating, she answered, "November 24, 1866."

"Ah, yes . . . the premier at the Crystal Palace." He paused. "What did you think of the performance of Alfred Piatti on cello?"

"He was wonderful . . . a perfect balance of technique and emotion."

"Yes, I agree. That night, he was a true master."

Geaxi frowned slightly. "You were there?"

A long moment passed. "Yes," the cellist said, rising out of his chair and turning to face us.

He was two inches shorter than we were, but wide-shouldered and long-armed, not unlike many of the tough street kids Ray and I had befriended when we lived in New Orleans. His cheekbones were high and wide, and his browridges were pronounced, but not any more than some of the pirates I'd seen while sailing with Captain Woodget, and certainly not as much as some of the illustrations I'd seen based on ancient skulls. He had a receding chin similar to that of a group of tribes I'd seen on our travels in western China. His lips were full, especially the lower lip, and his nose was broad, much like a prizefighter's nose after taking too many punches to the face. His eyes were dark and intense, and his hair was a reddish brown and cut short. He was dressed in corduroy pants, which were tucked into green rubber Wellington boots, and a well-worn green plaid cotton shirt. He looked like the son of the gardener, or the gardener himself. But he was no gardener. He was Neanderthal—a living, breathing Neanderthal boy, and without a doubt, he was Meq.

He rested his cello on a stand near the chair and walked across one of the Persian rugs until he was three feet away from Geaxi. He stared into Geaxi's eyes and she stared back. "Yes," he said. "I was at the Crystal Palace on November 24, 1866. And I was with you in 1927 at Caitlin's Ruby when you were trying to wake the aviator Charles Lindbergh. I heard your distress and sent my song to help."

Geaxi said nothing. It wasn't necessary. Her eyes said everything. They were exploding with wonder, joy, understanding, recognition, triumph, and surrender. I knew the look well. I had seen it in Opari's eyes in the first moment we saw each other. As sudden, unlikely, and impossible as it seemed, Geaxi had just met her Ameq. Finally, and almost as an affirmation to what she was experiencing, she whispered, "You . . . are the other 'Voice.'"

"Yes," he said, nodding once.

"And you know of Caitlin's Ruby?"

"Yes . . . since the beginning." He reached in his shirt pocket and retrieved something small, then asked for Geaxi's hand. She held out her hand and he placed a cube of salt in her palm, gently folding her fingers around it. "I believe your phrase is *egibizirik bilatu.*" He then made a few sounds unlike anything I'd ever heard and I realized it was the oral version of the "dream language." He said, "Welcome, Traveler."

Several seconds of stunned silence followed, then Ray couldn't help himself. "Damn!" he said.

"Damn, indeed," Sailor added.

"Indeed, indeed," Mowsel echoed.

The boy told Geaxi his name in the "dream language." It was impossible to pronounce and barely translatable, but similar in construction to the way we say Umla-Meq, Trumoi-Meq, or Zeru-Meq. The closest translation in English was "Traveler-All Directions," so Geaxi decided to call him West. He smiled, showing even white teeth, and told her West it would be.

The boy, or West, turned and shifted his gaze to the rest of us, focusing on our eyes and leaning his head forward. His nostrils flared slightly, and I was certain he was recording and committing our individual scents to memory. One by one, he greeted us and offered cubes of salt. As he did so, he made another gesture, which was touching hands palm to palm with fingers spread, then putting his hand over his heart. He seemed to know a great deal about all of us. He knew I was the Stone of Dreams and guessed correctly that I had been the one to "understand" and "teach" the others. He then said cryptically, "And just in time."

Staring into his eyes, feeling his touch, watching him move and speak, I couldn't quit wondering how old West must be. His age would have to be at least twice the combined ages of every Meq in the room. A being that old with that much experience is incomprehensible and unimaginable. Still, he was friendly, gracious, and comfortable with everyone. He joked with Ray and complimented Nova on her "long eyes," or her ability to have visions. He spoke to Mowsel in Cumbric, an extinct Welsh language, which delighted and surprised Mowsel, who was a scholar of languages. He traded Taoist poems with Zeru-Meq and exchanged greetings with Susheela the Ninth in the language of her childhood, which brought a smile. Sheela had not heard the language in forty-two centuries. He greeted Sailor with deep respect and complimented him for his part in the Meq escape from the Phoenicians three thousand years earlier. He then gave Sailor his condolences for what happened later in Carthage. After welcoming Opari, West told her she had always been the one he knew the least about, then he said the Stone of Blood was essential to the Remembering, which made all of us glance at each other. The Remembering had not been mentioned anywhere among the markings on the spheres.

The Fleur-du-Mal was the last to be greeted. The boy looked hard into the Fleur-du-Mal's eyes, scanning, searching, then folded the cube of salt into his palm. "For many, many reasons," he said, "I thought this day might never occur."

The Fleur-du-Mal stared back without expression, then with a hint of his usual arrogance, he said, "I have a question, sir."

"I assume you have several, and please, do not call me 'sir.'" The boy turned and glanced at Geaxi, who was following his every word and gesture.

"Of course. Tell me . . . West . . . how is it possible for you to know so much about us when, before today, we have never known of your existence?"

No one moved or spoke and the moment hung in the air. I felt like I was in the *Wizard of Oz* and the Wizard was about to be revealed. "A fair question," West said slowly.

"And one that deserves an answer." It was another high-pitched, raspy voice coming from somewhere behind us. We all turned at once. Walking into the big room and carrying a tray of finger sandwiches, scones, and berries, along with a vase full of fresh-cut yellow roses was a girl who resembled West in every way except her hair, which was longer and a deeper rust-colored shade of red. She wore blue jeans tucked into green rubber Wellington boots, like West, and a well-worn corduroy jacket over a white cotton shirt. She also possessed the most powerful essence, aura, and presence of Meq I had ever felt. Following her was the old man we'd met at the door. He carried a tray holding a teapot and a dozen cups made of finely decorated Spode china. They both set down their trays on the long coffee table in front of the couch. The girl looked once at West and the old man turned to leave. "Thank you, Mr. Morgan," she said after him, then began pouring tea into each of the cups. Speaking to us, but not looking at us, she said, "This is one of our special teas, very rare—Jun Shan Silver Needles. I hope you enjoy it. And you must try the blackberries." She filled the last of the teacups and turned her head, staring directly at the Fleur-du-Mal. "They ripened early this year," she said.

The Fleur-du-Mal stared back, and in that moment, in that split second between the angled shafts of sunlight, something so stunning and so unexpected occurred that it seemed imaginary. But it was real, it was a bolt of lightning, and it was "clear as a tear," as Ray would say. And as with Geaxi, there was no doubt. Xanti Otso, the Fleur-du-Mal, had just looked into the eyes of his Ameq for the first time.

Holding two cups of tea, she walked calmly over to the Fleur-du-Mal. Her hands and fingers were noticeably broader and stronger than our hands and fingers, yet she offered him a cup of tea with the delicacy, charm, and sophistication of a lady of the manor. Then, without warning, but with the exuberance of a football fan, she tapped her cup against the Fleur-du-Mal's, spilling some of the tea on the great Persian rug. She laughed like a schoolgirl and gave him a mischievous look, saying "Cheers!"

For a moment the Fleur-du-Mal stood mute and frozen, and so did the rest of us. He turned and looked at West, who gave nothing away, then turned back to the girl. Gradually, he awakened to something inside, and a smile began to spread across his face. "What is your name?" he asked.

"In the *Language of the Long Dream,* I am called by this name," she said, then made a series of high-pitched, unpronounceable sounds that looped and clicked and squealed together until she stopped.

The Fleur-du-Mal frowned and rubbed his chin with his hand. He glanced at me. I knew he had understood what she had said because he had learned the "dream language," but what her name meant was too complex to be a name in the same way that we use names. "Well, *mon petit?*" he asked. "How would you trans-late that?"

In a formal sense, the name meant "Traveler-All Spirits," yet it was much more than that. Contained within her name were other names—the Finder of Souls, the Singer, the Far Seer, the Long Listener, the Retriever, the Returner, and many others, all connected with complicated emotional and psychological nuances.

"Yes," the girl said to me, studying my eyes. "What would you have me called?"

"Fielder," I answered immediately, thinking of baseball. A good fielder sees and catches everything, including souls.

"Fielder?" the Fleur-du-Mal said.

"Yes. Fielder. It's as good as any."

"I adore the name," the girl said. "Fielder it is, then. I have had many names in the past, but never Fielder." She exchanged looks with the Fleur-du-Mal, then looked at Geaxi and nodded once, as if introducing herself. She turned to West. "And your name is now 'West'?"

"Yes, it is," he said with a smile.

"Good. It suits you." She paused, taking time to look into the eyes of each of us. "Now," she said, motioning toward the couch and chairs, "let us sit and share the tea and scones and discuss the last thirty thousand years, shall we?"

Events were happening too quickly to calculate and yet time seemed to slow down in every way. The curtains were opened even wider and we gathered in chairs surrounding the coffee table and couch. The view through the windows to the south and west revealed the steep cliffs and ragged coastline only a few hundred yards away, and the sea below stretching all the way to the horizon. And Fielder was right. The blackberries were delicious. Larger than the ones that would ripen later, they tasted pure and intense. I nibbled on them and sipped my tea and listened. For the next hour and a half we all listened. The old ones among us, Susheela the Ninth, Sailor, Opari, Trumoi-Meq, each heard things they had never heard before, and we all learned things about the Meq we could never have imagined.

West let Fielder begin, saying she would answer the question the Fleur-du-Mal had asked because she *was* the answer. Fielder explained by starting with her birth, which was approximately thirty-four thousand years ago in what is now Croatia. Although she was born with the ability to be a "tracker" and "finder of souls," she had to be nurtured and taught how to do it accurately and at greater and greater distances. Fielder's teacher was her own mother, who also was the head of their tribe of sixty-three souls, or "Travelers," as they referred to themselves. They were Meq, like us, but they were in the form of a human species we now erroneously term Neanderthal. And, like our unique and ancient relationship with the Basque, they traveled alongside several tribes of their "parent" species, who acted as protectors. And travel they did. Fielder told of some journeys lasting centuries and covering thousands of miles, which required much more mobility and technical skill than modern anthropologists attribute to them. During these travels, Fielder's ability to "find" and "hear" others was a valuable and necessary tool for survival. In time, she became known as "Keeper of Souls" because of her expanding powers. Intuitively, at any given time, she knew where every living soul of her kind was on the planet. Then came the newcomers, the ones we now call Giza. She had heard of them, but she had never seen them. And along with the newcomers there were us. There were not many of us, but we were there. Fielder said, "I could feel your arrival and count your numbers on ten fingers . . . just as I do now."

Though she was living far to the north, she followed the movements of our ancestors and the newcomers with her ability. Our numbers multiplied quickly, and our adaptation to the climate was just as rapid. Eventually, she heard rumors of trade and the exchange of gifts between the newcomers and her kind. At first, the reports were positive, and coexistence seemed to be evolving. But another wave of newcomers soon appeared, and their gift was something else entirely. It was not a tool or an animal skin or a beautiful string of beads and shells. It was silent, powerful, unknown, invisible, and no shaman could give it back.

"What was the gift?"

Fielder paused and West answered the question. "Virus," he said.

Within four thousand years the Travelers were virtually extinct. No one could withstand the effects of the virus, and distance between tribes was the only factor that kept it from spreading faster. The ones who were Meq, like Fielder, had always been immune to toxins of any kind, but this strain of virus brought by the newcomers infected everyone with equally lethal results. Fielder was the only Traveler to remain healthy and alive, or so she thought. For this reason she spent twelve years quarrying and carving the first of her granite spheres, telling her story in the *Language of the Long Dream* and leaving it behind. After living on her own for another two thousand years and exploring lands farther to the east, always staying south of the ice, she suddenly "heard" the souls of six Travelers. Five were old souls and extremely weak, and one was that of a young soul, a boy. All six were in severe distress.

She made her way south until she found the boy sitting alone outside the mouth of a large limestone cave. The cave overlooked a slow-moving river that emptied into what is now the Black Sea. The boy was watching the river and he was crying. Instinctively, Fielder could tell he had only recently had his twelfth birthday and begun what the Meq would later name the Itxaron, the Wait. He looked up as she approached and showed no surprise. Fielder thought that perhaps he was in a trance or in shock.

"Why am I not sick like the others?" he asked.

Fielder glanced around and saw no one. "Where are the others?" she replied.

"Inside," he said, pointing to the mouth of the cave. "They are too sick and weak to continue. They have decided to lie down and enter the Long Dream."

"When?" she asked.

"Tonight," he answered, then glanced at the pale, setting sun on the horizon.

Fielder turned and walked into the cave. There was a fire pit with a fire still burning, although it was down to coals. Beyond the fire pit she saw five Travelers sprawled out on animal hides. They were lying on their backs in a circle with their hands joined and their eyes closed. She could barely "hear" them. Their hearts were already beating as one, and their spirits were deep into the waters of the Long Dream. Resting on each of their chests was a pitted, egg-shaped, black rock that was attached to a leather strap, which they wore around their necks. Fielder knelt down next to one of them, a female with reddish hair like her own. She inhaled and filled her lungs with the girl's scent. It was different than any essence of her kind she had ever encountered, and it was ancient. Then, without opening her eyes or making a sound, the girl began to speak to Fielder telepathically. "Welcome, Traveler," she said. "We are the Ancestors. Take care of the boy. He is the last of us. Teach him the ways of a Traveler. Endure and survive. And take these five stones we carry. Live long and listen and understanding will come to you. In time, the stones will reveal their purpose, and the boy's, and yours." The girl's telepathic "voice" became a faint and broken whisper. She was far from shore. Her last words to Fielder were, "Endure, Traveler . . . endure."

Fielder and the boy, who would become the one Geaxi has named "West," stayed in the Caucasus long enough to shape, smooth, and carve a sphere, bearing witness to who and what they were, where they were, and where they were going. They then gathered the five stones and began their endless journey west across all terrain, interacting with the newcomers only when it was unavoidable, and never staying anywhere longer than a season or two. Millennia after millennia passed and they endured and survived, and along the way discovered the powerful effects the stones had on the consciousness of the newcomers, who were now spread throughout every land. West told Fielder his mother had once used a term for how long the tribe of the Ancestors had carried the stones. The term translated as a unit of time equaling two hundred and ten thousand years. With her ability, Fielder could also "hear" and "feel" us, the new Travelers, the ones who looked like the newcomers and called ourselves Meq, growing in numbers and concentrating in the Iberian Peninsula and northern Africa. And as the Ancestor predicted, gradually, almost like re-calling a long-forgotten dream or having an old memory unfold with new meaning, Fielder and West came to a clear understanding of their true purpose and destiny. It was the opposite of everything they had imagined. How could it be, and why? If there was a reason, it made no sense to them at that time. Yet it was so, and with this strange, unexpected understanding came another realization. If all events were to transpire as they had been revealed, then everything depended on the new Travelers' survival far into the future for more than thirteen millennia. To do that, Fielder and West agreed the new Travelers would need assistance. They would need the unique and ancient power of the five stones.

Before they could act, however, Fielder and West would have to wait another two hundred years for the right time to occur. The transfer of the stones had to be in conjunction with a cross-ing, or the Zeharkatu, and a crossing can only take place during what the Travelers called the "Empty Ring" and the Meq call the

Bitxileiho, or Strange Window. The Bitxileiho is the peculiar and mystical celestial event known as a total solar eclipse. Similar to birds that know instinctively when to migrate, the Meq know in advance when and where these events are going to take place. Whatever magic there is in being Meq is crystallized, energized, and reborn during this timeless phenomenon of cosmic geometry. To the Meq, a total solar eclipse is terrifying, wondrous, paralyzing, and transforming all at once, and only during the precious few seconds and minutes of totality can the mutual metamorphosis of a Meq crossing and marriage take place. This was essential for what Fielder and West had in mind.

Following traditional routes from valley to valley and river to river, they walked south until they reached the foothills of the Pyrenees. From there, Fielder "counted" the number of Meq living in the mountains among the Basque. The Meq totaled one hundred eighty-four souls who were in the Wait. There were no children under the age of twelve because there had not been a crossing in six hundred years. Fielder's ability also enabled her to locate the leaders within every tribe and she focused on one Meq in particular. At this point in her story, Fielder looked directly at Sailor. Calling him by his true name, she said, "It was your ancestor, Umla-Meq. He was the one we went to see."

There is no future without memory. Fielder chose the oldest Meq with the longest memory to distribute the five stones and give them names. Surprisingly, he welcomed Fielder and West without question, and their physical appearance seemed to inspire a mild curiosity rather than hesitation or fear. Their kind had long disappeared from the landscape and it simply made no difference to him or the rest of his tribe how Fielder and West appeared. He was far more interested in what they had to show him—the stones. And when he found out what each stone could do, he welcomed them for as long as they wished to stay. Fielder told him they had only come to present the stones as a gift and witness the Bitxileiho, which was about to occur over the Pyrenees and across the great sea to the south. Fielder knew she could tell him how to use the stones, but little else. That was the way it had to be. The inexplicable future event that had been revealed to Fielder and West could not be revealed to the Meq. The length of time involved was too great to comprehend, even for the Meq, and it had to happen on its own, if it happened at all.

Two days later under clear skies and shortly before midday, every Meq and Giza in the Pyrenees experienced a total solar eclipse. The smooth disc of the moon slid gracefully into place in front of the sun, and for the next two minutes and thirteen seconds a wheel of fire burned in the center of a black sky, while five Meq couples, who by coincidence were all Egizahar, crossed in the Zeharkatu. Sailor's ancestor and his Ameq were among them.

During the crossing, Fielder and West concentrated as one spirit and used the "Voice" to implant and imprint a future time and place in the collective unconscious of the five couples. This information would resonate forward in the minds and memories of every generation of Meq to come, even into Africa, and though the profound nature of this information would remain, the reason for it would elude them all. Eventually, this information would become the central mystery and sacred destination in Time for every Meq on the planet. It would be called the Gogorati, the Remembering.

After the crossing, the five stones were distributed to the five couples and given names: Blood, Will, Silence, Dreams, and Memory. Sailor's ancestor became the first Stone of Memory. Fielder and West stayed another day, then bid the Meq farewell and headed west. They wandered for months before they settled on a lonely and remote spot along the coast of what is now Portugal. Fish were fat and plentiful, as well as wild berries and greens, and though they were isolated, they felt at home. Twelve centuries later, West carved the last of the spheres and they left it behind, hoping for the best. Traveling north, they finally ended their journey on the beautiful coast of South Wales. There they would endure and learn to live among the newcomers, and wait, and wait, and wait, while Fielder "listened" and "followed" the lives of the Meq.

When Fielder finished her story, she looked each of us in the eyes, ending with the Fleur-du-Mal. "West is correct, Xanti. I am the reason we know so much about you while you know nothing of us. I have 'felt' you since you were born. I have 'followed' all of you."

"Why did you not simply come to us?" Geaxi asked. "You could have come to us. You could have . . . revealed this long ago."

"No, we could not," Fielder answered. "It must come from you. We cannot interfere. You must find your own way to us." She paused and smiled at me. "And because of the Stone of Dreams, you did."

The Fleur-du-Mal asked, "What if Zezen had not been able to read the spheres?"

"Yes," Sailor added, "I was pondering the same thought. We have only forty-three years until the Remembering occurs and—"

"Forty-three years?" West interrupted. He looked completely surprised. "No, no, not forty-three years, Umla-Meq." He held up his hand and spread his fingers wide. "Five years—what you call the Remembering is in a little less than five years."

I said, "That was what you meant when you said we were 'just in time.'"

"Yes," West replied, then grinned. "It seems that like a clock that has run on its own for a very long time, the Meq are a few seconds slow."

"But you have not answered my question," the Fleur-du-Mal said. "What if Zezen had not shown us how to read the spheres in time? What would you have done?"

"We would have continued waiting."

The Fleur-du-Mal raised one eyebrow. "For what . . . another Remembering? You have waited over thirteen thousand years for this one . . . and I assume for Geaxi and me. Is not this Remembering the only one for us? After what I have heard and what I have felt today, I am certain this Remembering was and is inevitable."

"Yes," Sailor said, "is it coincidence or destiny that we are here?"

"Both," Fielder answered. "For us, the Meq and the Traveler, it is both."

Out the windows to the west there was only a faint glow where the sun had slipped below the horizon. Inside the big room, West turned on a few lamps and Fielder leaned over to gather the empty teacups onto the tray. Ray, who had not yet made a sound or moved a muscle, said, "I got just one question. Is this Remembering gonna tell us why we are the way we are?"

No one said a word. No one had an answer.

In the space of a single afternoon the Meq had changed forever—past, present, and future. Now we no longer were the *only* ones, we were simply the *newer* ones. What this meant and would mean was still not clear, but we were on a path of understanding and the path led straight to the Remembering.

Fielder and West extended an open-ended invitation to stay at the manor and we accepted. Morgan Manor, as it had long been known in that part of South Wales, became our home for an indefinite period of time. Koldo said his farewells and drove the

tour bus back to Cornwall and Caitlin's Ruby. He had never asked
what we were doing or why. He was just acting as his father and
his father's father would have acted. He was the last Aita of the
tribe of Vardules, protectors of the Stone of Dreams.

In the first few days at Morgan Manor, we learned its history
and that Fielder and West had a relationship and connection to
the Morgan family and their estate much like the Meq had at
Caitlin's Ruby. And the connection, or coincidence, went even
deeper. It was rumored that an ancestor of the current Morgan
family, Mr. John Dawes Morgan, had known Caitlin Fadle inti-
mately and was possibly the father of her son, though it was never
proven.

Fielder and West had established similar relationships with the
"newcomers" in the area going back in time to the end of the last
ice age. West said they had also lived nearby but farther inland,
twice for a period of time on the River Wye and for a few thousand years or so in the Lliw uplands. He spoke of whole millennia as if they were minutes or hours on a clock. In the months
that followed, listening to West and Fielder was mesmerizing, ex-
hilarating, and enlightening. We not only heard about times,
places, and animals barely imaginable, but we learned the living
history of the planet itself. Within their lifetimes, Fielder and
West had seen and experienced entire geological and climatic
epochs come and go. They had long known of the ecliptic path
and had witnessed the entire twenty-six-thousand-year cycle of
the precession of the equinoxes. They knew the causes and effects
and they had endured and remembered it all. There were no living beings more connected to this Earth than the two long-living
Travelers.

Now they were connected to us in the deepest and most intimate ways, West to Geaxi and Fielder to the Fleur-du-Mal. During the first few months at Morgan Manor, I watched Fielder and

the Fleur-du-Mal become closer, although they did not display
the kind of physical closeness that Opari and I shared, as well as
Nova and Ray and Sailor and Sheela. His arrogance would probably not allow it. Neither Opari nor I could fathom why they
were each other's Ameq. How could Fielder love a cruel and
cold-blooded killer, and how could the Fleur-du-Mal love at all?
Even in her presence, he never denied or regretted a single act,
yet that did not seem to concern Fielder in the least. One of the
contradictions in the Fleur-du-Mal is that he is as honest as he is
evil. Maybe that was their connection. Both their natures were
contradictory and unpredictable. She ignored his arrogance and
he ignored their physical differences and each embraced the
other's intellect. Watching West and Geaxi interact was similar in
that Geaxi's personality did not seem to change—her droll wit
and blunt manner remained—but in her eyes there was a brand-
new understanding that was universal and joyous. In her heart,
Geaxi had come home.

Five years. For the Giza five years can prove to be a long stretch
of time, even a lifetime for some. For the Meq five years is nothing. Sailor once told me that in the past it was not uncommon for
the Meq to discuss the brightness of a single star for a hundred
years or more. It was that way at Morgan Manor. With so many
of us living in one place, long walks along the coast and treks
inland among the barren and beautiful foothills of Black Mountain were common and frequent and usually filled with discus-
sions that always led back to the Remembering. Seasons ran into
seasons and time passed around us unnoticed and barely felt.

Mowsel enjoyed his stay in South Wales perhaps more than any
of us. He had always had a great desire for knowledge of all things
Meq, especially our history and our secrets. Every day he learned

from the Travelers what was myth and what was reality. In his nearly five years at Morgan Manor, Mowsel probably spent more time in discussion with West and Fielder than did Geaxi or the Fleur-du-Mal. Zeru-Meq was equally intrigued and intoxicated with the Travelers and their stories. He asked them endless questions about ancient cultures and routes of travel that had only been fairy tales and fantasies to him until he learned the truth through their own histories and journeys. Zeru-Meq had once been indifferent about the Remembering and its importance, and he and Sailor had feuded about it for centuries. But now Zeru-Meq and Mowsel, along with Sailor, had become the true caretakers of the Meq and our destiny. Early on, it was Zeru-Meq who recognized that this Remembering, whatever else it might be, was all about the Zeharkatu. "It is self-evident," he said. "The five Stones are here, as they must be, and the five are now here with their Ameq. It is no coincidence. The five are here to cross in the Zeharkatu during the Remembering."

"You are correct," Fielder told him. She glanced at West, then looked hard into the eyes of the Fleur-du-Mal. "Those of us who have met our Ameq are meant to cross now. What is within us is within the Stones and must be returned and renewed. The five Stones must cross in this Bitxileiho during this Gogorati, this Remembering."

The Fleur-du-Mal did not move or give away his thoughts, but if anything when I looked at him, he seemed pleased with the idea. Ray muttered "Damn!" and grinned and winked at Nova. Geaxi turned her head and locked eyes with West. Sailor and Sheela didn't make a sound or look at each other, but I saw her hand move closer to his. I glanced at Opari. She didn't say a word. Her black eyes were bright and inscrutable.

• • •

On January 1, 1979, West lit fires in each of the three fireplaces in the great living room of Morgan Manor. A long oak table was placed in the center of the room and the curtains were pulled wide open to allow everyone a good view of the sea. The table was stacked with dozens of breads and cakes and a plate full of good Welsh sausages. As West played an impromptu concerto by Vivaldi on his cello, the rest of us sat at the table feasting on the sausages, drinking mulled wine, and toasting the New Year. It was only fifty-seven days until the Remembering. Because of Fielder and West we had learned the correct and exact time and place where we were to be for the event. It was set to occur on the morning of February 26, 1979, near the town of Grass Range in what is now the state of Montana in the United States. An unlikely and inauspicious time and place, but that made no difference. The Meq would be there, all of us, including the five Stones.

The next six weeks passed without incident. Our routines and daily life remained the same, yet there was a slight tension in the air, even among the old ones. The anticipation of the singular event was palpable, and everyone was anxious to begin our journey. Our plan was to leave the United Kingdom together on February 17, flying by charter into New York, then on to Denver, Colorado, where we were to transfer aircraft and fly into Billings, Montana. From there, we would be driven north to a hunting lodge twenty miles east of Grass Range near where the Box Elder and Flatwillow Creeks converge. Through contacts established by Mr. Morgan, we had leased the lodge for the last ten days of February, and it was there that we would wait for the morning of the twenty-sixth. Our "chaperones" for the entire trip were an older couple from Cardiff, and they would serve as our grandparents. Fielder and West had hired them before for international travel, and West said the couple was friendly, efficient, and could be trusted implicitly.

Opari and I had little to pack for the journey, but on the afternoon of February 16, while we were folding and packing our clothes, Mr. Morgan knocked on our door and handed me a telegram that had just been delivered to the manor. It was for me. It was from Koldo, and as I read it, I knew I had no choice but to act immediately.

"What is it, Z?" Opari asked. "What is wrong?"

I stared down at the telegram. There were only three lines. "It's from Koldo," I told her. "It says, 'JACK DIAGNOSED IN DECEMBER WITH PANCREATIC CANCER. FAILING FAST. BETTER HURRY.'"

Opari and I looked at each other. I didn't have to say a word. She said, "I will come with you."

We left that same night. Before leaving I told the others of the situation in St. Louis and said we were only taking a detour. Opari and I would meet them at the hunting lodge. They all understood. Ray even tipped his beret in respect to Jack, but Sailor remarked, "Make sure you are both in Montana by the morning of the twenty-sixth. The Stones must cross." I assured him we would be there. Mr. Morgan was gracious enough to drive us to the Cardiff Central Railway Station, where we caught a train for the two-hour ride to London. The next day at Heathrow we purchased tickets and boarded a nonstop flight to Chicago. The ticket agents and flight attendants were all more than helpful after I explained that we were brother and sister traveling home alone because of a family emergency. We used the same story going through customs, then caught the last flight out to St. Louis, landing at Lambert Field in a cold light rain, almost a mist. It was well after midnight by the time our taxi pulled into the long driveway and finally came to a stop under the stone archway of Carolina's house. I paid the driver, and Opari and I walked through the rain and around to the side kitchen entrance. There was a light on in-side, and two women, one in her early fifties and the other in her late seventies, were playing cards at the kitchen table. They both jumped and dropped their cards when I knocked. "It's okay," I said through the window. Antoinette and Star stared back. "It's just me . . . Z."

It was Antoinette who opened the door, giving Opari and me a long, tight embrace. "Come in, come in, both of you. You're wet," she said.

"Just a little," I told her and followed Opari inside.

Star was still sitting at the table staring at me, and she was smil-ing. "I knew you would make it," she said. "I knew you would be here."

"Is he . . . ?"

"He is sleeping . . . for now. He's in a great deal of pain." I walked over and embraced her, holding her head close to me. "Mama would be glad you're here, Z," she whispered.

We stayed up another hour talking with Antoinette and Star. We were told Caine was in Chicago giving a series of lectures, while Georgie was living in Berkeley and working on her doc-torate. It was only the two of them in the big house, and they said they often played cards late at night just in case Jack might need something quickly. We learned that his cancer had spread rapidly and viciously throughout his body. His mind was sharp and clear, but his body had failed. Jack was dying and he knew it would be soon. "But please, do not pity him," Star said. "He will literally try to kick you out of his room if he senses pity of any kind."

"That sounds about like Jack," I replied.

"Believe me," Antoinette added, "Jack is still Jack."

· · ·

The next morning, after Antoinette informed me he was awake and had even eaten a little breakfast, I walked unannounced into Jack's room. He was lying in his bed, propped up with pillows to a sitting position. He had a tube in his nose and another tube in his arm, which was connected to a morphine drip. His face was gaunt and he weighed less than a hundred pounds. His once dark hair had turned snow white. He still had his hair because Star told me he had stopped chemotherapy after only one round of treatment. I dragged a chair up next to him and sat down. He didn't seem at all surprised to see me. Because of the morphine his eyes had a slightly dull and lazy focus, but he was there. Behind those eyes, Jack was very much alive. He looked at me and smiled. "I saw Bob Forsch pitch a no-hitter last April, Z. First one in this city in fifty-four years."

"Jesse Haines, July 17, 1924, right? We went together, remember?"

He laughed. "I do remember. I was just testing you. You know, Z, you have a pretty good memory for a kid."

I looked him in the eye and said, "Thanks, Jack, but I don't feel much like a kid anymore."

"Neither do I, Z." He paused and adjusted the tube in his nose. "What do you say, let's talk some baseball for a while and maybe we will? I have nothing against Star or Antoinette, but they can't talk baseball. It's a shame, really."

I smiled and said, "I agree. I pity them."

"So do I," Jack said, "so do I."

It was a privilege and a pleasure just to sit with Jack. Every second was filled with humor and wisdom, the kind that is earned, not bestowed. During the next five days and nights, when he was conscious, I sat with Jack and we talked about a lot of things, but mainly we talked baseball. And when we talked, Jack seemed to rally, physically and spiritually. We talked about the great players we'd seen. We talked about pitching, hitting, fielding, strategy, and we talked about the great moments. Only in baseball can you witness a situation, a crazy play, or a wonderful and unique event that you have never seen before and will never see again. In baseball, there is no certain destiny, only circumstance. The ball is hit, or not. The play is made, or not. The run is scored, or not. The player determines the outcome. Jack likened baseball to his own life and regrets. He told me, "I don't have regrets, Z. I've had my share of luck, good and bad, but I don't have regrets. Right or wrong, all my decisions were mine alone. Nobody made them for me. If there is one thing I regret in this world, it is not finding what you and Opari have together. That's one play I never got to make."

On Saturday, February 24, Jack had a bad day. He was in and out of consciousness throughout the day, and his breathing was often shallow and uneven. The morphine helped, but when he was conscious, he looked to be in agony. By sunset, the pain had finally relented and allowed his mind and body to relax into a deep sleep. He was worn-out, helpless, and beaten down. But he had not yet given up or given in.

Later that night Opari and I were lying in bed. We were on our sides and she was facing away from me. I had my arm around her waist. I whispered, "We have a decision to make."

"To stay with Jack or leave for the Remembering," she whispered back.

"Yes."

"I do not think it is a decision. I think staying with Jack is what we must do. You and I are Meq, my love, but he is your family."

"I love you, Opari."

"I know. I love you, too."

I started to say something else, then realized it wasn't necessary. Opari took hold of my hand and raised it to her lips, silently kissing the palm of my hand.

Sometime just before dawn I awoke from a strange and compelling dream. My first impression was that it was not a dream at all. It began at night. Opari and I were following the steps of a stone path along the cliff's edge at Morgan Manor. The path was unknown to both of us. Each of the stone steps was carved in the shape of a hand, and the path was only visible because of the full moon overhead. We seemed to be in a rush, although no one was chasing us. The path was dangerous, with a sheer drop of two hundred feet on the left side. The steps began leading down a hidden niche in the cliff face. At the bottom of the steps there was an entrance to a cave, which would have been covered by the sea at high tide. A faint, flickering light was coming from somewhere inside, and we heard voices chanting or singing. We followed the peculiar hand-steps into the cave and toward the light, finally coming to a larger space where a boy was bending over a table and writing something on a strip of papyrus. Along with the papyrus, the five Stones were lined up on the table. The flickering light emanated from two lit candles on stands next to the table.

In the dream, I knew the boy was Meq. He was darker than Opari and me but lighter than Susheela the Ninth. His oily black hair curled over his collar, and he wore two jade loops for earrings. The jade was the same color as his eyes. I instinctively knew what he was writing and I knew his name. He was called "the Thracian," and he was writing the text of the *Nine Steps of the Six,* the writing I had translated from the papyrus that Susheela the Ninth and her family had carried for millennia. Surrounding the table in a spiraling circle stood Trumoi-Meq, Zeru-Meq, Ray,

Nova, Sailor, Susheela the Ninth, Geaxi, West, Fielder, and the Fleur-du-Mal. They had their eyes closed, and they were chanting the *Nine Steps of the Six*.

"The Thracian" turned to me and pointed at the papyrus. His gold bracelets jangled on his wrist. He spoke in his ancient language, which I understood. "Read it again," he said. He then picked up the five Stones, one by one, and began juggling them in the air, creating a perfect moving circle of Stones, and repeating, "Read it again." I leaned over the table. The writing was in red ochre. It said: *Nine Steps of the Six. The First One shall not know. The Second One shall not know. The Third One shall not know. The Fourth One shall not know. The Fifth One shall not know. The Living Change shall live within the Sixth One. The Five shall be drawn unto the Source Stone. The Living Change shall be revealed. The Five shall be Extinguished.* When I looked up to ask "the Thracian" what it meant, I awoke from the dream.

Jack rallied again on Sunday morning. When he woke, he did something he hadn't done in weeks. He asked Antoinette for a hot cup of coffee and a piece of toast with butter and blackberry jam. Caine arrived home from Chicago around noon, having flown himself in the Beechcraft King Air he had inherited from Willie Croft. Jack was glad to see him, and all of us gathered in his room while he and Caine talked and laughed about the difficulty of being a Cardinals fan stuck in Chicago. But the excitement was short-lived. By three o'clock Jack had taken a downturn and went through an hour of relentless pain, then slipped away into a sleep that seemed more like a coma. As day turned to night, Jack's pulse became weaker, and he didn't respond to Star's touch or her constant whispering in his ear. Opari and I held hands and sat next to Jack. Antoinette and Caine sat in chairs on the other side of the bed. We spoke little and time passed slow and thick as fog. Then, just after eight o'clock Jack's eyes fluttered and he squeezed Star's hand. It took him a minute to do it, but he willed himself awake and looked up at Star. "Where's Z?" he asked.

"I'm right here," I said, taking hold of his other hand.

Jack turned his head and stared into my eyes. "Tell me about Mama as a girl, Z. Tell me what she was like."

"That's easy. Where do you want me to start?"

"At the beginning."

"All right." I pulled my chair in a few inches closer. "The first time I ever saw Carolina was at old Sportsman's Park. It was a Saturday in late summer." I kept talking and I told him about her stringy blond hair and her face full of freckles, and I told him about how we played every game we could think of while we explored Forest Park and all of St. Louis in the early 1880s. I talked and I continued talking and when I finally stopped, Jack's eyes were still staring at me, but Jack was gone. I let go of his hand and closed his eyes. "Farewell, Jack," I said. "Travel far."

While Caine called for an ambulance to take Jack's body away, Opari and I went for a short walk outside. We walked slowly into the "Honeycircle" and stopped next to Baju's sundial. It was bitter cold and the ground was frozen solid. My arm was around her shoulders and her arm was around my waist. I looked up at the sky and broken clouds obscured the stars. We had not yet discussed the decision we'd made to stay with Jack, if it had been necessary. The Stone of Dreams and the Stone of Blood simply do not make decisions like that. I turned to look at Opari. I reached up and held her face in my hands and we stared deep into each other's eyes. I said, "Everything is different now, isn't it?"

There was a long moment of silence, then Opari kissed me on the lips and said, "Yes."

Half an hour later, after the ambulance had come and gone, we all sat in the kitchen talking about Jack. Star sipped her coffee and let the tears run down her cheeks without wiping them away. I waited for the right moment to do what I had to do next, then realized there was no right moment. I turned to Caine and said, "I know this is an inappropriate time, Caine, but I have no choice." I glanced at Opari. "Opari and I need to get to Montana. Can you fly us there?"

"Where in Montana?"

"Billings."

"Of course, Z," Caine answered. "When do you have to be there?"

"By dawn."

"Dawn?"

"By dawn tomorrow. Can you do it?"

Caine looked at his watch. It was 9:20 P.M. on a Sunday. "The King Air can cruise at 280 mph," he said. "If I can still get someone to service the plane and fuel us up, we can make it easily."

At 11:20 P.M. we were taxiing out on a runway at Lambert Field, loaded with fuel and taking off, heading north by northwest. Caine had called in a few favors owed to get everything done so quickly, but we were in the air and on our way. He had also called ahead and made arrangements in Billings to have a car and driver waiting to pick up "a boy and a girl who are in a hurry."

We climbed easily to twenty-six thousand feet and leveled out. Above the cloud cover the night sky sparkled with stars from horizon to horizon. As we flew on I asked Caine if he was going to be able to stay awake and he said he'd have no problem until we got to Billings, then he'd rent a room and get some sleep be-

fore returning home. Somewhere over South Dakota the drone
of the engines began to lull me to sleep, and I drifted off while
thinking about Opari and me and the Remembering. I now
knew we were going to make it, but I kept thinking, what if we
didn't . . . what if we didn't?

In the dream I was sitting on the same train in the same seat I'd
been sitting in when the train crashed on the way to Central City,
killing my mama and papa and dozens of others. As the train
picked up speed, I was rubbing Mama's glove and watching Papa
at the front of our compartment. Then I looked down at the
glove, and in the palm, or the pocket, there were words written
in red ink. The words were the last three lines of the *Nine Steps of
the Six*. They read: *The Five shall be drawn unto the Source Stone.
The Living Change shall be Revealed. The Five shall be Extinguished.*
Just then, Mama screamed, "Yaldi! Yaldi!" I looked up to see my
mama and papa lock eyes and go somewhere in this universe
where only they were allowed. As the train went across the bridge
and on to its destiny, Mama and Papa were at peace and together
inside their own destiny.

"Z, wake up."

I opened my eyes. It was Opari. "Where are we?" I asked.

"We are approaching Billings. You were talking in your sleep."

I watched Opari's mouth move as she talked, and her eyes
seemed to be lit from inside. She was so beautiful. "What did
I say?"

"You said something about 'the answer.' "

I smiled and took her hand in mine, then kissed her fingers. "I
know what to do now."

Opari looked at me carefully. She wanted to be sure of something. She touched my lips and said, "Tell me."

I leaned over and whispered in her ear, telling her everything.

Opari listened until I was finished, then whispered back, "Yes, yes, yes, my love. Yes."

Before we landed, I thanked Caine again for all that he'd done for us. I told him that I hoped Jack didn't mind, and at that precise moment a pair of sunglasses dropped from a clipboard on the copilot side of the cockpit.

"Maybe he came with us," Caine said.

"What do you mean?" I asked.

Caine laughed and said, "Those are Jack's sunglasses."

I looked out the window to the east. It was still dark, but there was a hint of a faint glow just over the horizon. Caine executed a perfect landing and we taxied to a private hangar adjacent to the main terminal. Idling inside the hangar with its headlights on was a blue van with the name Lewis & Clark Limousine and Shuttle painted on the side doors. Caine swiveled the plane around and came to a stop, then turned off the engines. As he unlocked and opened the door, I told him he might not see us for a while, but I promised to stay in touch, somehow, some way. Opari said to give her love to Star and Antoinette. We stepped out of the plane into the frigid Montana night. Opari ran ahead to the van and I turned back to Caine.

"Good-bye, Caine."

"Good-bye, Z. Good luck."

"As a great friend and a wise man used to always tell me—'Zis is good business.'" I waved and ran to catch up with Opari. We had half an hour until first light and another hour and a half until the Remembering.

Our driver was a heavyset man in his fifties who looked at us in the mirror and talked incessantly. Before we had even turned out of Billings onto Highway 87, he said, "I suppose you kids are flyin' in and tryin' to beat the eclipse, am I right?"

"You sure are," I said. "All our cousins are waiting for us."

He winked in the mirror. "Don't you worry. Lewis and Clark'll get you there."

But he was nearly wrong. Fifty miles north at Roundup, he missed a turn and didn't realize it for several miles. The mistake and turnaround cost us forty miles and another thirty minutes. As dawn began to break, we were still miles from our destination, and our driver couldn't increase our speed because of patches of black ice on the two-lane highway. Finally, just south of Grass Range, we turned onto the county road that led to the hunting lodge twelve miles away. Thin gray clouds in the east hid the sun. It was 7:32 A.M.

The entrance to the lodge was marked by a split-rail fence and an open gate, over which there was an eighteen-foot arch made entirely of antlers, spelling out the words "BLACK ELK RANCH." We sped down the gravel drive another half mile to a compound of buildings in a wide semicircle. Our driver stopped the van next to the largest, an adobe Spanish-style ranch house with a red tile roof. A jeep was parked nearby with its motor running. Before we could get out of the van, Ray Ytuarte burst out of the jeep. I opened the side door just as Ray got to us. He grinned and said, "Damn, Z! Cuttin' it kinda close, ain't you?"

"It's complicated," I said.

"Always is, my friend, always is." Ray glanced at Opari, then back to me. "There were some of us, I won't name names, who thought you might not make it. I was not among them."

"We're here now, Ray. That's what counts."

He gave me an odd look. "Well, come with me and I mean quick. We only got a few minutes."

I thanked our driver and Opari and I hopped into the jeep

with Ray. He could barely reach the gas pedal, but he set out cross-country toward a rock outcropping in the distance, a small promontory in the middle of a cold, vast, and barren landscape.

I looked up at the sky, and the clouds obscuring the sun had vanished. I thought to myself, it might have looked just like this thirteen thousand five hundred years ago when the Stones were distributed. They were somewhere south of the ice, but close to it. They would have been close to the ice wherever they were. I thought about what Sailor had said last, "The Stones must cross," and I felt for the Stone of Dreams in my pocket. I turned to look at Opari, and she was staring straight ahead with the hint of a smile on her face.

After a rough ride, mostly along a dry creek bed, Ray brought the Jeep to a jolting halt. He glanced at the clock on the dashboard. "Eight-eleven," he said. "We got five minutes."

We leaped out and Opari and I followed Ray as he scrambled around boulders and climbed up the south slope of the outcropping. At the top, standing in a ragged line, the others were waiting for us, all wearing heavy wool blankets around their shoulders. Against the empty sky and desolate landscape, they looked like abandoned children at the end of nowhere.

Opari and I ran to greet them with an embrace and the words *"Egibizirik bilatu."* Sailor and Sheela were standing together, as were Geaxi and West, and now Nova and Ray. Mowsel and Zeru-Meq stood alone.

"I never had a doubt," Sailor said calmly.

"Neither did I."

"Are you ready?"

"Yes, but there is something Opari and I must do." We had not yet greeted the Fleur-du-Mal and Fielder. We walked over and I embraced the Fleur-du-Mal for the first time in my life. *"Egibizirik bilatu,"* I said. He stiffened a little, but returned the greeting and added, "I must admit, *mon petit,* I did not think you would be here."

I nodded to Opari and she took the leather necklace and the Stone of Blood from around her neck, while I took the Stone of Dreams out of my pocket. I reached for the Fleur-du-Mal's hand and placed the Stone in his palm. Opari slipped the necklace and Stone over Fielder's head and around her neck. Fielder was not surprised. She looked Opari in the eyes and smiled, nodding once.

"After you have crossed and carried this," I told the Fleur-du-Mal, "you will understand."

Sailor shouted, "Zianno, wait—"

Just then, Mowsel said, "It is beginning. It is beginning now."

Although no one gazed directly at it, we could all feel it happening—the cold dead disk of the moon sliding into place in front of the burning disk of the sun. Simultaneously, we began to feel something rising inside us—fear, yes, but something more, something overwhelming. Mowsel had a grin on his face and Zeru-Meq had his eyes closed. Nova looked at Ray and Ray looked at Nova. Susheela the Ninth took hold of Sailor's hand and entwined her fingers with his. Geaxi removed her beret and West wrapped his arm around her shoulders and pulled her to him. The Fleur-du-Mal glanced at me, giving me an enigmatic grin, then took Fielder's hand in his and turned to face the sun. Darkness spread rapidly and the shadow bands raced across the landscape in a surreal dance toward the horizon. Twenty seconds to go. Ten seconds. I turned to Opari and we embraced. I held her so tight and close I could feel every part of her. I whispered in her ear, "We are on our own now."

She whispered back, "I know."

Totality!

We both looked up and stared at the beautiful and terrifying burning black hole in the sky, the Strange Window, the Empty Ring, the Bitxileiho, and we became suspended, weightless, nowhere and everywhere. Where was where? *What* was where? I was so far away and small, centuries of light-years from anywhere or anything, falling without falling, drifting into nothing. I knew nothing, there was nothing to know, nothing to remember. There was no remembering, only returning. I felt the pull of the current, the inside tide of darkness gently pulling me into the waters of the Long Dream. Then came the voice, so faint and so familiar. "Beloved, wake . . . wake."

Even though I was not aware I had closed them, I opened my eyes and realized I was on my knees, and so was Opari. I glanced over at the others and everyone was on their knees. The sun was still in partial eclipse, but totality was over. It had lasted only two minutes and forty-nine seconds, and I thought it was odd how something so anticipated, complex, and fundamental could pass so quickly. Fielder and the Fleur-du-Mal, Geaxi and West, Sailor and Sheela, and Ray and Nova, each looked the same as they had two minutes and forty-nine seconds earlier, but they were not. They had crossed in the Zeharkatu, and during that time every cell in their being had been changed, altered, and restructured. That which in the past had made them invulnerable to age and disease was now gone, along with the mystical Meq ability to heal, repair, and restore all tissue, fiber, sinew, and bone in a matter of minutes or hours. They were now more like Giza than Meq, but each one could also do something they could not do before. Like the Giza, they could now mature and reproduce. Of course, Mowsel and Zeru-Meq remained unchanged because they had no Ameq and could not cross. But everyone else had crossed—everyone except Opari and me.

· · ·

It had long been assumed that Opari and I would cross during the Remembering. Even Opari and I had assumed it, though we rarely discussed it. In St. Louis, when we made the decision to stay with Jack while he was dying, even if we missed the Remembering, we both knew something essential had occurred. Betrayal is too strong a word, but Opari and I understood that we had separated ourselves from the others in some way, and it was irreversible. After Jack died and we felt we might still have a chance to make it to Montana in time, I realized what we must do with the Stones and with ourselves. The solution was absurdly simple and seemed meant to be. For us, it became the key that unlocked the whole purpose of the event. Ray and Nova were the first Egipurdiko and Egizahar Meq to ever cross. It wasn't thought possible before. Susheela the Ninth was Sailor's second Ameq and they crossed. That also had never happened. West and Fielder were a completely different species, and they crossed with Geaxi and the Fleur-du-Mal.

For some reason, the Meq were evolving, changing from the inside out, and this Remembering was all about that evolution. Sailor had said "the Stones must cross," and now they had. By transferring the Stones and their mystery to Fielder and the Fleur-du-Mal, Opari and I had made sure the Stone of Dreams and the Stone of Blood became part of that evolution. But for Opari and me, this Remembering was not our moment, not our time to cross. The Meq are blessed with destiny *and* free will. We decided to continue the Wait.

Back in South Wales, Ray had asked if this Remembering would "tell us why we are the way we are." I didn't think so, but I was hoping it would. Who are the Meq? I don't know. Why are the Meq here? I don't know. Where are the Meq going? I don't know. Opari and I had not found these answers. Instead, we had found each other.

It was a cold Monday morning, February 26, 1979. Below us the earth was turning, and overhead the sun was shining. Along with the others, Opari and I stood on the small outcropping of rock and turned in a full circle, staring at the barren beauty around us and remembering it. That's all we can do with any moment. We can do that and we can endure and survive. Moment to moment to moment.

EPILOGUE

There is a lot to be said for traveling in a twelve-year-old body. First, there is your height. You are halfway between a little kid and a big kid, or teenager, both of whom are highly visible in public. But the twelve-year-old is invisible. No one pays attention to the activities of a twelve-year-old, or even two of them. With the right resources, time, and imagination, any kid could do it. In the years following the Remembering, Opari and I traveled this way, generally unnoticed and always unannounced, and never stopping long in any one place. We had only one criterion for choosing the next destination—it had to be a place where neither of us had been.

Using a complicated system of drop boxes and postcards, we kept up with the whereabouts of most of the others. Ray and Nova had moved to Veracruz, Mexico, which was the city where Ray was born. They were the first couple among those who had crossed to have a child. In 1984, when Nova turned seventeen, she and Ray became the teenage parents of a healthy baby girl, seven pounds eleven ounces, named Eder Zuriaa, and she was born with a rare and unusual characteristic—her left eye was dark brown and her right eye was green. Ray reasoned that this would make her a good switch-hitter when she learned to play baseball.

I didn't understand the logic, but Ray said, "Damn, Z, it's clear as a tear to me."

Geaxi and West returned to live on the south coast of Wales at Morgan Manor. Two years after Nova, when Geaxi turned nineteen, she also gave birth to a baby girl after being in labor for thirty-three hours. It was a trying and traumatic experience, but Geaxi never complained. She told me, "It was no worse than playing chess with you, young Zezen." The baby was named Iza, the Meq word for "first," because Geaxi said she was the first of a new species of Meq.

Sailor and Sheela settled in Cairo, living with a wealthy family of traders Sailor had known and trusted for centuries. Mowsel and Zeru-Meq lived with them for a few years, then left suddenly, heading in separate directions, Mowsel going west and Zeru-Meq going east. Both of them had no fixed plans and were not intent on arriving anywhere in particular. In the late spring of 1988, Sailor and Sheela had their baby, a beautiful boy with sharp features and dark skin. He was given the formal name of Zubi-Meq, but Sailor called him Jack.

The following year Opari and I stopped in Cairo for a visit and to see the baby. It was bizarre to see Sailor as a young man. He and Sheela were twenty-two years old and looked just like any other young, modern, handsome couple. It was also odd to be so much smaller than Sailor. However, the most surreal moment of the visit was an act that is completely common and mundane, but something I never thought I'd witness. Early one morning I happened to see Sailor shaving.

Before we left, I asked about the Fleur-du-Mal and Fielder. Sailor said he thought they were living somewhere in the United States, but no one knew their exact location, or if they had a child.

In 1990, six months after the accident, Opari and I received the tragic news that Koldo and Arrosa had been killed in a car wreck in Cornwall. We had missed the funeral, so we sent our condolences and best wishes in a letter to Kepa and Yaldi.

For the next ten years, as Opari and I continued to travel, I called St. Louis on a regular basis. Except for the usual aches and pains of old age, Star, Antoinette, and Caine remained healthy. Georgie had moved back from California with her border collie, Carolina, and was now running the household and taking care of her parents and Star when they needed it. Then, on New Year's Eve, December 31, 1999, Star died peacefully in her sleep. She was ninety-nine years old. Three years later, Caine suffered a massive stroke at the age of eighty-four. At the moment of his death, he was writing a book on his theory of the origins of the Basque language. He was in midsentence when the stroke hit, and Antoinette said the pen was still in his hand when she found him. His death must have been difficult for her because afterward her own health began to deteriorate rapidly. Six months after Caine, she developed pneumonia and never recovered. Georgie said she passed away on February 1, 2003. She was seventy-six years old.

Opari and I kept moving. Year to year, country to country, continent to continent, avoiding war zones and tourists with equal disdain, we kept to ourselves and we kept moving. Traveling without the Stones was a new experience for both of us. Many times in potentially dangerous situations, I unconsciously reached in my pocket for the Stone that was no longer there, and it wasn't until 2012 that I finally broke the habit. That year we were in Argentina, and we crisscrossed South America for two more years, then followed the sun and headed west, stopping to live in the middle of the Pacific on the Marquesas Islands for another year.

By 2016 we were living in Australia, where we spent a year

wandering through the cities of Sydney and Melbourne. We then began a slow journey across the Outback for the same reason we went anywhere—because we'd never been there.

On my birthday, May 4, 2017, we decided to visit Ayers Rock, or Uluru, the massive, solitary block of sandstone standing in the middle of the Australian desert, sacred to all aboriginal tribes in the area. The big rock changes color with the changing light and weather, and parts of it are covered with ancient paintings, dots, and handprints. There were dozens of tourists there with us, some to climb the rock, some to study it, and some to just look at it and wait for sunset, when the rock turns red in the falling light. While the sun dropped silently below the horizon, Uluru came alive, and as it seemed to glow from inside something happened to Opari and me. It happened quickly and quietly, unasked and unannounced, and was as gentle and effortless as an angel's touch. We weren't sure when or if it would ever happen, and neither of us expected it, at least not so soon. I looked up and saw the Southern Cross hanging like a kite in the sky.

I turned to Opari and Opari turned to me. "Let's go home," I said. "Let's go home for good."

We bought tickets in Sydney and flew into Los Angeles using the same family emergency story we'd used hundreds of times in the past. We then flew on to Dallas, where in order to change planes we had to use the internal tram system connecting all terminals. Opari and I took our seats on one of the crowded trams and turned to look out the window. Across the platform another tram going the other way came to a stop. Just as our door began to close, the door of the other tram opened. Among the first out were a man about fifty years old and an unusual but striking-looking boy about twelve years old. The man was impeccably dressed, and he had his arm around the boy's shoulders. The boy was dressed in a black T-shirt and black jeans. They were in a hurry. The man had a perfectly trimmed beard that was showing a bit of silver, and even from a distance I could see his red ruby earrings. It was the boy who saw me, or should I say "felt" me first. He stopped immediately and stared at me from across the platform. In the next moment he reached in his jean pocket and pulled something out. He held up his arm, waving it at me, and in his hand I could see the Stone of Dreams. He smiled a bitter smile, showing off his perfect white teeth, and in a matter of seconds our tram was gone.

St. Louis is beautiful all year round, but in the spring, in May and early June, it is especially so. We landed in the afternoon. The sky was blue and clear, and the temperature was seventy-five degrees. It felt good to be alive and good to be in St. Louis.

Georgie was sitting in her car waiting for us outside the airport, along with her new border collie, Solomon. Sadly, she told us she had put Carolina to sleep two years earlier. "But you never knew Solomon," I replied.

"Oh yes I do, Z," she said with a smile. "He is everywhere in that house." Georgie was fifty-eight years old and had taken over her father's position at Washington University. She also resembled her mother, Antoinette, more than ever. On the drive back to the big house, I asked Georgie if she could take a slow detour through Forest Park and as we were driving through she asked Opari, "How long will you two be staying?" I had my head out the window smelling and feeling the air just like Solomon. "As long as this place is here," I shouted back.

. . .

A day later Opari and I bought bicycles and began exploring St. Louis the way two twelve-year-old kids should in the summertime. We went everywhere every day and at night we usually went to the ball game if the Cardinals were in town. June and July passed by and Opari and I hardly ever talked about what was approaching; however, we did discuss how many children would make a good family. She wanted three. I told her that was fine with me.

August started hot and has stayed that way. Yesterday was one of the hottest. Today is August 21, 2017. Right now, it's 1:14 in the afternoon and I'm sitting with Opari next to Baju's sundial in the "Honeycircle." Today, a total solar eclipse is occurring along a path from Oregon to North Carolina, passing directly over St. Louis at precisely 1:15 P.M.

Georgie had to work today, but before she left this morning, I told her Opari and I would be growing up now. "Sure, Z," she said, "and I'm going to be getting younger."

I just glanced up and it is beginning. The moon is sliding into place. It is getting dark. There are no birds singing. Opari's hand is waiting for mine.

"Now, my love."

"Yes. Now."

"It's clear as a tear, ain't it, Z?"

—RAY YTUARTE, on many occasions

PHOTO: © JIM MAYFIELD

ABOUT THE AUTHOR

STEVE CASH lived on the West Coast while attending college, then returned to his birthplace of Springfield, Missouri, to become an original member of the band the Ozark Mountain Daredevils. He is the co-author of the seventies pop hits "Jackie Blue" and "If You Wanna Get to Heaven." For the last thirty years, he has played harmonica; written songs; performed all over Europe, the United States, and Canada; raised his children; and read books.